PROHIBITION

ANDREW MICHAEL YEAGER

This book is a work of fiction. Any references to historical events, real people, or real locales are used fictitiously. Other names, characters, places, and incidents are products of the author's imagination, and any resemblance to actual events or locales or persons, living or dead, is entirely coincidental.

The text for this book is set in Electra LT & Betty Noir.

Editing by Joe Calamia & Amanda Tuzinski.
Biography by Lauren Gullitti.
Additional Editing by Lauren Gullitti & Lee Grant Yeager.

ISBN: 9781791625665

For my mother and father. Whose taste in music became my tastes and inspired the events of this book in a way I never dreamed possible.

PROLOGUE | THE STAGE

I was caught in a blaze of nerves as I arrived at Eddie's. It was a building that only lit up at night. Its door only opened after giving a secret password to a large man wearing a bowler. The words felt like a ticket that would take me on an unchartered journey.

From my first step through the front door, I felt a sense of unease. It was pitch black. I heard my heels clicking against the floor six more times before the light of the next room hit me. It was set up like a restaurant foyer with old seats arranged in circles with no tables in between them. Everything had embellishments that would have felt more commonplace in the mid-eighteen-hundreds. It was hauntingly elegant.

There were eyes of patrons glistening in all directions. Strangers were shimmying and swaying to the music coming from the band. A spectacle took place each time my eyes blinked.

Before I got to the doorway by the stage, another gentleman yelled from the bar, wearing an identical outfit to that of the doorman. “Anything to drink?” I shook my head in response and continued to my destination.

I felt a strange sensation as I pushed through many bodies to arrive safely behind the stage. The place was dark and disorienting and the only comfort I had was my oldest friend, Robby, waiting for me. I was about to do something that I had never done before and in front of one hundred strangers.

“You ready?” Robby asked, with little word.

The acids in my stomach battled in my body for dominance. I regretted not taking a drink from the gentleman at the counter. “Sure.” I gulped before I felt Robby’s hand pushing me through the curtain, onto the stage, and into a blinding light.

Two things happened at once. The music changed and I felt a bewildering sense of relief as the light made it nearly impossible to see anyone beyond it. I sighed as I approached the microphone. I gently wrapped my fingers around the mic like I was handling a precious pearl from the sea and belted the beginning words of the song. I forced my mind to think that I was back in my mother’s home, singing along to one of her old songs.

There were semitones in the guitar playing that felt almost like the folk music my mother would play on records. As the music careened in directions beyond my volition, I imagined the two of us dancing and laughing but mostly creating our own world with the color sounds. It wasn't easy but somehow, I was able to act as if the people weren't even there. I was back in that imaginary world with my mother.

The song finished and my face turned and met Robby's. There was an unrealistic smile splashed across his face. I looked out at the sea of faces. They all looked like they were ready for a swim. Each face had a completely different, yet, very satisfied expression. For whatever reason, my adrenaline was maddening to my perception.

Before I could leave, I felt a cold hand grab my right shoulder. When I turned, it wasn't Robby.

"Hello." He was wearing a suit that I would have never pictured on anyone. It was bright and colorful. Slightly shorter than me, he had a smile that could have been painted magazine ads. "The name's Tony. I own this place."

CHAPTER 1:
SLOW FOR A SPEAKEASY

Gray walkways below my feet went by at a pace that made my eyes spin. My vision traced up the pinstripes of my wardrobe to make sure that my bowtie was still tied tightly around my neck. I figured it was fine, considering my airways were already constricted so badly, that I had trouble breathing.

I passed a street-side diner when I heard a man shouting from an automobile to my left. I stopped square in my tracks and turned toward the road. "Do want a ride?" It was Tony Reynolds.

"No thank you, sir. I'd much rather walk. It's such a lovely day. Besides, the streets are littered with automobiles." I explained.

"It's truly not a problem. Jump in." There was a sense of excitement in his voice. "I wouldn't feel right if you were to lose your— Uh— What is that exactly?"

"It's a portfolio, sir." I told him, formally.

"Please, call me Tony." There was a smug smile forming on his face and his eyes creased as he did.

"Sorry, Mister Tony." I stuttered out.

"No, no, no, kid. That defeats the whole purpose of dropping the sir." He chuckled. I couldn't help but stare at his huge, silver watch as it caught the light of the sun. "Now, get in this automobile."

Without further hesitation, I opened the door from the curbside and sat next to him. Our legs were touching just slightly. The cab of the vehicle smelled like cologne and cigars. "I'm sorry, Mister Tony. I'm late."

"You did it again." His smile was off center and sarcastic. "Late for what exactly?" His face grew serious as he focused on the slow-moving traffic in front of us.

"I have a meeting with a gentleman about my work." I explained vaguely.

"And what kind of work is that?" He lit a cigar with a pack of matches that he pulled from his pants pocket. "You're still singing or playing the piano tonight, right?"

I coughed out of instinct. I was a rare breed; a non-smoker. Feeling rude I said "I am sorry," through my coughing. I stopped myself and began to unzip my shabby portfolio case. Then I pulled out a small painting I had blotted together just this morning. “Yes.” I answered him, placing the painting between us.

“What’s this?” He rushed out. There was quickness to his voice that was unwavering. Sometimes when he asked questions, I had to make sure they were intended as such.

“This is my hobby.” I tried to make it sound like it wasn’t a big deal when in fact it was the biggest of deals. I was an aspiring painter behind my musical venire.

“Hobby?” Tony spat out disgustedly. “This is brilliant! I’ll give you sixty smackers for it.”

I tried not to act excited. “Sixty dollars?” I was completely blown away. I had never sold one of my paintings. I was an abstract artist. So, most of my work was not in high demand.

I watched the New York buildings move past us slowly as we drove. It was quite a spectacle. There were sites of construction scattered on every street corner we passed. This was only my fourth or fifth time in an automobile.

“Still intend to make your meeting?” He asked sarcastically, referring to his purchase of my work.

“I suppose.” My mouth barely moved.

Tony flicked his cigar out of the window and floored the gas pedal while he spun the wheel to the right. The automobile hit the curb and it bounced onto the sidewalk. We zoomed through the walkway, avoiding any traffic that stood between us and the gallery.

I braced myself against the inner-frame of the vehicle. As I pressed my body subtly against the dashboard and the window, I tried not to look at Tony, for fear he would think ill of me. Instead, I watched as pedestrians leaped out of the way in panic.

It came as no surprise to me that *the* Tony Marlon Reynolds would be able to pull off something as illegal as this. From words whispered of him, he had to be the wealthiest man that I had ever come in contact with. He was also, quite simply, the most interesting. He was slightly shorter than me and wore thin-framed glasses and always dressed to the nines with colors of vivid style. He was what they called an extremist or free radical to the prohibition movement. It probably contributed to his unshaven facial hair that was left in a thinly shaven beard and goatee.

With his money and power, he persuaded the community into taking part in his nightly speakeasy, which was becoming more popular than Sunday Church. It was big, bright and flashy with live music and booze as far as the eyes could see.

As we continued to zoom past other vehicles and pedestrians, he asked, "When were you born?"

"July twenty-seventh, nineteen-hundred." I said quieter than I intended.

"What was that?" He asked.

I repeated myself as I looked him in the eyes for a split second. I'm sure the question was intended to ask my age. I didn't elaborate further.

"That makes you twenty-six then?" He smiled a strange smile.

"That's correct, sir." I looked out the window, realizing that we were nearing the destination.

We pulled back onto the street by the gallery and he put on the brakes, which stopped traffic behind us. "Well, Guy, you said that you wanted to make your meeting on time." He jeered.

I couldn't help but laugh. We had just met last night after a fellow of mine suggested that I take over for a singer that dropped out last minute. That same fellow told me not to take it personally if Tony didn't recall my name for, he never did with anyone. Yet, he just did.

"I sure did." I smiled in concert with his. "Well thank you, kindly." I ran my fingers through my coarse, blonde hair to make sure that my part wasn't disrupted. I opened my door.

"Ah." Tony sounded off as he placed his hand on mine. I looked down as my face turned a dark shade of red. I was in no fancy to be embarrassing myself around Mister Reynolds. "The painting?"

My head jolted in his direction. "Oh, you meant now?"

He let go of my hand, which was holding the painting in question, and held out his palm like he was waiting for a wad of cash. I handed him the eight by ten canvas and smiled solemnly.

Thinking that I was to expect no immediate payout, I started to exit the vehicle. “Wait a moment.” I heard him say from inside the cab. I turned around and poked my head back inside. “Here you are!” He held out a closed fist. I put my hand underneath and he dropped a load of bills into it.

“This is…” I was at a loss for words. “Thank you.”

“Wait, Guy, do you know ‘Bye Bye Blackbird’?” He asked.

“Of course.” I smiled. It was a song by Gene Austin, whom Tony compared my singing to just last night. He told me that I was a singer who improvised most of my lyrics, which he liked. It was a trick that no singer in New York could pull off.

“Could you sing it tonight?”

“It’s a little slow for a speakeasy, don’t you think?”

“I think everyone will enjoy it so.” He pulled a lever and spun away from me on the sidewalk, leaving me still holding a roll of bills that I couldn’t believe.

My meeting didn’t go quite as planned. The owner of the gallery was looking for someone who didn’t have so much going on in their work. He called my paintings “ill attempts that are best kept behind closed doors", which I took bothersome.

No, my work was not meant for galleries just yet. I lived in a day and age where surreal work was more attention-grabbing. Even paintings of androgynous nudes set against fantastical backdrops were quite a shaker. My work did not fit the mold.

The walk home was brisk. The changing seasons left me cold in late autumn. I wished that I had brought my flat cap but nothing would go well with my pinstripes.

I opened the door to my third-floor apartment, which sat in a layout similar to a broom closet. I pulled out my copy of "Indiana" by MacDonald and Hanley and placed it gently on my phonograph surface. The main area of my apartment was painted a faint blueish white and had neat piles of newspapers by the window. Pieces of clothes littered the handles of the doors as well as the floor. I was without a fancy sitting room chair that was comfortable, so I sat in my windowsill and peered down into the world below me.

My day was, in large part, over but people continued to wheel and deal up and down the streets. New York was a town of constant movement so I looked upon its residents as instruments of the music I was listening to. It was an experience that often times inspired me to paint something of similar nature.

For fear that I would wear the record I stopped the needle early and put it away. I wasn't made of money, so buying music was rare. Sometimes I would go a day or two without eating just to afford a new record.

I should have been looking for work like a normal class stiff. However, I was not one for Wall Street like a fellow of mine, nor being a newsy like another fellow of mine. No, I was a man of integrity. If I couldn't make money doing what I loved then I would settle for the title of a starving artist.

I grabbed a newspaper off of the top of the stack. It had been days since I traced through one and I was curious as to what I was missing out on. The title, "ASL takes New York by Storm" caught my attention.

> *"The ASL (Anti-Saloon League) makes its presence known in New York for the first time since 1922. This weekend, five of its members, including newest member Ella Hastings, threw a speech-filled rally that crowded the streets of Manhattan. Almost two whole city blocks were affected by the event.*
>
> *'We are here, making our march through these filthy streets until the people of this great city listen to our words.' Cried spokeswoman Hastings at the opening of the congregation. Her mixed sentiments of New York alienated her from the audience. She then continued to degrade New York by stating that it is one of the few cities that is continuing to fight the Anti-Alcohol amendment. An uproar broke from anti-protestors proclaiming that New York was doing no such thing. 'Ah, but listen, sinners. It*

may not be taking place during the light of day but rest assured, there are men and women paving the road to hell as we sleep!'"

I dropped the piece of newspaper back onto the pile and rolled my eyes. There was quite a bit of the anti-alcohol movement that I had missed while shutting myself in during the beginning of the twenties. I couldn't believe that it was still a running problem.

After a short nap, I shot up and dressed myself for another night at my favorite new joint, "Eddie's". It was quite a walk from my home on Bedford Street in Manhattan. Tony bought out an old blacksmith shop and turned it into the most popular speakeasy in all of New York.

I stumbled into my bathroom to make sure I was cleanly shaven before I departed for the night. The room was so small that I usually left the door open. I had no curtain for my bathtub; so, I never spent more than ten minutes in the shower at a time. My eyes kept making quick glances to the floral tiled wall. It was slightly faded and stole my mind from time to time when I was deeply lost in thought.

I left with enough time to walk at my usual pace. I half wished that Tony would show up and offer to drive me there but alas, no such luck. I observed the faces passing me as I made my way through the New York hustle and bustle. I wondered where everyone else was heading.

I could feel the cold on my fingertips. I dug them into my front pockets. I often did this even when my hands weren't cold. It was the reason why I didn't get my job at the bank. The man interviewing me said he saw it as impersonal.

I watched a merry couple approaching from twenty feet in front of me. The man was flicking his cigarette into the street and laughing at something that his wife had said. I looked at the two in awe and wondered if I was to expect a future like that.

Upon my arrival, I saw my name, above the bar, beyond the gate and into the secret entrance, "Guy Linister." It practically glimmered on a board just above the door. I was officially listed as a featured singer. Butterflies swam through the basin of my stomach. "What do you think about that?" Tony's booming voice pounced from behind me as his hand draped the base of my neck.

"I'm speechless." I responded with great candor. "You're making it very difficult for me to feel humble, Mister Reynolds."

"That's Tony." He corrected. Our bodies turned to face each other. His hand jotted out and I took it with mine. We shook briefly.

"But how did you ever figure my last name?" I asked him as I looked up at the sign.

"I know things." He insisted with his thick Italian accent.

"Honey." A lady in a flapper getup came out from the bar and moved between us with a beautiful smile. She had a slight gap between her front teeth. Her hair was short and a band pushed down just enough to see most of her forehead.

"Oh, Guy Linister, this is my wife, Laurel." He politely swung his left arm out so that we would shake hands. "You're going to be the calm before the storm, my friend. You're all set to open the night."

My nerves shot through me like hot mercury. "I'm starting now?" I gulped.

"Any moment now." He was smiling.

"So, what'll you have to drink?" Laurel asked me in a voice just as pretty as her outer appearance. I could smell the scent of jasmine and wild flowers wafting from her as people passed us. "My treat." I could see why he was with her. She was bedazzling.

She led me past many people on our way to the bar that I felt dizzy. I hadn't seen anything like it. It looked even more packed than yesterday. There were round tables sitting on the edge of the dancing area by the stage. Each had three chairs surrounding them and a vase of flowers as a centerpiece.

I tried to remember my performance from yesterday and concluded that there weren't quite as many decorations as there were now. It was like the entire place had a huge transformation since. My eyes roamed in every direction. I instantly understood the appeal of the speakeasy. It was flashy and bright and had smiles in every direction. It felt as though I had walked into a place of complete peace as well as organized chaos. It was miraculous.

Everyone was talking and laughing so fast that the whole joint seemed to be a blur to me. I kept pace behind Laurel, her perfect smile looking back at me every few seconds. The music grew louder and louder as people swayed in all directions. I dodged three of them to keep up with her.

I watched Laurel take a seat and make eyes for the bartender. He was preoccupied, so, I continued to watch her for a few minutes. She twirled her hand in circular motions and turned to look at me with a charismatic smile. Every action that she made was like magic, it had me entranced and mesmerized. She had endless curves and an iconic smile.

Eventually he came to take her order. "A lemon martini, please." I said in a meek voice when she finally turned around to address me with her question again.

"That's sissy stuff." She shot and placed my ordered.

When she handed me the hourglass filled with liquid, I responded with, "I'll show you sissy stuff," and took to the stage.

I had to shimmy my way through the packed room to get there. The mingled faces were looking at me with mixed and drunken expressions. Everyone seemed to be transfixed on my movements in the crowded silence.

The spotlight cast upon my face, and within seconds, the band began to play "Bye Bye Blackbird". I swam through the song like nothing. My nerves were a thing of the past with the glorious liquid that filled my veins. Afterward, the band leader Robby whispered in my ear, "Are you ready to improvise?" He was smiling a devilish grin.

Robby wasn't just the band leader, he was also my best friend. He was the reason why I was here to begin with. He stood next to me on stage, towering over me with his all black suit and tie that matched his hair, which was pushed back and out of his face. It normally hung over his forehead and cluttered his sight. The sight of it being so tidy completed the perfect atmosphere of the night.

I simply nodded and begged for the band to continue. I was relishing in my spotlight. The song I began to sing was one with lyrics of rain drops and floral numbers on blonde women. I was singing about Laurel and for a few brief seconds I sang it to her as well. She picked up on my words and began to blush.

I didn't intend for the lyrics to sound like I was trying to pick her up for myself. I just wanted her to know how impressionable she was. I was jealous of Tony. Her dreamy eyes weren't breaking focus with mine. She bobbed back and forth but never relinquished eye contact. I began to blush back but the spotlight luckily hid it.

The crowd was eating up every last word I sang. I didn't

understand where this side of me was coming from. I could do anything at this moment. I watched as the lights danced in the joint. Everything was spinning slightly from the booze. The people in the audience reminded me of the New Yorkers below the window of my flat; crazed and spinning in directions of their own devices.

As the music began to grow from a slower ballad to a tiptoed beat, I watched Tony approach me from the audience. People were dancing much slower. I swung over the side of the stage with the inkling that he was trying to speak to me. "Follow me!" He yelled above the crowd and pulled me off of the stage with one hand.

He was leading me to a stairway off to the side of the dancefloor. He walked through the doorframe that had no door, up the stairs and into the darkness. I followed, nearly falling twice. I could begin to hear his heels clicking as he neared the top. We reached a balcony area that stood above the rest of the hall.

"This place is incredible. I didn't even know that this was here." I shouted to him, peering down in to the intoxicated faces of the crowd.

The view from this balcony was amazing. There were lights from the crowd dancing on the rest of the room as people moved in perfect unison to the music. I couldn't help but watch as I had from my window, every day, at the citizens of New York, hustling and bustling.

I had heard among friends that Tony Reynolds wasn't one to dance but he began to sway slightly. Dancing was a big deal. I had often heard of people who didn't dance and not the other way around. So, I followed suit and shook my hips to the music. "So why are we up here? Was there something you needed to tell me?" I inquired.

"Sort of." He responded. I watched as he tore his tie loose and unbuttoned the top two buttons of his shirt. We were men, so this wasn't a big deal. With women it would have been considered a social faux pas.

I waited in the music for him to elaborate on his statement but he sat back in his sway for comfort. It was minutes before he continued with, "I think that you are a very talented artist. I think you're really going places. How would you like to perform weekly here?" He asked.

"I would love to." I responded in hardly a second's time.

"Good. We'll start here. Then, as soon as I open my next few clubs, we'll take New York by storm." His eyes were gliding along the room behind me as he shouted to me from a foot away. I watched as his body moved to the music.

"You're planning on more places like this one?" I asked as my head felt like it was falling into a fish bowl. This was the first time I drank alcohol, besides using it for medicinal purposes in the past. I wasn't sure what was going on.

"Why yes! These speakeasies will take New York by storm. This ban on alcohol will never know what's coming!" He smiled like he was enjoying a private joke.

We continued to dance along to the music and before long, the song was over. There was a cheer from the crowd and the place went dark. As the crowd's hollers began to die, I could hear the sounds of people moving around below us.

I felt warm, nervous hands pull me in and lips lock to mine. In a sudden instant, I realized that it was Tony and this whole situation was a game changer.

CHAPTER 2:
THE NAME OF THE GAME

I had a weird taste in my mouth when I woke up at home. I felt dizzy and didn't bother trying to make myself presentable. This was just another day, after all, and I had no one to impress. I was a dewdropper. But what happened last night? I had no memory.

Visions blazed through my mind. I recalled drinking and performing and Laurel. Her smile drove circles in my head. Then I remembered Tony and suddenly rolled over, falling out of bed.

I got up and sipped water from the faucet and swished it around my mouth until I came to the conclusion that I didn't need to freshen my breath. As I stared at my reflection, there was a loud knock at the door.

I walked up to the front door and looked through the peephole for a second before collecting my thoughts. It was Tony

Reynolds. All of the events from the night before rushed back and I wondered if he remembered as well. "Good morning, Mister Reynolds." I said as I opened the door slowly.

"Good afternoon, and you can call me Tony." His face was serious but still carried a sense of softness.

I looked down to find that I was still in my night trousers. "Will you excuse me for just a moment?" I didn't want to be rude and shut the door but I also didn't want him to see me in all of my morning glory either. I invited him in with a motion of my hand and quickly dug through my wardrobe in a hurry as not to come across disheveled.

"It's quite alright, Guy." His spoke calmly. "You can stay as you are. I just wanted to take you out for the day. I had a few things that I wanted to go over with you."

"How could I possibly stay as I am?" I was being figurative. I continued to pull on some slacks and grabbed a white button up. I wasn't sure where he would be taking me but I assumed by his character that it would be high class.

I wanted to tell him to "beat it" after last night's fiasco. I thought "What was a little bit of fame with sacrifice in return?" After all, wasn't I asking for something ludicrous? I threw on my clothes as fast as I could and put on my best tie, a satin black. My favorite.

He was sitting on the only chair that I had. It sat right next to the front door. It was a piece of furniture that I inherited from my mother. She had great taste and loved the Victorian era, so it was a piece from that period that had lots of embellishments and dim coloring of off blue and gold.

"Can I offer you something to drink?" I asked, trying to be polite. I didn't want the only person interested in my work to think ill of my hospitality. Deep down though, I had no drink to offer.

"I don't suppose you have anything dry, do you?" He spoke with a sarcastic undertone.

"I do not. I'm sorry." I gave him an expression that said that I wasn't kidding. This whole situation was new to me.

"Well what *do* you have, exactly?" He was judging my income with this question. I didn't understand this about people of wealth. They assumed everyone leads the same lifestyle as they do and when they discover that you don't, they were instantly turned off.

"I have water." I said, honestly.

I was at a point where I couldn't make any mistakes. My head constantly replayed everything that was said. I had a lot to lose but I was afraid to admit it to myself. I knew that if I let Tony out of my life, I would not only lose my chance at selling my artwork but I would also lose his wife, Laurel.

So, truth be told, I didn't completely understand my feelings for her but she was an added bonus to my dealings with Tony. As I began to piece together last night, she became all I thought about.

A feat that even Tony wasn't doing.

"It's fine." Tony said. "I'm not thirsty anyways."

I was afraid to ask about his situation with Laurel. I had heard, once before, that some men had preferred the company of men. However, it wasn't anything that was considered normal. If Tony really was that way then I had to find a decisive way out of working with him, but still make money for my art. So far, he was my only lead, so, I decided to play the game.

"Alright, I'm ready." I smiled as I finished buttoning myself up. He returned the smile and I opened the door of my apartment for him. I walked out before him, but turned to lock it behind me. My neighbors were untrustworthy and I never cared to take any chances with them.

We walked silently down the few flights of stairs to the landing. I knew that he preferred the elevator but I didn't bother asking his preference. His hands went into his pockets as he followed along behind me.

As we left the building, I smiled at my landlord. He was sitting in the lobby with a deck of playing cards before him as if waiting for an opponent. I always played nice with my landlord because I was often late with my rent payment.

We walked into the brisk, New York air. I took a deep breath, mostly in attempt to try and get over my hangover. Tony waved his hands for a second and motioned towards the black automobile sitting on the curb.

"You sure like to park wherever you deem suitable, don't you?" I asked sarcastically, admiring his choice of parking.

"Why should I care? If the feds have a problem with my parking, they'll just take the bribe." He sounded quite demanding in his statement.

Tony wasn't perfect. He gave the impression that he could get away with anything so long as he paid for it, or at least that was what he thought. I didn't have a problem with this perspective. His attitude, however, I didn't agree with. I was a man who tried to be fair with everyone, while Tony believed that he could purchase happiness from people whose jobs it was to provide as much.

We got into his vehicle and he drove north to Bryant Park. There wasn't anywhere to park so he left his vehicle on the curb once again. He was fearless. We walked to the Lowell fountain and sat at the benches.

"I didn't even know that this was here." I confessed.

Tony explained where we were and what we sat in front of. A round, golden disk that emitted water from it's top, it sat on a foundation of beautiful embellishments. Each end had spouts jetting water into a small, strange-shaped pool. The entire area was encased in a square of trees that blocked us from the rest of the city. By the time I focused my attention back on Tony, I had missed a large chunk of what he had said.

"I come here to think from time to time." Tony paused to check and see if I was listening. Then, he began to talk with his hands. "That is, when there aren't people about. I like my privacy and, on busy days, I don't bother."

I was envious of his freedom. He didn't bother with anyone's thoughts of him. I wished that I could live like that. As an artist though, it wasn't a luxury that could be afforded. I was constantly judged. It was the only profession that couldn't be mathematically put to paper in any way, but was the first to be placed under a microscope.

"So, what did you bring me here to talk about?" My bluntness took grasp of my better judgement.

"I wanted to let you know that I really think you are quite a talented person. I believe that you don't realize just how powerful your work is. You might be afraid to be outspoken and tell people that your work is worthwhile but it is. You see," he continued, "if you don't tell people what they like then they will have mixed feelings. You have to convince them that what you do is what they like, otherwise you're wasting your time."

I had never heard anyone put it that way and it took a second to comprehend it fully. As I sat and ingested it, I realized he was right. If I sat back and waited for others to understand what I did then no one would take the second needed to truly enjoy it. I would have to interject and make them think that it was a trend, something that others have already discovered. That way, I'd make them feel like they were missing out.

"Wow. I never thought of it that way." I said, completely flabbergasted.

"No one does. You see, that's why very few of us have made it in this field."

"What field?"

"The field of chumps. You have to remember that other people are not as bright as you and I. As long as you believe that you have something over them, you'll always be on top." He smiled as the words escaped his mouth.

I didn't quite agree with what he said, but his success stood as a reminder that I wasn't in the right frame of mind to make it. Maybe I was looking at life from a completely different perspective. What if all artists had to do was think that their material was worth the pitch and then actually make money doing it? If I wasn't one of those people, who would actually buy my paintings?

We sat in silence as I contemplated asking about last night. I was curious as to why he would make a move on me. I knew that he had been drinking. I tasted booze on his breath but I was afraid to bring it to light.

Instead I took the conversation to a less abrasive place. "So what night are we deciding on for my weekly performance?" It was a question that wasn't worth asking but steered attention away from the few topics that I was avoiding.

"Friday and Saturday." He answered after little thought. "Speaking of which, this is yours." He handed me a handful of cash that I wasn't expecting. It was rolled up tightly and meticulously.

"Tony, I can't accept this." I told him as I tried to push the money away.

"Tony? You just said my name without a 'mister' or even saying the entirety of it." He was astonished. "You must accept it." He continued to place the bills in my hand. This was the most money I had made in any month of my life. "You did a great job last night. I can't wait until this weekend."

The weekend came quicker than I had hoped. I didn't bother picking up shifts at the mill like I usually did to garner extra cash. Thanks to Tony, I had enough money to pay for half a year of rent. I went out and bought two whole outfits and a couple records that I had been dying to own.

I painted some, but I mostly sat in my happiness and became quite lazy. I looked out my window more at the world below me and wondered where they were headed. Where I was headed? What I was doing?

I somehow reflected my own personal growth onto the world around me. How I had gotten myself into this predicament? I wondered even further into the complications of its worth. Sure, I would be making money, but I would feel like I was degrading myself with any action that I took.

It was such a nice day out, that I decided to go for a walk and catch some sunshine before the winter began to kick in. I threw on the breeziest outfit that I owned, a full suit of beige and fluffed my hair in a direction that I deemed suitable. I left the house, nearly forgetting to shut the door.

I didn't have a lot of time before Tony wanted me to meet with him, but I felt like a walk was something I needed to do. I wanted to breathe in the air of the changing seasons, one of my favorite sensations.

I reached a dock that I used to visit with Robby and began skipping stones. It was a great way to clear my mind, though, I never made a habit of it. I hated the idea of killing a fish by hitting it in the head with a rock.

There were cars behind me, honking up and down the streets. I tried not to focus on it. The water was crystal clear in the parts closest to me. In the distance, the waves sang a deep, dark blue that was inviting me for a swim, but I wasn't prepared to do any of the sort.

"Are you contemplating swimming as well?" A soft voice murmured to my right.

I turned to see a man around my age, who was slightly shorter than me. He hair was a light, red-brown color. He wore a white button up with a dark drown vest and pants that matched his hair. His face was round, though his physique was skinny. He had an innocent look on his face and his hands were nervously in his pockets.

"Actually, for a second there, I almost did." I responded truthfully. It was a rare occasion that a total stranger could ever guess what I was thinking.

"I could tell by the way you were looking in the water." His voice was a deep, popping bass. It had a strange somber tune; however, that made it seem less deep and manly.

I smiled in amusement but didn't say anything back. I looked back at the water with a similar pallor to the one I had before he had interrupted my train of thought.

"I'd be willing to jump in, if you are." He took a second and waited for me to look at him. "I'm Markel." His smile was nervous, like he was talking to a ghost and he kept blinking like I would disappear.

"Alright, I suppose it wouldn't hurt." I replied, looking at the water again.

He began to take his vest off and then his white button up. Then he began to undo his pants.

"What if someone sees?" I asked. This was not something anyone did during the light of day. This was a risqué thing a lower-class person would attempt.

"We're the only two people here. Who do you think will see?" He laughed as he pulled his trousers off.

I too, began to take each article of clothing off until I was in my undergarments. "After you." I swung my arm towards to the water and waited for Markel to protest.

Before I could react, he threw his body into the water with an immense energy and created a huge wave running in all directions. I jumped in behind him. The water engulfed me as the world went blank. I emerged from by the banks and grabbed the side of the dock.

"What are you doing?" Markel called from where I had just been.

"I can't really…" I coughed out water. "Swim."

He laughed and swam up to where I was, grabbing me by my sides and hoisting me on the land by the side of the dock. "Then what in the blazes are you doing in the water to begin with, you nutter!"

I stood, freezing now in the wind that blew through me. "I don't know. It seemed exciting." I wrapped my arms around myself to keep from chattering my teeth. "When I would swim in the past it was close to the shallow parts. That way, I wouldn't be afraid of drowning."

"Get back in here before you freeze." His eyebrows showed concern. "I'll teach you how to swim." His voice was confident, so I slowly entered the water and paddled in his direction.

"I'm Guy, by the way." I pulled my wet hair back and off my forehead.

We spent a few hours in the water, swimming and laughing about completely usual things in life. This was exactly what I needed.

"Do you ever get tired of having to get up and go to work every day? Do you ever just want to live in the middle of the woods and ignore society?" He asked, clear out of nowhere.

"Actually, yes." I replied in amazement. At least I wasn't the only one.

"I'm a finance advisor for a bank. What do you do?"

"Something similar." I responded, wondering what it is that I do now.

"Well," he huffed after a few seconds of silence, "if you ever want to swim again or even grab a drink, let me know." His, now confident, voice said. My eyebrows raised in question. "Oh, come on! Everyone in New York drinks." I noticed the right side of his mouth smiled wider than the left.

I smiled back. "Alright, come to Eddie's tonight."

"Isn't that one of those illegal joints?" He asked. His face became unreadable.

I realized that I might have said too much. "Well, it's more of..." I paused, thinking of what to say. "Yes." I came out with after a moment.

"Bees knees." He grinned, nodding his head. Each side of his smile reached the ends of his freckled face.

Later that day, I got dressed up and walked over to the home of a fellow Tony knew. He wrote the address down for me on a folded piece of paper. His handwriting was far from neat, almost illegible. After I deciphered the address, I noticed that it was twenty minutes from my apartment on foot, but I had promised to be there for a card game.

When I arrived, I had to be cleared by the security in the lobby. I gave them my name and hoped that I would be let up. I couldn't tell from the building's set up if it was an apartment or hotel.

There was a man that had to escort me through the building. He was tall and didn't speak. He acted like a policeman rather than a doorman. It felt like a long time before arriving at the destination.

The front door swung open after a short tap. "Ah, Guy, this is Morgan. He's an old-time friend of mine." Tony talked like he was really old but I was pretty sure that he was in his mid-thirties. I wouldn't have said it aloud but I was taken aback by the fact that Morgan was a dark man who lived in such a lavish place. As I shook his massive hand, I peered into the glint in his brown eyes. He was one of the most intimidating men I had ever seen. Yet, as he practically broke my hand with his grasp, he returned my reluctant smile with the most welcoming and warm expression.

We shook hands and I was introduced to everyone at the table as we sat down for a friendly game of poker. Morgan tipped his bowler hat to me with his left hand, and shook with his right hand. I felt misplaced as I looked at the faces around the table.

Three other men sitting with high shoulders and straight expressions. Everyone was quiet and intimidating. I sat at the only open seat at the table and looked at all of the strangers in front of me, trying not to catch Tony's glimpses.

The cards were dealt and I looked at my hand as if I had never played a game in my life. I didn't even know the rules so I sat back in silence and watched my opponent's faces during the game. I bet very little as I figured this was just a friendly game anyways.

Everyone looked at me. It must've been my turn to say something so I uttered the only words I knew in this situation. "Hit me." They all looked at me like I was a foreigner. I didn't bother asking how I was out of line. I should have mentioned that I had never played poker before but I was already out of place here.

"No, kid, you have to put down a hand. Make a bet!" Morgan

told me as I looked down at my cards. I wished that I was simply bluffing, but I was honest to God terrible at this game. I set my hand down except for a couple cards.

"Aren't you going to bet?" Another member of the game asked me.

I took a big gulp of the beer that they handed me before the game and said, "Oh no, I'm fine." I was hoping that I sounded intelligent. No one questioned my intent after that, which was good. I tend to learn quickly and made assumptions based on everyone else's actions.

The game wrapped up by nine o'clock and then we headed for the speakeasy. I was fortunate that there wasn't real betting involved because I had lost every hand.

I rode with Tony. His hand was placed on my thigh the whole way, although, I didn't bother saying anything. After all, part of my job was to make him happy, even if it was at my expense.

I walked in front of him and opened the door. He walked in and uttered the words "thank you" as he passed the threshold. I followed behind him and couldn't wait to hit the bar.

I sat down and ordered a beer in a tall pilsner glass. I figured I should stick to the same alcohol just to be safe. I just craved the feeling of being able to escape my mind. It was the best way to handle my situation.

I knew that if anyone was going to put me on the map it would be Tony Reynolds, so I didn't make a peep on my regard. I took large gulps and waited for my cue. I had heard that tonight, I was singing with a female named Peggy. She was from the Bronx and sang duets with other class name acts. I assumed that she was paid heavily to come and help up my appeal. We were to sing "By the Beautiful Sea". It was a hit from 1914 and a personal favorite.

I slammed my beer down and waited for Tony to introduce me to her. He was nowhere to be found, though, so I ordered another drink. This time I asked for a martini.

"Another Lemon Martini?" Laurel asked me as she sat at the bar stool next to me. She seemed even more interested in me than last time. Her outfit was somehow even shinier. It was a bright white in contrast to the silver she was wearing last night. It was angelic.

"Why yes, do you have a problem with that?" I asked in a teasing manner.

The band played in the background. They slowly transitioned into a slow song that I had never heard before. I listened intently in the silence of our conversation.

"No, I don't. I actually find it quite amusing. You're different from other men that I have met. You don't think about social graces. You do what you please and wait for convictions later." She spoke like a poet and captivated me in ways that I didn't wish to admit out loud. I wondered how she got caught up with a creep like Tony to begin with.

Tony was inviting with every nature of his actions but there was this sense of cynicism to his principles. He went places and did things solely for self-motivation, which got him where he wanted to be. But was he happy? Was Laurel happy?

"I'll take that as a complement." I told her as our talk began to take serious avenues. "Make that a gin and tonic." I told the bartender as I kept my eyes on her. "So how did you and Tony meet?" I asked.

"Believe it or not, I used to dance for a club in the Upper Eastside. He convinced me that I could make more dough in a speakeasy and slowly paid my way into the spotlight. We became an item shortly after and he popped the question. After that, I didn't bother keeping up appearances. I could simply use his finances to do as I wished."

So, it was the money then. She must have wanted more than that. She couldn't be a person of luxury and physical possessions. *Could she?*

I wanted to ask if she was happy but I knew what position she was in so I zipped my kisser tight and changed the subject. "I'd love to sing with you."

Her face turned red for a few seconds. "Wouldn't you?" Her attitude mirrored to that of Tony's. It was as if she picked up a thing or two from him. "Nah, I don't belong on stage anymore. I'll leave the performance art to professionals like you."

"But I don't even consider myself a performer. I'm more of a painter." I told her. "This is something that Robby got me into."

"Ah, the band leader." She smiled. "He's quite the looker." I instantly felt jealous. I had known Robby my whole life. He was quite the lady's man, and he got away with murder with even the prettiest woman. It was a gift I wished I had.

"Yeah, that's Robby." I agreed. "He's the one who convinced me to take the stage the other night." I told her.

"I'm glad." She said as her eyebrows rose. "You're quite the talent."

"Thank you but like I said, I'm more of a painter." I told her. At this point, we were both on our second drink. I wondered if I was going to be able to sing.

"Well I'd love to see your work." She was smiling in a way that made me question her intent. I pondered Mister Reynolds' intent with her and considered the possibility that she wasn't really satisfied with him.

I wanted so badly to tell her the truth about her husband but instead I replied, "Maybe one day you will." I returned her smile but I wasn't too convincing.

"Guy, this is Peggy." Tony came up half a minute later with a gorgeous redhead with wavy, curly hair. She curtsied instead of shaking my hand and laughed. It gave me chills, but was playful and teasing. The stage light struck her eyes and the brilliance that emanated from them was an indescribable hue. It was as if I had just discovered color for the very first time. She was magnificent.

"I'm Guy." I felt like an idiot and held out my hand for a return of favor. I was not used to meeting women. I was pretty anti-social growing up. I kept to my family and close family friends. No actual girls or even guys from school.

"I'm Peggy." She said mockingly.

Tony saw the way we looked at each other and ushered us to the side of the stage to await our cue. He took to his wife's side and swayed to the end of the song that was playing. As I stood against the side of the stage, I noticed a familiar, round face looking at me from the crowd. It was Markel. I waved politely.

I had barely a second to interact with Peggy before things picked up. She gave me a strained expression and I didn't know how to react to it. Instead, I stayed quiet.

They announced our number and we both stood side by side and began to sing. We mesmerized the crowd with our voices and didn't even have to harmonize. It was a magical moment. I knew everyone was here for her but I sang my heart out and tried to out-win their favor. Part of me wanted to leave the joint with her and forget about it all. It was the side of me that was already drunk.

We finished to grand applause. We fulfilled our purpose. I

left the stage and tried to exit the Speakeasy. I wanted no more of this game. I was ready to pay the piper and move on with my life.

I caught Peggy's attention as we walked off the stage in unison. I tried to say something to her but she shrugged me off. I couldn't tell if she was being rude or if she had even noticed me.

I kicked a nearby waste bin and hobbled my way past the bar. "Where are you going?" Tony asked me as I opened the front door.

I looked him square in the eyes and gave up. There was no argument to his question. I knew that if I continued with my lifestyle that I would have to work the streets again and try to convince people to like my work. But was it really any different here? Who really knew who I was? After all, they were here for the booze. The only one who was really looking out for my interests was Tony and deep down he was only looking out for himself.

CHAPTER 3:
SHE'S SOMETHING, AIN'T SHE?

"Come on. Follow me." He announced after seconds of battling with our eyes.

I followed him up the same stairwell that we had visited before. I already knew what to expect this time but I followed anyways. I didn't question his intent as I did so. I was too far gone to think for myself.

The band played as he danced. "I know you like to shimmy just as well." He said in an attempt to get me to follow suit. I did and he was right. I loved to dance, but I wasn't used to doing it and I didn't bother mentioning it to anyone.

We danced on for a few minutes as the song lasted longer than expected. I let go of all sense of control and danced moves that I didn't know I had. It felt good to let go. My mind raced, my arms moved, and my senses soared as my feet stepped in all directions.

Every once in a while, I glimpsed at Tony. His expression was deep and drunk but he was still smiling. His marriage with Laurel was everything that I could ever dream to have, yet, he was here dancing with me. I wondered what Tony's intentions were. The inner-ticking of his mind seemed to be one of the most interesting things.

After the song concluded, his hands found my backside once more and his mouth met mine. I didn't fight him away, even though his tongue dug deep into my throat. My mind was lost in workings that I didn't fully comprehend. Besides, if I pushed away, I would be pushing away any meaningful future that I had. I was a hopeless mess.

After minutes of his advances, I finally pushed him off just slightly and asked, "What about Laurel?" It was a bold move but we were both drunk, and I had nothing to lose. I needed resolve.

"She would kill me if she found out." With that, he drove his tongue back into my mouth.

I felt a sense of excitement in the situation. I didn't want to admit it but no one had taken as much interest in me before. From the looks of outsiders, I knew that I was appealing aesthetically, but I never saw anyone act upon it. I was too chicken shit to do so myself. It made me feel good even though I knew it was wrong. Men didn't like men. It was a fact. But did I?

His hands caressed my back and I felt a strange sensation take over me. In that moment, I knew it wasn't what I wanted. I pulled away to see the look on his face and caved again.

He pulled me into another embrace and didn't ask for forgiveness. I felt his hands move south towards my behind. I tore away once more and gave him a glare that I never would have thought could escape from me. "What? I like to make my friends happy." He said with little to no explanation.

"What would you think tomorrow?" I asked him trying to provoke guilt.

"Sex." was all he replied with. It was vague enough to get away with murder but answered enough for me not to ask further. I was stuck between a rock and hard place.

I tried to embrace the moment for what it was worth; to drop every stereotype I had picked up in the course of my life and embrace Tony for the being that he was. It wasn't an easy feat but the feature that stood out to me was his attention to risk. He had made his living on the outcasts of the government and won. Which meant that I was one of them. Was my work really worth its salt?

I kissed him back with the same velocity that he solidified within me. Was I kissing back because I felt passion or lust in what I wanted to achieve? In that moment, I wasn't sure but I did know that if I wanted to make anything of myself, I would have to do what Laurel did with marrying him. Luckily, there was no court that would have our marriage.

I excused myself to the restroom in an attempt to find Markel. He was sitting close to the bar, alone. "You made it." I smiled.

"Yeah." His eyes looked drunkenly back at me. There was a smile mirroring mine in his face. "Boy, you can sing!"

I thanked him and gave him my address. "If you ever want to accompany me again, let me know. I'm sure we'll have more time to talk next time."

I liked Markel. He was easy to be around and didn't talk a whole bunch. He kept life simple. Which was something that was becoming hard to come by nowadays.

A few weeks went by in similar fashion. Being someone's play toy grew tiresome. It was a Sunday morning and I was flipping through newspapers when I heard a brief knock at my door. I wasn't expecting company.

I made sure that I was fully dressed before cracking the door open. It was Robby. This was quite a surprise, considering the last time he had shown up unannounced was the day that he needed someone to stand in for his singer who went AWOL. Before that, it had been two years since I had seen him. He used to show up at my place, trying to get me out of the house. I had a long bout of depression at the time. He eventually gave up and quit coming.

"Well, hi." I said, awkwardly. We didn't have a speaking relationship, really. Even as children we were boys of little word.

"Hey. I wanted to stop by and see how you were." He spoke slowly as if he was worried I would close the door on him.

"Please, come in." I offered, noticing his reluctance to make the first move. He was wearing short shorts with a striped tank top.

"Actually, I was wondering if you wanted to go for a dip in the bay, like old times." His voice sounded hopeful.

Maybe I was through being alone. Maybe there was more to life that I was missing out on. Four years had passed since I found myself with a social calendar.

"It's a tad late in the season, don't you think?" I was apprehensive, even though the day looked sunny from my windows.

"It's hot as blazes out there, trust me." He was smiling an old, familiar smile. "And it's not like you swim anyway."

We went to our favorite spot on the lower west side. There were docks and with a sandy beach that had the perfect amount of shade. Trees littered the shoreline. It was a hot and sunny day but we didn't swim.

"So, tell me something." He began, intent on hearing my every word. "Do you plan on doing this full time?" He asked about the music gig.

We were sitting on the docks with our feet grazing the top of the water. "I'm not entirely sure. You know that I— "

"You want to be a painter, I know." He broke in. "But Guy, you're the only person I know who can improvise the way that you do. I used to come over to your house, back in the day and find you and your— " He paused. "Well, you're just... You have a knack for it. That's all." He looked a little nervous. I could tell there was more on his mind.

"Your singer disappeared, didn't he?" I asked, wanting to cut to the chase.

"Guy, that's not all." Robby was folding the frays of his shorts in an attempt to not have to make eye contact with me. "I think you've spent too much time, wasting away in that house. You need to get out. Make some friends." He paused. "Make some money. I think that taking this gig with Anthony Reynolds is your best bet. We just started this weekly set three months ago and I've had no money troubles since."

That was more words than he had spoken in a very long time. I could tell he had been thinking about talking to me on this occasion since our last performance or even since the first one. "Robby, I don't want to give up my painting to be a showman."

"Then don't!" He stammered. "You only have to do two performances a week. You have plenty of time to do your painting bullshit." I shot him a glare. "You know what I mean." He raised his eyebrows. "I like your paintings. I just think that if someone's paying you to do something as simple as singing nine or ten songs a week with a tall bill, you should oblige." He continued to shrug. "You could even use the money to fund your painting."

His words were convincing. I couldn't argue with his statement. I just wanted to make sure that I was making this decision for me. That I was performing every week because it was in my own interests and given everything that has followed since I started, I wasn't entirely sure of it.

"Well I appreciate you looking out for me." I patted his thigh, lightly.

"You're like a kid brother to me." His smile pulled up on one side.

"Robby, we're the same age." I reminded him, despite him always calling me that.

"Oh, I know." He continued to smile, looking out at the boats in the bay.

A few days later, Tony invited me to an outing with his high-class friends on a boat in the harbor. I dressed as neatly as I could in layers just in case it got cold. I wanted to be able to take some of them off, if needed.

I was picked up by a taxi that was employed by Tony. The driver spoke maybe four words the entire way to the docks and dropped me off in silence. I wondered why he wasn't the one who drove me this time.

My question was answered when I arrived and saw a handful of people dressed similarly to Tony, all talking and rubbing elbows with clear glasses in their hands. They must be in the same social circles as he was. One clue was the fact that they were drinking in broad daylight on the most popular private dock in New York.

I strode up to them with an expression that left my demeanor open to interpretation. My hands were concealed in my pockets and my shoes were anything but freshly polished. I was clearly out of my league.

I got lucky when Robby came up from my left side and swung his arm under mine and locked our elbows. "Oh buddy, how I am glad to see you." His voice flew by quickly.

I was a bit taken aback by the fact that he was here. Did Tony invite him? Why? "Me too." I mirrored, but it was obvious that I was saying it for cosmetic reasons. "Why *are* you here?" I cut to the chase.

"Laurel invited me." My heart sank. Of course she did. If anyone had to choose between Robby and I they would clearly choose him. He was not only more handsome but his way with words was more natural and always worked in his favor. He was what they called a cake-eater.

Speak of the devil. Just as he said it, she walked in between us. "Good morning gents." Her voice was deep and quick. "Ready for some sailing?"

I wanted to answer but Robby's perfect words found themselves out quicker than mine. "Only if you're ready for some music." He made a quick hand motion towards a couple of carrying cases against the inner railing of the boat. I assumed they were instruments. Maybe she invited him for entertainment purposes. Suddenly my heart steadied because I knew that had to be it.

We all boarded the ship and I found within an hour that Tony seemed to be ignoring me. I talked on and off with Laurel and Robby but waited for the moment that Tony would try and make his dig at me. After all, wasn't that the reason why I was there?

"So, you write?" Laurel asked me during a one on one that we began to have on the very backend of the boat. We were alone for the first time during the trip and I figured that she was just making casual conversation which, for some reason, excited me.

"Yes and no." I responded, thinking hard about the question. I watched her blondish hair sway in the wind. It caught the sun with each curve.

Her eyebrows rose slightly as she went on to ask, "What do you mean by that?"

"I guess I'm not very good at writing. I'm more so a poet on the spot." I didn't know how to explain it, which was obvious but I didn't want to look like a phony. "I used to listen to a lot of early records that my mother had. Mostly ones with little to no singing. I learned from those, how to sing off of the top of my head." I had hoped that the explanation that I had come up with was good enough for her.

"So then, you don't write any music at all?" She looked disappointed. Why did she seem so content with asking me?

"I mean, I guess I could." I was stuttering.

"Oh goodie!" She smiled like a high school girl. After a few seconds of silence, she followed up with, "you know, if you were looking, we have some giggle water downstairs."

She was, of course, referring to the alcohol they had on board. I wasn't so sure about getting gussied up, however. I had enough of the juice as of late. "Oh, no, I'm good, thank you." I told her with quite a few pauses. "Why were you asking?" I was tracing back to her questions about music writing.

"I've always thought about working with a songwriter to make music. I cannot write for myself, you see, and I want to do something that people aren't expecting." She explained.

"So then, you want to take to the spotlight again?" I asked in contradiction to her statement from the other week.

"I suppose if I have the right writer and duet partner." She winked at me. I wasn't sure what she was trying to do so I didn't bother asking.

"I'm in." I smiled a wide, hopeful smile as she patted my head and walked off.

Just as my heart began to beat incessantly, I noticed a redheaded figure through a mess of people to my left. It was Peggy. It was like my insides were being torn in two different directions. On one end, Laurel was prancing into the distance on my right and, on the other, my curiosity was pulling me to the left.

So, I swallowed my fears and wished I had taken up Laurel's offer of booze. I found myself in her presence within uncountable seconds. She was giggling to something unknown that a gentleman next to her must have said. Again, I found myself unable to speak to her. Her eyes found my face and her expression turned curious, almost whimsical. "Can I help you?" Her eyebrows rose slightly as she asked.

"I was just wondering if you cared for a dance?" I blundered.

"Not at the moment, thank you." Her facial expression deepened and she turned back to the man on her right.

I walked back to where I had been standing before and started to mentally kick myself. What possessed me? Walking up to a complete stranger. A famous stranger at that. I must have been the stupid man alive.

Tony walked up a few moments later and put his arm around

my neck. I was looking out at New York from the couple hundred feet distance that we had made. "Here you are!" I found myself saying like I had been waiting for him.

"She's something, ain't she?" He asked me, presumably about his wife, who was walking in front of our view.

"Yeah, she's quite the bearcat." I replied without thinking. My mind stared blankly at her as she continued through the doors in front of me.

"She was my first big purchase. I had always wanted a boat, growing up. Care for a jorum of skee?" He asked, bearing a flask with his initials on it.

"I'll have to pass." I smiled to be polite.

"Then, perhaps, you'd like some wine." He didn't bother waiting for my response. He turned around and walked inside and out of sight.

He came back moments later with a globe of a dark, purple red wine. I took it from him and said, "I thought you were going to be getting me today."

"All more of a reason that I should get you a blower." He said quickly.

"A blower?"

"Yes. A telephone. That way I can let you know when plans change. Granted, I wasn't planning on stopping by your place."

I almost asked him why but then I reminded myself that I wasn't the one who was looking for attention from the other in this situation. "You know that I don't need all that fancy stuff. I'm happy with what I have." I told him.

"Nonsense. I'll get you a telephone along with an updated radio. You can't play records for the rest of your life. You'll have to join the rest of us and listen to what's sizzling." He lit a cigar and looked at me like he was holding in a secret. I didn't bother asking what it was.

Music began to play in the distance. I knew that it was Robby so I graciously walked past Tony, looking him in the eyes as I did so and continued to the other side of the ship. I wanted to see how content Laurel was at watching him. I had a sneaky notion that the two of them might have something going on. And with how absentminded Tony was with her, I wouldn't be the least bit surprised.

I reached the back of the small crowd that was forming around Robby and his two horn players. He sat at an upright piano that they must have wheeled out to the deck just before the performance. As I stood there, Tony came up from behind me with the bottle of wine and poured more into my glass. He must have guessed that I wouldn't waste wine.

I voiced my thoughts on wine quite stupidly as it was beginning to kick in. He responded with, "That's why I do it," and winked.

I watched as Laurel's eyes watched his performance like a sailor's wife awaiting a ship in the distance. She was so focused on him. I began to grow a tad jealous. It was just minutes before I jumped between the members of the crowd and stood in front of the band.

Everyone looked at me like I was crazy but my tipsy-soaked mind begged me to take the spotlight. I began to belt out something guttural that matched the music flawlessly. It was a song about clear days and fair-faced dames. It was a sure-to-wow them type of lyric that I was storing up my sleeve while watching Laurel's eyes just minutes ago.

When the song ended, everyone clapped. Robby grabbed my shirt and yanked me down the stairway, towards the cabin. "What on Earth are you trying to do, buddy?" He asked me. I could tell that he was slightly irritated.

"What do you mean?" I asked back, playing the innocent role.

"They billed me for this show. They didn't mention anything about singing." He paused and looked long and hard at me. "Especially from you."

"What's that supposed to mean?" I looked him dead in the eyes. Our glares were enough to start fires. He was very typically condescending. I decided to pry on his illicit problem with alcohol. "Everyone knows that you're a cellar smeller."

"Excuse me?" He blew in my face. "I'm clean. If anything,

I'm here for Laurel." His words were like knives.

"Laurel?" I asked, dropping the charade of hurting his feelings.

"Yes, she asked me to be here. I think she fancies me and to be honest, I kind of fancy her as well." He explained.

I thought about it all for a second and took a breath. "I'm sorry, my friend, I just wasn't expecting you to be so angry with me."

"It's completely fine. To be honest, I don't know what came about me." He replied. "I guess I just want to make sure that she sees me."

"Boys? Everything okay?" A mousy faced, brunette came down the stairs and glared at me with piercing eyes.

"Everything's fine, Ruth." Robby's face looked a tad bit shocked.

As she turned to walk back up the stairs, I whispered, "She's married, you know… Laurel." I was hoping that there wasn't something that he knew that I didn't.

"I know. Oh boy, oh boy, I know." He said, half-delusional.

"What the hell's the problem down here?" Tony pushed past the lady and came between us on the stairs, shooting me a look that I couldn't place.

"Everything is alright, Mister Reynolds. How are you, sir?" Robby asked him with his lip turned up. He was trying to play it cool.

"Fine, thanks. Just wanted to make sure you were good to go for another few songs."

"Yes, of course, sir. One moment." Robby replied.

"Make it snappy." Tony clicked his fingers a few times and left in a rush.

"Show time." Robby smiled, jokingly. Then he ran up the stairs to locked arms with the dark-haired lady and returned to the stage with Tony and I following behind.

They played a couple more songs and I watched as Laurel's eyes stayed put on Robby. There was this burning in my chest as I downed two more glasses of wine. I couldn't help but feel betrayed by my own friend. But how was he to know that I even had feelings for her?

After his set was over, he unbuttoned his shirt and went below deck. I watched as Laurel followed. I got up from my seat and went to follow but I was stopped by Tony. "Where do you think you're heading?" There was a faint smile on his face but I wasn't sure what I could get away with at this point in the evening. I thought, in the back of my head, about how many drinks he had had and decided to sit put for the time being.

We sat down and talked briefly for a minute or two when I

said casually, "Where did Laurel run off to?"

His head swam in every direction and his eyes roamed about the boat. "I don't know. Probably sleeping with someone." I wasn't sure whether he was being sarcastic or not. Was that something that she did often?

"You don't seriously think that she— "

"No. I'd like to believe that I married someone with more class than that." He spoke with a sarcastic tone and got up from his seat to walk to the entrance of the cabin.

I followed with my hands in my front pockets. As we entered the dining area of the boat, Laurel and Robby came out from a back hall with smiles on their faces. "Laurel, what in the hell is going on?" Tony's voice was sober. This was the angriest I had ever seen him and sadly, the least liquored. At least, he seemed pretty sober when he spoke.

"Tony, what is your deal? Robby and I were working on a song." She shouted in a soft voice.

"Yes, that was all Mister— " Robby began.

"You, be quiet and get out of here." Tony grabbed his collar and yanked him forward to shout in his face. Then he let go and threw his hands in all directions.

Robby didn't hesitate. He left the room with his horn in hand.

"Tony, don't do this, please." She pleaded. I kind of felt bad for her but I didn't know what really took place and I didn't want to write her out as a saint just yet.

"You're a whore." Tony spat. "I don't want to deal with this right now." He put a few fingers to his temples and turned to walk in circles. "Do you want a divorce? Is that it?" He continued yelling.

"No, Tony, common' you know that you're the only guy for me. I'm not fooling around with the bandleader." She tried to convince him.

I sat back and awkwardly watched the two of them. I felt like I had perpetuated this fight. I wanted to leave the room but I thought it would appear rude, so I just stood there in the background like a shadow.

For some strange reason, watching the two of them, I couldn't decide whose energy felt more thrilling to me. I instantly thought that Laurel was more physically appealing. But now, watching Tony with his fire after seeing how offputtingly charismatic he usually is, I felt dazed. Sure, I thought that Tony was pretty much a creep on the surface but my artist side wanted to know what was fueling that flame.

I wanted to know exactly how the pair met and what it is that I found so irresistible about them. I also wanted to know how I fit between the two.

Just as I thought the storm had struck and all that was left was the debris, there was a loud bang that seemed to be coming from the other end of the ship.

"It's the booze buggies, guys!" Shouted a voice from upstairs. Everyone in the hallways began to scramble to get to the upper decks and out of the dining halls. Screaming began to erupt.

Tony & Laurel looked over at me, their faces instantly drained of color. Tony walked over to the wall and pulled a bowler hat off of a rack. "We have to get to the spare life boats on the south end of the ship without being caught by the booze bashers." He spoke in a clear, yet frantic tone of voice.

"Let's be sure not to split up." Laurel followed and drew her jacket across her breast.

I could tell that the two of them had done this before. It was a very spot-on strategy. "How do you know what side is south? Should I cover up as well?" I asked the two frantically, just realizing that my jacket and flat top were with the coat check on the upper deck.

"Don't worry 'bout it. We may need to swim." Tony half joked.

"Don't listen to him, kid. We should be fine." Laurel's voice took on a motherly characteristic.

We bustled through a door behind me that I didn't know existed. It was a long hallway that led to the north end of the ship.

"Aren't we going in the wrong direction?" I asked the two of them.

"Yes," Tony began in a hushed voice, "but this is the only way to the upper decks that are probably free of anyone waiting to detain us!"

"Where are we—" but before I could finish, I realized that we were at the foot of a long ladder that led up to a hatched exit way whose door had gleams of light shining down from its four sides.

"Ladies first." Tony spat bitterly.

"Just go!" Laurel pushed me in front of them.

I wiggled my way up the later. It led to a dark corridor that continued forever. There were beams of light peeking through in small circles on the way to the end of the hallway. I pushed a door open at the end and found a police man tracing paths in circles in the room. He was banging a long black object against his left hand. I retracted my steps to the right and Tony pushed passed me with his fists raised.

Before I could even blink the copper was on the floor and more light bellowed out of the doorway to the left of where I was standing. Everything happened so quickly. I didn't even have two seconds to compose my thoughts.

"The life boats are gone!" Tony shouted in frustration. "We'll have to swim."

"You can't be serious!" Laurel yelled back. "This is an outrage!"

Before any of us could object, a policeman came up from behind us with a gun. "Stand right where you are!" He shouted in nervousness.

"You don't wanna do this, fella!" Tony reasoned. "Do you know who we are?"

"I don't know nothing!" The cop shouted back at the three of us, pistol in hand. "You're going to follow me back to our boat and we're going to put you in custody." The cop sounded like a ball of nerves.

"I don't think so." Tony said in a very rational voice, trying to keep the calm.

Just as we thought it was all over, the copper went cross-eyed and fell to his knees. "Howdy!" It was Robby.

"What the hell are you doing here!?" I yelled at him.

"Saving your ass! Now common', we gotta go!" He slurred.

"We have to jump!" Laurel shouted. I watched as she tore the sides of her dress off.

"I don't think I can swim!" I exclaimed as Tony belly flopped into the icy blue.

"Aw, well, I guess you'll learn, bucko!" Robby grabbed

Laurel's hand and flopped into the water as well.

I closed my eyes and dove into the water with parting hands. I pushed and paddled and combed through the cold, wet water with all the strength I could muster. I tried not to think about all of my fears. If Robby could glide across the water with a goddess like Laurel in his mutts then I surely could pass feats beyond my own comprehension.

It felt like ages before I reached the shore. I didn't think that I had the capability to pull it off but I did. It was strange to see Tony and Laurel drenched in their evening wear.

Tony alone, surprised me. He always struck me as a man who would rather have others do things for him. Yet, he didn't need assistance when swimming.

The Arguments from the boat rocked back in forth in my head like the illness of disembarkation. Every other word was Tony's, reminding me that there was only one way out of it all: to swim.

CHAPTER 4: NEW PRODIGY

I had been dreaming a lot lately. One in particular was about taking a motorcar into the countryside. There were lights in the front of houses. There was this particular white colored two-story house in the middle of farm land. I didn't know what it meant because I haven't been there but it meant something to me.

I longed for the complete feeling that this dream brought me. It was a longing that I had never quite felt before. I could taste the evening air at this dreamscape.

I woke up wanting to know where this dream was coming from and why it seemed oddly natural, but nothing rang a bell. Maybe it meant that life was supposed to be simpler. Maybe I was supposed to live in the country. I had never really needed anyone and this dream echoed that. I just wanted to be left alone.

Why did I ever feel like I belonged in New York? Was it because this was all I knew? If so, then how come I knew of this country place that I could not understand? I had thousands of questions rattling through my brain.

If I hadn't been such a success, would I even be thinking like this? I didn't have to worry about rent anymore. I was moved into a penthouse that Tony thought would suit me more. It was in the upper-west-side. It was rich city. My clothes were tailored and fit for the first time in my life.

I hated it. I hated it all. I wanted so badly to get to this point but now that I was here, all I wanted was sanctuary. I had never been myself in this position. This crazy world has always made me think I was supposed to be a certain way. Even my own mother had tried to straighten me out and make me realize my own dreams within this society.

I did not belong. The last thing I wanted to do was be usual. I was anything but that. You were expected to be someone worth only a few mere words of description. That wasn't me. I was more complex and even more so, I wanted to be free.

That night, the air was refreshing from my new balcony window. I put a record on as I danced to myself on the other side of the double doors. Any minute now, Tony would be picking me up for a night out in a neighborhood known for its thrills, Harlem.

There was a slight knocking on the door. I barely heard it from the balcony as I walked back into the living room. Without invite, Tony entered the room with a tall man that I had met once before. "Guy, you remember Morgan, right?"

Morgan flashed a grin from the doorway and walked over to take my hand. He didn't speak as I shook it. "I'm ready." I raised my eyebrows.

"Alright, the cab is waiting outside. You're going to love the place we're taking you. It has some incredible surprises in store." Tony's voice was exuberant with excitement.

"I can't wait."

Tony wasn't kidding, and may have undersold what he had in store. We arrived at a small brick building in a grimy neighborhood where each street lamp was a different shade and everyone walked around the streets in completely different manners from one another.

"Is this the place?" I asked, incredulously.

"Don't judge a book by its cover." Morgan's booming voice spoke to my left as he helped me out of the vehicle.

"Thank you." I bowed in thanks to him and we walked to the entrance, single filed.

"Name?" The man behind the hole in the door asked.

"Tony Marlon Reynolds. I'm here with Morgan Gains and Guy Linister." There was an obvious smile on his face. Even though he was turned away from me, I could hear the pride in his voice.

The man opened the door from the inside and admitted us into the passing darkness. I held my hands out in front of me to try and grab ahold of anything to guide me through. We were taken into a dimly lit waiting room with a large, black curtain on the other end. From what I could make out in the darkness, there was a film of dust covering all of the fixtures. There were three other people in the room. Their faces turned from one another to look at us with brief disinterest but then immediately went back to each other and began to toss back the drinks in their hands. "Gentlemen, this way." A lilted voice called from the curtain.

I could feel my nerves bouncing around in my stomach to the slight pitter-patter of the music on the other end of the large veil. "Is it too late to leave?" I asked, feeling like I was going to be killed.

"Nonsense." Tony laughed. "Take my hand."

I looked around at the other men in the room. "Are you sure about that?"

"Of course. You're safe here." He smiled, looking up at me.

I grabbed his hand and walked with him through and into a bright room, full of people. There was a large stage and a band behind it. There were two women on stage beginning a song. They looked strange like they were wearing too much make up. I gulped and sat in between Tony and Morgan.

"Don't worry, they're harmless." Morgan whispered in my ear. "You've never seen one before, huh?"

"Seen what?" I asked, bewildered by the spectacle before me.

"They're men. They dress up for performances... Expressions." Morgan giggled in my ear.

"Why?" I asked, confused.

"Why not?" He continued to smile, shout and applaud to the performance.

I turned to find Tony's face fixated on them as well. He began throwing bills onto the stage. Others were throwing flowers and other shining objects of silk and clothing.

I watched Tony and Morgan having the time of their lives. This was something that had been going on for a long time, I could tell. I was missing this. I was missing everything. I couldn't wait to experience more.

"Are there more bars like this one?" It was a question that was burning in my mind.

I could have been asking anyone but Morgan was the one to answer. "No, boy. This is my bar."

"You own this place?" I couldn't hide my astonishment.

"Of course not… I wish." Morgan's smirk made me believe him.

"He means that Harlem and its Renaissance belong to him and his people." Tony's smile was overwhelming with pride.

"Could you blame me for asking?" I smiled back. "So, does this mean that we'll only find these types of performances at Speakeasies like this one?"

Morgan's face fell. "Unfortunately, yes."

"Not just these performances, kid. The social acceptance as well." Tony placed his hand on mind.

"And it's less a Speakeasy as it is a normal bar. We can do our business a little differently here." For some reason, Morgan's voice was even deeper than usual.

It wasn't for another twenty minutes, that Tony had me alone in the dusty sitting room. We were waiting for Morgan to use the restroom. I was positive that Tony was going to lay a move on me. When he opened his mouth to speak instead, part of me felt deflated.

"I've been pretty proud of you, kid. That's why I think we should hit the road. I got a good chunk of places we can hit in Chicago. What d'ya say?"

I tried to focus more on his question than my feelings. Damn booze. I kept it simple. "Sounds great." My smile wasn't convincing.

"Something a matter?" His tone changed.

Before I could answer, Morgan came out from the dark hallway behind Tony. The three of us walked back into the dancehall in silence, Tony glancing over at me every couple of seconds.

I made my way to the bar to slam down two drinks before my performance. It was at the hottest new joint in Chicago. I was beginning to do shows in new cities, per Tony's request. I had gotten lucky, in the sense that, his advancements seemed to take a backseat lately. I wasn't sure if it was business getting in the way or the unraveling of his and Laurel's marriage. Though, I didn't want to admit it to myself but part of me missed the attention.

I didn't think about any of it as I rolled through my usual upbeat starting number and glided into the ballad of the night. It was a somber lament of losing love and all its grandeur spoils. The lights in the joint turned to a dim blue to give the space a tone that matched just perfectly.

Quickly, after finishing my set, I threw on my jacket to leave for the hotel when a hand grabbed my upper right arm and swung me off my feet. "Hey, what the—"

"I'm so sorry." A small, deep voice spoke in my ear. "I didn't mean to knock you over."

I gained my balance and turned to look, drunkenly into the face of a man that I had never seen before. He was just as blonde as I with sharp, crystal blue eyes and a smug grin. I straightened myself and stood tall. "What's the big idea? D'you know who you're dealing with?" I flared my nostrils.

"Guy Linister." His lips curled. "Anthony Reynolds' new prodigy." He spoke smugly.

"What?" I was at a loss for words. Not most drew a connection between Tony and I. Not anymore.

"I know you, Guy." He paused to scale me up and down with his eyes. "I used to *be* you." His words felt strange in my stomach.

"What?" I repeated.

"Tony is a monster. Just please tell me you didn't let him... You know." He grabbed my low neck and short sleeves. I pulled away.

"What the hell is your kicker, buddy!?" I asked in outrage.

"You know exactly what I'm talking about. Tony doesn't just give this shit away for free."

"I'm not like that, kid. Let me loose." I shook him off.

"Sooner or later it will be too much and at that point, there will be nothing you can do about it. He's a killer and you'll see it soon enough. Just be sure to drop me a line before that happens." He crumpled a piece of paper into my hand. "I live in a big house in Louisiana. You should pay me a visit some time and I'll tell you my story." And with that, he walked into the shadows.

I wasn't one for patience. I found my body propelling towards him, into the darkness, when Tony's hand grasped my shoulder.

"Where the hell do you think you're going?" His voice was playful. "You really won them over tonight, kid. Common' I'll get you a drink."

As we entered the silence of the bar area, my thoughts filled the quiet space with the stranger's words. What did it all mean?

A few days after returning home I found myself on a street all too familiar to me. It was in the nice part of town. There had been a restaurant, just a block from here, that I had been longing to dine at for the longest time. It was a beautiful brick building with a gorgeous interior that I had admired from the other side of the windowpane. It was one of those fancier and pricey places but I decided that, with my recent income, I would take a peek and have a bite.

The place was pretty empty for the evening time. I thought that I was possibly arriving too late and that they wouldn't seat me but a man came up to the podium and found himself at a loss for words. "Are you—?"

I smiled in response and he showed me to my seat. "Dining alone, are you?" He asked, as if he would like to sit across from me and drill me with more questions.

"Yes." I forced a smile to try and get him to leave me alone. It worked. He sent my waiter afterward and I ordered a steak. My favorite.

After my food had arrived and I finished eating half of it, I watched as a woman past me, heading in the direction of the restrooms. I was fairly certain that I knew her. I removed my napkin from my dining wear and got up from my seat. From behind, it didn't make any difference if I had known her or not. The only thing that gave me any indication was her fiery red hair that matched her illusive and defiant demeanor.

I had to know if it was her but I felt it best to sit down and mind my p's and q's. I dug into my steak again and finished within a few minutes. As I took a sip of my glass water, she walked in my view again. "Peggy?" I called, curiously.

"Yes?" She turned to find my face and turned a little pink as she did so. "Oh? Guy? What are you doing here?" Her voice seemed a little caught off guard.

I wasn't expecting a regal response. So, I choked for a second before finding my words. "Just having a steak." I wanted to laugh at myself. I found it so hard to speak any time she was around.

"That's nice." Her words seemed forced and her face turned

surly. "Well, Enjoy." She tipped her head and continued on.

I felt so embarrassed that I didn't bother touching the rest of my potatoes. I took another big gulp of my water and left without saying another word to anyone.

I peeled through hundreds of headlines on my boring Sunday afternoon.

I was obsessed. I looked for anything that mentioned my name. I heard the same paraphrases over and over when it came to my singing. "Pitchy and winey," "no true grasp of the genre," and "Why doesn't Guy just give up?"

"You have made it big time!" Tony declared. It felt like pity, considering the newspaper he was holding had the large, bold title "Guy Should Say, 'Goodbye'".

"Tony, these articles are bullshit!" I spat back at him.

"Only the bullshittiest ones hit the headlines! They LOOOVE you!" He blew.

"They what!?" My eyebrows kicked up. "You're ridiculous… They *loathe* me."

Sitting in my new bedroom, I rolled over and over in my satin sheets as I looked at the most recent headlines, "Peggy Plays for the Troops!" There was an incredible photo with Peggy's cherry curls glowing in the black and white stillness. Though the photo was black and white, it somehow did not remove the indescribable, impossible color of her eyes.

I hadn't seen her in months. I feel like every time Tony got me close to any pretty lady, he quickly realized the mistake he was making and quarantined us from each other.

"You just need to use their fame until you gain enough popularity." He explained to me. "Who needs 'em anyway?" He patted my hand.

I always just thought of myself as an investment. Sometimes Tony acted as if he couldn't live without me and other times he acted like my manager. There was this strange line between the two men that I thought I knew and I would never ask questions.

These were the moments, in which, the words from the gentleman in Chicago would echo in my head. "He's a killer." Part of me thought it was because he let him do it to him. Another part of me thought it had happened in time. I wasn't going to let him have that much time with me.

Two men walked into the diner just as the tab was left on the table. They were dressed in black suits and had bowler hats on. The taller of the two bent down and whispered something in Tony's ear.

"Excuse me, kid. I've got some important news to attend to." He slapped a wad of bills onto the check and strode out of the diner in a quick pace.

I sat for a few minutes in the humdrum of the café. Before I got up to leave, our waitress drew in close to me and said, "You know that gentleman at the bar over there?" She pointed to a man not five years older than myself. He was a brooksy with dark brown hair and a chiseled face.

I nodded simply, still looking at him. When I turned to look at her, she continued, "He would like to buy you dessert."

"Why?" I asked her rudely, like she would even know. She shrugged and cleared the table. I was still looking at him. He was glaring back with big blue eyes and a dincher in his mouth. His expression was one I could not read.

I slowly grabbed my trilby and jacket, pulled up the overalls on my oxford bags and took small steps. I sat next to him with my brows furrowed. "Care for a lap?" He asked with a British accent so smooth, it could grease a skillet.

"In public?" My eyebrows shot up.

He pulled out a silver flask and poured a clear liquid into two glasses that already contained coke. "Gutsy. You pull trains for a livin?" I asked him as I took one of his cigarettes and lit it with a match.

"Cyril." He took out his hand to shake mine.

"Guy." I took it and shook with a firm grasp. If there's one thing I learned from Tony, it's that you must always shake a man's hand like you have already driven his car.

"I know who you are. Even across the pond, you're quite the... What do they call it? A shaker." His smile lit up the whole diner.

"Is that why you insist on buying me dessert?" I asked incredulously.

"Ah, yes, dessert. Drink up!" He steered the cup closer to me. "Guy Linister, what is your favorite drink?"

"Right now, I am fond of anything with Gin." I answered honestly.

"What is your favorite genre?" There was this air of playfulness to his tone.

"I'm into stride at the moment." I slammed the drink down and gave him a look that showed I was being serious again. His cryptic attitude was wigging me out. "Why am I being Edisoned?"

"I mean no injustice or cruelty. I simply know of a place that has both. Care to join me?" He raised his eyebrows and gestured to the front door. Outside was a limousine.

"Who's cake basket?" I asked with severe casualty.

"Mine, obviously." He smiled. "Common, we're going to miss the act I want you to see."

"Just who are you?" I asked, confused but slightly tipsy.

"I told you. I'm Cyril. Cyril Bassit." He continued smiling as he got up from his stool, grabbed a cane from his side, placed a flat top on his head and walked out of the diner. I followed reluctantly.

The joint he took me too was a dusty number on the Eastside that I was unfamiliar with. The place looked like it was barely keeping up. There was a tap on my shoulder once I found a spot by the bar. I turned to find Markel.

"Hiya, Guy!" His voice was exuberant. "Whatcha doing here?"

I took a second to answer. "Just grabbing a drink with a fellow." I turned to Cyril. "This is my friend, Markel." I introduced them.

"Hello. I'm Cyril Bassit." His British accent stood out even more amongst the two of us.

"I'm Markel Hamburg." They shook and I saw a strange look exchanged between the two of them. Not a look of indignation but certainly one that told me they were sizing each other up. "I've been meaning to tell you that you have an incredible voice." He complimented with a polite smile.

"Thank you." I said after a few moments. I was terrible at receiving compliments.

"Who knew when I met you that I would be meeting someone in the makings of becoming famous." He continued.

"Certainly not me." I said, in honest.

There was another tapping on my shoulder. It was Cyril. He gestured me away from Markel. "Could you excuse us for just a moment?" I asked.

Markel nodded without saying a word. Then, continued to watch me as I swung away from him.

"What do you think?" Cyril asked with a sinister grin painted across his face as we walked into the crowd of people.

I look about the room with its tattered wallpapers and draperies. There was a small, square stage at the far end of the bar. A waitress came between us with a tray of drinks. "Thirsty fellas?" She sang with her pretty voice.

We ordered and sat at a table close to the front of the stage. There was a card sitting atop it that read, "Reserved for Cyril."

"I like it here." I said after a few minutes of listening to the band. For a second, I could swear that I saw Robby in the corner of my eye, talking to someone much taller than he but I didn't have much time to think about that. "But why am I here?" I asked to get to the point.

"How would you like to do a performance here?" Cyril asked through the small slit of his mouth. His smile made it hard to see his lips.

So that was his game. He wanted me to headline a

performance at a bar that was losing its edge. "No thank you." I set my drink down and began to walk out.

Before I got to the door, he scrambled to his feet, ran up to me and grabbed my arm. "Please? I know the owner. He wanted me to help save his bar. I thought if there was anyone who could do it, it would be the famed Guy Linister."

I don't know if it was the liquor or the sweet talk but turned around again and leapt onto the stage, grabbed the mic and began to sing a number off the top of my head.

The band master called, "Guy Linister everyone!" There was a roar from the crowd and I continued on to the second number in the set. There was a little bit of movement from me when they went from stride to rag. I grabbed another drink, slammed it down moved onto song number three.

There was a loud bang several seconds later and the music stopped. Everyone began screaming and running in all directions. "It's the boozies, buds!" shouted a man from the bar.

My alcoholic mind stirred in crazy circles as I tried to jump off of the stage. I landed on my feet but fell over a table. As I got up, I felt the stone-cold clasp of metal rings around my hands behind me.

CHAPTER 5:
TALK OF THE CENTURY

I grunted and panted and tried to swing my body in all directions. I was not going to the slammer. Not tonight.

I heard muffled shouts and a man trying to give direction to the dance hall as they heaved my body from the floor and carried me into the fresh, night air.

They pushed me into the back of the squad car and slammed the door on my face as I shouted obscenities at them. Everything was still a strange blur to me. It was like the rest of the world was running at a quicker pace.

The front door to the vehicle opened and closed. Then the car started and we began to drive backwards. My head was reeling from having too much to drink. "You alright back there?" It was a familiar, British voice.

"What the fuck, fella!" I yelled at him.

"Calm down. I'm busting you loose, buddy." I could tell from his voice that he was smiling. It pissed me off.

"You think this is funny, do ya?" I pulled leaves out of Tony's book.

"Listen, I have to admit something to you. First of all, I'm a cop." He was still smiling. "Second, this was more than just a saving grace for my gent's joint. It was also a new light for your career."

"What in hell are you talking about?" I tried to reposition myself in the backseat. My hands were uncomfortably folded behind my back in a way that my body was not used to.

"Guy, you're the first celebrity to be arrested. This story is going to hit the newsstand tomorrow morning and make you the talk of the century!" Even though I couldn't stand him, I still loved his accent.

"Is that so?" I spat, agitated from falling forward with the swing of the car stopping. "Then, would you mind pulling over and taking these goddamned cuffs off me!?"

We arrived at a place closer to my penthouse. "Where are we?" I asked as we walked into the lobby.

"This is my dwelling." He looked at me as I gave him raised

brows. "I'm still getting used to your lingo." He half smiled.

"Better question, why are we here?" I asked as I pulled my jacket off and straightened my collar. I must have looked a mess after being pummeled into a squad car.

"Listen, I think with my understanding of the media and connections with the government, I could make you the most famous man on this planet." His words seemed less like a proposition and more like a command.

"That's absurd, why would I want that much fame? I don't even want to be a performer." I said in contrary, trying to beguile his offer in my favor.

"Nonsense!" He raised a finger in the air. "You are a talented gentleman!"

"That doesn't mean anything to me." I shot a glance of disinterest.

"It would help you sell your paintings."

There was a long, silent moment. Instantly I knew that Cyril knew more about me than he was letting on. I never told anyone of my ambitions to become a famed painter. Was he a friend of Tony's? "What's the bargain, broomer?" I asked through tough skin.

"There is no bargain. I simply want to see you succeed."

"Horseshit. There's always a price." My mind raced to the

thought of Tony on the night of my first performance at Eddie's. People never did right by anyone without it being a selfish endeavor.

"Would you believe me if I told you, simply, that I like you?" His question had a great deal of honesty in it. I wanted to believe him but I've been slowly learning not to trust anyone in this world.

"Would you believe me if I told you that I don't believe that is all?" Was he going to be just like Tony with his offer? Was I just some strange target for this lousy nonsense?

"Fine. You're free to catch a ride back to your place to think over the details but my offer will always stand." He held out a white card with his name printed in gray, spaced lettering and a series of numbers below it. "One day in the distance, you'll encounter something not quite as surmountable as your usual day-to-day dealing. When this day comes, you will need me."

I blew through many thoughts over the course of a week. Who was Cyril? What kind of connections did he have? Why did he have those connections? I needed to know as much about him as he knew about me before I made any deal with him.

The complications of his presence made my life even harder to sort out than before. I spent a lot of time deciding what kind of fame I really wanted. It was true that I was beginning to like the attention if and when I did shows. The money was always a pleasant addition but the things that bugged me the most was my privacy, followed by favors. It seemed like every stranger in New York had the need to ask me for something from time to time.

I just wanted people to leave me alone. I wanted the solidarity of my life back. I wanted my empty weekend evenings. I missed having nothing to look forward to doing. I was a pretty boring person and did not care much for entertaining. Especially at my own expense.

He was right. My name was plastered over every newspaper the next morning. Headlines like, "Guy Linister caught at an illegal night gathering" or "New York's hottest singer or head of the booze conspiracy?" littered the pages. In some magazines, I was a saint who managed to get away from the police and, in more religious printings, especially those that donned the headlines with the ASL, I was the second-coming of the devil. Here to collect our brightest youth and march them into the flames of Hell.

I pitted most of my favorite clippings onto my dining room table and tossed the rest of them into a trash bin in my kitchen. The dining room seemed like such a waste of a room to me. I hardly had company and I mostly ate my food, standing in the kitchen once I had finished preparing it. I wasn't the greatest cook but I managed when I needed to.

I hopped out of bed on a brisk spring morning and threw on a pair of shorts and a shirt. I passed the concierge on the way out of my building. I had held myself up in my loft for a week. So, a morning run was just what I needed.

There were muffled voices in the distance, ahead of me. It sounded like a crowd of people taking turns talking in and out of a speech over a megaphone. I ignored it and pressed on through my run.

The beautiful buildings of my new neighborhood went by in a flash. The world was a mass of people that I found myself disconnected to. My mind was clear to adventure other avenues of thought. For the first time in weeks, I was able to collect my cognition and focus on some deeper details. I was beginning to believe that Tony had to know Cyril. The coincidence was too precious. I would need to ask him the next time I saw him. Which, considering his strange absence as of late, could be a day or two or even a month's time.

The voices that were seemingly in the distance just moments ago grew louder. There was a screaming sound that began to fill my ears. It was a woman's screams. I felt my ears tickle with the volume of her calls. I couldn't ignore it.

I found myself in the middle of a small group of only a few people. All of which had eyes narrowed and brows drawn together in outrage. There was a single, black haired woman, standing in the middle of them with a horrorstruck expression painted across her face.

"Is everything alright?" I directed my question to the woman with the pained face.

"This woman is a sinner." Called the voice of a woman from the head of the group. I turned to find a sallow face filled with the most unreadable expression I had ever seen.

"And who are you to judge her?" I asked, suddenly swept up in the midst of the social battle.

"I am Ella Hastings." The woman's deep, choral voice replied.

I took her appearance in. She was a pale woman with dark hair, standing a few inches shorter than myself. She was wearing an all-white dress with lace flowers and non-matching black boots. I couldn't help but notice how many buttons adorned her dress and I wondered if I had ever seen an outfit as strange.

I repeated my question, staring her in the eyes.

"I am here in New York as part of the active Anti-Saloon League of America. I have the authority of the eighteenth amendment in stating that this woman is a heretic." Her words were so well practiced that I could have puked right there. This was something straight out of the newspapers.

"And what has this woman done so recently to earn this grand trait?" I asked in wonderment.

"She was caught just last night at an illegal gathering, right here in this city!" She shouted to great applause. "It is my duty as a high-ranking member of the ASL, to turn her in to the proper authorities." With every word, I wanted to punch her. No woman had ever infuriated me in this way.

"Not under my watch." I grabbed the woman's hand and pulled her out of the crowd. We were lucky, no one was following us. Her low sobs were continued as we found ourselves in an alleyway nearby.

"What do you think you're doing?' She asked. "They have already pegged me. They won't stop." Her words were shaken and uneven.

"Listen," I paused, "just get out. Leave." I told her without thinking.

"My name is Elouise Margery. If you ever need anything, please, don't hesitate to look me up." With her words, she took off through the alleyway.

Within a few seconds, I heard a harsh voice coming from where I had just been. "You may think that you have evaded us, but know, Mister Linister, that we are always here. Watching every move you make. Waiting for you to screw up. Waiting to be there when you slip and make an absolute ass of yourself." Ella was pattering through her words like a priest at the pulpit. She had traced our way with a large group of people, including a woman who was the same height as her. She had tan skin and long black hair. She had an angry expression on her face and she was dressed in an outfit similar to Ella's but in all-black.

I didn't respond. I liked the silence of disposition to show her how idiotic she sounded in front of all of those people. "Bug off." I said through my teeth, after a long silence.

"You'll wish you never said that one day." She gave me an ugly smile and backed away out of sight.

I continued my run with so much more running through me. I was so lost in my own head that I almost missed it when I heard the words, "hop in!" It was a familiar female voice calling from a street buggy. I turned to find Laurel sitting suspiciously behind the front seat of a vehicle with her head wrapped up like a Christmas present with a peculiar, sapphire colored hat.

"What on Earth are you doing?" I asked her as her hands nervously found my face. She pulled one hand away to remove her sunglasses then poured her face into mine.

"Hiya, stranger." She giggled after our kiss had ended.

"Laurel, I'm confused. What's going on?" My voice cracked.

"We have to be very careful right now. A stool-pigeon has been peaching the coppers of your involvement with Tony. That's why you've had bulls patrolling the neighborhood." She explained.

"Bulls? You mean coppers dressed in normal clothes?"

"Yes, sheik, please keep up with me." I was already flattered that she had kissed me. Now she was giving me compliments.

"So where are we heading?" I asked.

"We're going to give the cherry-toppers the slip and meet up with Tony." She paused as she turned a corner. It was strange watching a woman drive, especially so well. "They're saying that you're the kingpin of the operation and you're using your booze connections to gain public appeal and fame."

"That's absurd!" I stammered.

"Yes, honey, I know but you have to look at it through their eyes. You have close connections with an underground society. You gained popularity very quickly. Mostly in places outside of the public eye. You moved into a penthouse and you were almost arrested the other day for being at an elicit club, partaking in the consumption of alcohol."

"Wait, I'm confused." I spat. "That doesn't make any sense. If I was arrested but didn't end up in jail…" I trailed off thinking of Cyril and his secret operation. "Why would they still be following me?"

"I don't know exactly how you gave them the slip but apparently they have nothing on you… yet. This is exactly why we're meeting up with Tony."

"Well, where is he?" My words rolled out in what sounded like a drunken stammer.

"Morgan's joint. You remember Morgan, right? Tony's alleged poker pal." She smirked and pulled out a cigarette. "You know," she began, with the fag between her lips, "you're severely underdressed, my friend." She pushed the hope chest back into her pocket and spun the wheel in a frenzy.

"I know! I was trying to run!" I exclaimed.

"It's not my fault the only time you leave your apartment in days happens to be when you're dressed to go swimmin'!" She grinned. "Listen, you're fine. Want to pick up some glad rags on the way?" She stuck her tongue out after letting out a big puff of smoke.

"I'll pass." I replayed her words again in my head and thought of how funny she seemed to be acting. "Laurel." I said softly with my eyes squinting hard.

"What's that, honey?" She turned to see my expression.

"Have you been drinking?"

We arrived at what appeared to be a rundown meat packaging company. "This isn't Morgan's place." I said.

"Oh, you thought I meant his penthouse? No, honey. This is Morgan's old business before the booze cruise crisis."

"It's eerie." I spoke in a soft tone.

"It's business." She said flatly.

"Do we knock?"

"Go ahead." She swung her arm in a lazy gesture.

I began to knock as Laurel grabbed a crooked board that was nailed over what looked like a window to our left. Her body flopped onto the other side of the structure and into the building.

"How did you—" I followed behind her quickly.

The inside of the building smelt like something dead. I plugged my nose and crept through the passage ways calling for Laurel. "I'm right in front of you, silly." I replied every thirty seconds or so.

It was dim and there was a smoke in the air. We finally came to a clearing to find Morgan, two henchmen, Peggy, and Tony. All congregating in a circle around a large wood table.

"Welcome." It was Morgan who spoke in his large voice. He was standing there, tall, dark with wispy, short, black hair and a bowler hat. "Please, have a seat, princess." He was addressing Laurel. You could tell there was an obvious discourse between the two of them.

"D'ya got anything to drink?" She said with a smirk.

"Is gin okay?" Peggy said in a tiny, but defiant sounding voice. This was the first time in a long time that I heard her speak besides our brief exchanges of words here and there.

"I'll take some gin, straight. With just a tad bit of ice, please." I raised my finger from the chair I began to sit in.

"What is this? The four seasons?" Morgan spit. "Just give him a big swig! We don't have much time." He talked with his hands. An obvious trait of someone who was friends with Tony.

"He's right. The best way to defuse the situation is to—" Tony began but was cut off by Laurel.

"He's right? He's always fucking right, ain't he, Tony?" She cursed.

"Can you calm down? Almost everyone in this room is wanted for somethin' or nother." Tony blew back at her.

"I'm tired of this shit, Tony. Getting so tired. I don't get it anymore." Laurel paced in small circles. It wasn't until this moment that I realized that she was pretty lit up like a store window.

I tried to jump in and help. "Laurel calm down, there's no need to—"

"Fuck you! Fuck you, Guy! You're just another queer! What would you do if your husband was a lounge lizard out to vampire New York?" She was hysterical.

"Listen, Laurel. None of this concerns you." Tony spoke in a soft tone to defuse the situation.

"Excuse me!?" She yelled.

"Guy, Peggy. Drive into the country and buy a house somewhere where no one will think to find you. Lay low for a few months and come back to New York when this whole scene has found its cake." Tony blurted in a hurry, not wanting Laurel to interrupt.

"What?" Laurel looked at me with a pale expression. "Guy and Peggy?"

"Yes. They are both singers. The newsprint won't think twice about it. If anything, they'll think they're on tour er somethin'."

"He's right," chimed in Morgan. "If we all split and show ourselves in new places, the feds won't have any proof that there's something going on. Right now, we're the only targets in an ever-growing industry." I never realized how well-spoken Morgan was until now.

"I like the idea." Peggy said to my left. "Let's go." She blushed. My heart sank.

"How are we going to know when to come back, though?" I asked.

"We've got a plan in order, kid." Tony shot. "Shouldn't take more than a month's time. We just have to misdirect the feds." His face was on the edge of a smile.

Laurel looked between the two of us and turned to the table. She slammed a gulp of gin and sat down. "You should probably go before the bulls find us." Tony suggested, patting his hand on

Laurels shoulder and her head sank to the table top.

Morgan, who's hand was clasped around the handle of a large brief case, walked up to the two of us and handed the leather-bound casing to me, said, "Think of this as motivation." As I grabbed the case, he lowered his bowler hat and gleamed at us with his bright, white smile.

"Is Laurel going to be okay?" I asked as I looked around the room. The whole spectacle looked quite confusing. There must have been something going on that I was unaware of.

CHAPTER 6: ARE YOU JEALOUS?

We took Peggy's limo to my place to pick up a few things. She had already gotten her things ready. I had her wait outside while I threw my most important belongings and clothes into a leather bag. I pulled out a piece of paper from a tattered pair of pants that were hanging on my folding screen. I hadn't worn these particular pants since the strange encounter I had with the man who had an intricate past with Tony.

I pulled the crumpled-up piece of paper from the back-left pocket and read it aloud to myself: "Oliver..." followed by an address. It was a Louisiana address. The heart of Dixieland. My blood quickened.

I had Peggy relieve her limo and we took my car. I had seldom driven it anywhere. Mostly because I did not know how to drive well. Still, the adventure was one of momentous excitement. We were handed a large case of money and told to head anywhere unpredictable. I had never been on a road trip and I don't think that with her rich-up-bringing, neither had Peggy.

The first couple of days were very awkward, considering our few, chance interactions. She didn't speak much but I could tell that she was having a good time. I still found myself saying stupid things in her presence. Sometimes, I didn't think that she minded. Other times, her silence spoke volumes to my idiocy.

We danced our way through New York. Then Philly, Baltimore, D.C., Fredericksburg, Richmond, Atlanta, and Montgomery. A new city, a new Jazz scene every night. Our favorites were Atlanta's night life and Montgomery's lightning route and Empire Theater. It took us a very long time to get from one city to another and we constantly found ourselves getting lost and asking for directions.

It was a bit of a challenge to make sure that no one noticed the two most famous jazz singers of our time, so we made ourselves invisible. Peggy had a keen sense for the booze, so we mostly kept to the underground. Every once and a while a jocker would pick us out of a crowd or the doorman would alert the band leader and we would sing a number and escape during a light dimming moment. After all, our movements had to remain a secret and we were creating an obvious path to follow. If we were fugitives on the run, we were doing a lousy job of it.

We stayed in Atlanta for three days. On the second day, we took a walk through a park. That's when the real talk started. From the second Peggy began to answer my questions, I was rapt, surprised at the fact that she was beginning to open up to me.

"So," I began, "how did you get caught up with Tony's gang?"

"I was part of the booze crew before you, actually." She snickered. "Tony was the one who thought up the idea of the speakeasy. With music and booze and men and women getting together for it all. His vision was so beautiful that I couldn't help myself but try to get in on the operation."

"I thought the speakeasy started in Chicago." I mused aloud.

"Did you ever bother asking Tony where he's from?" she retorted.

"Good point." I paused. "How did the two of you meet?"

"Through his wife… I was her best friend in high school." My jaw dropped. "Trust me, this story goes back far." Her eyes rolled and flickered. "She was the valedictorian. I was the class clown. Both practical dropouts. Both wanting to hit the big time."

"I didn't know that Laurel wanted to be famous."

"Of course! She and I both! We sang and danced. She can play a mean piano… Or at least, she used to be able to. Now that she's with that… womanizer, she's become vengeful and frustrating."

That would explain her wanting to get back into music with me. "You two don't seem to get along." I said.

"We had a major falling out when her husband put me on tour and she stayed home. He doesn't let her do anything. I honestly think that if she tried to leave him, he'd have her killed."

"You don't seriously mean that." I offended.

"Of course, I do! You haven't seen Tony at full force yet. You've only been around for a short while compared to the three years I have under my belt. He's very controlling. You have to do things exactly how he wants them or you're finished." She took a breath. "It's just very fortunate that he's an incredible business man. His ideas work, if you listen."

"You don't think he'd have another person killed though? That's just insane!" I exclaimed. People were looking in our direction. We were beginning to start a spectacle.

"You bet." She smiled a grim smile. "If you think that he wouldn't, it just goes to show that you have a sweeter heart than most." She turned her head to stare at me with an awed expression.

"So then, what do you want out of this whole thing?" I asked. Wondering why she continues to put up with it.

"I want just enough money to move to Paris. I've always wanted to visit and experience the jazz over there. It's much different than it is here." She paused. "They whole world is different over there."

I had never really thought about leaving the U.S. The only thing I ever had time for was making sure I was living week to week. "I wouldn't mind visiting another world." I told her on a whim, with a fantastical tone.

"Maybe that will be our next vacation." She winked.

We were at the Empire Theater grabbing a quick drink before heading back to our hotel. The jazz of the south was something that I had never dreamed of before. It did things with its pace and tone that I wished I could convey in my music. Perhaps I would work with Robby on perfecting it when I returned to New York.

I began to explain some of the differences to Peggy with excitement when the bartender picked up on our identities. "Why yes, sir." Peggy said smugly. "However did you figure?" Her upper-class tone stained every syllable of her words.

"I knew it!" The man cheered in reserved celebration. "Well, would you grace us with a number or two!?" He spoke loud enough for the band master to hear.

"Well common' up, folks!" The man shouted from the stage.

I looked into Peggy's drunken eyes with a smile. "What do ya think, cowboy?" She said in the strangest voice.

"I don't need no convincing." I said, happiness staining my

voice.

She grabbed my hands and swayed me from side to side until we reached the stage. The band master welcomed us up and noticed in an instant just who we were.

"Ladies and gentlemen!" He announced. "The famed, the talented, Mister Guy Linister and Peggy Austrait!" He looked between the two of us with wonderment. "Here to sing a number for you!" He interlocked his fingers and shook in all directions as the band began to play.

"You ready?" Peggy's smile curved into an unfamiliar, catlike smile.

"I don't know this number." I pulled back.

"Make it up." Each word was slow and quiet as she whispered into my ear.

"Alright." I said, drunkenly and pulled her into a dance with my arm placed strategically on the small of her back. She dipped and we swayed for a few moments before she broke in with an incredible belt.

She sang of a day sweeter than the present and I echoed with some oo's and ah's until she gave me the floor. I sang in parallel with her lyrics. Trying to make my position believable.

I thought of Tony. I thought of Laurel. How their marriage must have formed during a time when they both made sense to one another. Was my relationship with Peggy making sense because neither of us wanted it? Is that all that life was? A big coincidence. You meet certain people and they ascertain a specific place in your life because of timing?

I couldn't believe it. I wouldn't. There had to be a better explanation that the one standing before me now. If you were to ask me about my position in my life about nine months ago, I would have told you that I felt affection and desire for women. But was it their placement in my life, currently?

I always had a fire in my stomach for Peggy from the first night that Tony had introduced us. Though he kept us apart for reasons of his own devices, I still felt a strange longing for her presence. Though, now, I'm here. Faced with her ever present longing for me. I could feel it. We had spent the last six days together. Laughing, dancing, singing. We were one entity.

Did I want this anymore?

What was happening to me?

I finished my singing and Peggy ended with embellishments. We were finished with. Our place in the night over. I helped pull her from the stage and shook our way back to our seats but before we could sit down, a parade of people pulled us back into the mess of dancers in the middle of the room.

For a long, beautiful moment, the world felt like a colossal, choreographed dance. Everyone was in sync and aligned in a tapestry of motion. Like dressed and ordained instruments playing symphonies in circles. I watched Peggy's face light up with excitement and wonder as we twirled in and out of passages of people.

My intoxicated eyes tried to keep up with the pace of the room but after minutes of losing my balance, I was beginning to grow nauseous. I grabbed Peggy's hand and led her back to our seats.

That's when the band leader waltzed over to Peggy and said loudly in her ear, like a secret, "My name's Charlie." He pulled out his hand for hers.

She pulled out her dainty hand and placed it in his. He kissed it wryly. "Please drop me a line." He smiled and the fires in my stomach blazed.

We were somehow able to get to our hotel safely. I pulled the car into a dark spot on the edge of the lot. "That guy was flirting with you." I said, trying to keep the jealousy out of my words.

"Poppycock." Her face was turning red in the dark, gray light.

"What do you mean poppycock? I could see it with my own two eyes."

"So, what if he was?" She started to grind her top-front

teeth against her bottom lip in a playful manner. “Are you jealous?”

“Are you saying that I have no right to be?” I asked on a whim.

“That all depends, cowboy.” Her eyes stared deep into mine.

“On?” I drew out the O.

“Would you have rather been the man giving me his telephone number?” She giggled.

“At least he has a ringer!” I jousted.

“You didn’t answer my question!” She retorted, still giggling.

“Yes. Yes, I would.” I giggled back. “From the day that I met you.” I paused and tried to sober myself. “But I was nothing back then. I had nothing. I didn’t have a chance with you.”

“Silly cowboy. All you needed was a horse and some spurs.” She chuckled and pulled my head in for a kiss.

My head started to spin and she pulled away, leaving me dazed. “Why do you call me cowboy?”

“Because you’re a go-getter. You always push yourself to do things.” She continued to stare into my eyes. “If I weren’t drunk, I probably wouldn’t admit this but I’ve always used your success as a model for my own business ethic."

"What do you mean? You're incredible."

"Thank you." She paused. "You don't understand how hard it is for a woman though. It was hardly seven years ago that we began to vote. We can't really work. There's not a whole lot we can do."

I never thought about it before this conversation but she was right. Women didn't have the same rights as us. "I'm sorry." I said. "I never knew. To be honest, I spent a long period of my life being alone." I took a long pause to consort myself. "My fundamental years after high school, pondering what life would be like if my mother didn't pass away. Those four years I can never get back."

"I'm so sorry. I didn't know that you lost your mother. That must have been terrible." She looked like she was going to cry.

"I'm sorry. This is an awful time to bring that up. I guess, I just never felt like being social after she died. Everything went grey for a very long time. Honestly, she's the only reason why I even have the ability to get on stage. Sometimes, I feel like I'm two people in one body. My mother used to play records to me when I was a child. That's how I know how to sing random words to every song. She taught me. It was something that we had always done together.

"When she died, I locked myself away from the world for a

long time. It wasn't until Robby made me get on stage that night, that I decided not to let go and be part of the world again. In some ways, it's my only way to connect with my mother again. When I'm on stage, I feel like she's there, singing with me. It's the best feeling in the world. Much better than the grey feeling. Though, It's still kind of grey."

"Is it bad?" She grabbed my hand. "Right now?" She glared into my eyes.

"No. You're the first person to make it go away. I feel like a whole new person around you." I wasn't lying. It was the complete, honest truth. I never knew that she looked up to me. I never thought that every move I was making in the music scene was that important. I was just doing what I had to do to survive. "I'm very thankful to have you here with me now. You take away some of the crazy."

"Life does get crazy sometimes… That's why I drink!" She joked.

"That's why we all drink." I said, laughing.

"Hey, cowboy, there's a bed calling our names. Isn't the night old?" She hiccupped.

"Older than us." I jeered.

I opened her door for her and grabbed her hand softly, leading her to the motel room that was four doors to our right.

I opened the door with the rusty key and found a beautiful, queen bed before us. "Is this the honeymoon suite? It's gorgeous!" She squealed.

"I told them I wanted the most expensive room they had." My eyes focused on the three bouquets of rose laying on the pillows.

"I love this room." Her eyes swam around in circles. "And I love you." Her eyes met mine in a long lock.

"I love you too." The words escaped my mouth before I realized what I was saying. I never thought of myself as the falling in love type. I never thought I'd even find someone that I cared for as much as I did Peggy. She and I didn't have to spend much time together. For some reason, things with us just clicked.

My mind couldn't help but refocus on our history though. "It's funny... I never thought you liked me very much." I smiled, trying to keep myself from ruining everything.

"You silly boy." She shook her head. "I was playing hard to get." Her face lit up in a beautiful smile, making her eyes shine brightly in impossible colors.

I grabbed her waist and pushed her slowly onto the bed. I whispered things in her ear and she slowly started to pull off her dress. Everything started to spin after that.

. . .

New Orleans was on my marker of places to crash. At this point, we gave up trying to stay under cover. Which was perfect because I was getting sick of driving through the country in the tiny vehicle. I began to see the road when I closed my eyes to sleep at night. We decided to get gussied up for a joint downtown called The Raven. It was a dark and well-hidden place that was rumored to have the best underground jazz.

Peggy wore a red dress in contrast to her bright, flashy hair and a black feathered boa. I fitted myself with a suit of all black with a loud, red tie. We finished our ensembles with black face masks to partially disguise ourselves.

We left the car parked in a dark, dirt lot. I grabbed her hand and we moseyed into the place like we owned it. The gentleman at the door didn't appreciate it much. He asked us a million questions before letting us in. We had to slip who we were before entry. It was one of those rare places that required a secret word to pass the door man.

"We could have just bribed him." I scoffed at Peggy after passing the threshold.

"That wouldn't make things as fun." She smirked. "Besides, I thought we didn't care about secrecy anymore." Her sentence was more of a question.

"Eh." I shrugged and we approached the bar. "I'll take a mole skitter, please." It was a current favorite.

"Two." She shot with her lips pursed. Her eyes never leaving mine.

"What do you think about jumping up there and announcing ourselves?" I suggested as she sipped her strong drink.

"That would be a change of pace." She smiled a sneaky smile. "Or what if you jump up there and start to sing. See what they do. Then I'll join in." Her eyes were blazing with courage.

"That sounds exhilarating!" I shot back and downed my drink in one giant gulp.

"Show off!" She shouted and followed suit.

"Shall we?" I winked.

"We shall." She stood, awaiting my queue.

I jumped up, onto the stage, grabbed the mic and began to ditty along with the music. There were a few people in the audience who looked at me like I was crazy but when I turned to the band mates, they all seemed to be enjoying my additions.

"Hey buddy, what do you think you're doing?" A voice slurred in my ear.

"Singing." I jabbed back at him, away from the ear of the microphone.

I started to dance and grabbed Peggy by the hand from the audience, pulling her onto the stage with me.

"We are Guy Linister and Peggy Austrait. Welcome to a night at The Raven." I began to laugh off mic and sang a bit of something that I was working on in the car earlier today.

Peggy swam in afterwards, adding bit of fluff to the music. She wasn't quite as versed in the art of improv singing but she was keeping up quite nicely.

When the performance was over and the crowd was in a perfect state of bliss, we sat back at our place at the bar and a large, dark man came over to us. "That was one of the best performances I have ever heard." He said, mostly to Peggy. "Darling, I heard you came from the streets of the Harlem Renaissance but I never expected you to be quite as good." His voice sang on the last word as his lips pursed.

"Why thank you, sir. I do appreciate the sentiments!" She jostled her necklace shyly. "I have always dreamed of performing in the South!"

"Well we're very glad to have the two of you." He smiled. "Can I ask, are you a couple? I heard the two of you were heading south and wondered if you were looking to hold up permanent residency here."

We looked at each other, quiet. "Do you own this place?" She asked. He simply nodded in reply. "Yes. We're together. No, we may not stay but nothing is definitive." She continued to smile. I beamed. I loved a gal with a big vocabulary.

"Lovely, well we do hope you do!" With that he paced off into the darkness.

"What do you think that's about?" I asked her.

"Well, because we've been doing shows off the light of the streets, we haven't been stopped by any usual paper publication. He must have just heard a bit of fuss about us and wondered. That's why I didn't mind."

"What do you think Tony will do once he hears that we're a couple?" I asked back.

We arrived just northwest of Baton Rouge in a city called Amite. There was a large, white house waiting for us on the edge of marshland, in the middle of the country. It looked strangely familiar to me. Like I had been to this house before. It was two-stories and swam in my mind like a memory that didn't belong to me.

I parked the car next to the entrance gate and asked Peggy to wait in the car while I talked to an old friend.

"Bullshit." She spat. I had never heard her swear before. "I'm not waiting outside. How do you even know this fellow?"

"I can trust you, right?" I asked, as if there were any doubt.

Her response was a facial expression I've never seen her use and one word. "Absolutely." She raised her eyebrows with every syllable.

CHAPTER 7:
DEAL OF A LIFETIME

"Where to begin." I rolled over and over in my head before finally coming out with, "Remember what we were talking about the other day? With Tony and Laurel?"

"Of course." She rolled her hands in a gesture to continue. She was wearing a floral day cap and light blue, jeweled earrings.

My mind swam. There were so many things that I was on the verge of saying but felt that if I found the wrong words to use, my point would be lost. I was a sensitive person but the last thing I wanted to do was let anyone suspect that of me.

I dug through the pockets of my mind, picking out just the right things to continue with. "Well I met this fellow a few months back." I took a dramatic pause, wondering where to go next. "He claims to be one of Tony's original... Play things." She gave me a look. "For lack of a better explanation." I had a feeling that she would get what I was talking about. After all, as much as Tony would like to keep things secret, Laurel must know. Especially after the things she told us before we left. "I just wanted to meet with him and figure everything out."

She fidgeted with a handbag and took a minute to respond. She was glancing out the window like her words were coming from beyond the car. "You mean, you wanted to before we had talked about it?" She asked.

"What do you mean?"

"Don't you understand? We've all been through this. We've all been affected by it. We know our onions. Why do you need justification? You're just going to hear another story like Laurel's and mine." Her voice had a sense of worry to it. I wasn't entirely sure why. She wouldn't break eye contact with me.

"You're right. I just wanted the full scope of things. Maybe he knows something that we don't. Maybe he knew Tony at a point of his life that can help us." I felt a little nervous with continuing. I didn't want her to think less of me.

"What are you saying?"

"I'm saying that there's got to be a way to use everything we know so far to our advantage. Do you want to be a puppet for the rest of your life?" I asked her as she repositioned herself in her seat. I was trying to take a more confident approach.

"No, of course not." She said through her perfectly white teeth. "But Laurel's never been able to successfully leave."

"Exactly. He has. He got away." I pointed in the direction of the house for emphasis. "That's exactly why I think he's one of our last options." I paused. "I'm beginning to feel trapped myself."

"We still don't know this guy." She breathed as she pulled a cigarette from the bow on her hat. She then grabbed a small set of matches from the floor of the car and began to light it. "This could be a huge trick." She finished with her lips wrapped around the cigarette.

"But why would it be? Tony isn't elaborate enough to make something like this up. Besides, it's been months."

"So?"

"So, if it were a trick, don't you think this man would have tried to make another presence in my life?"

"You have a point." She blew out a huge ball of smoke with her words. "I'm going in with you." She smirked.

"No, you're not." I said simply.

"Why not?"

"Because, I get the feeling that he won't tell me everything with another person in the room." I thought on the subject during the entire ride down.

"Fine." She said, through gritted teeth. "How about you go in. I'll give you thirty minutes. But after that, if I don't see you exiting the house, I'm coming in with a gun."

"With a what?" But before I could even get the words out of my mouth, she pulled a handgun from her bag on the seat behind her. "Peggy, where the hell did you get a gun? And do you even know how to work it?" I asked, exasperated.

"Can't be too hard, sugar." Her voice still wrapping itself around the cigarette as she loaded the gun with bullets from a small leather poach on the side of her bag.

"Just, please," I began, "promise that you won't come in shooting that damned thing. I'm trying to get as much information as I can out of this fella and I don't think dead bodies can talk." I teased.

I cut the engine, pocketed the keys and hopped out of the vehicle to begin my slow pace to the front steps. I couldn't help but think about my old apartment in the run-down part of town. How simple my life was at one point and now everything was running at a different pace. I used to dream about my future. I used to think that I was an incredible person. I thought that if my mother thought the world of me, that it must be true. I had plenty of things to offer this world.

I was at a crossroads. Everything that began to change in my life as of a short few seasons ago was drawing to a close. I was about to confront a man for a story that would ultimately decide what I was going to do next.

If his story was true and torturous, I would plan my escape. I would get as many people out of Tony's way of destruction. I wouldn't sick the Feds on Tony, but I would find a peaceful way to leave it all behind. I didn't want to ruin anyone's life. I just wanted to leave the scene with what little control I had left.

I almost made it to the door before turning back around to look at Peggy's glaring face from the car window. She was not happy about this decision, but I had to know for myself. I somehow felt responsible for everyone who was caught up in the dealings of Mr. Tony Marlon Reynolds. After all, I was his most recent investment.

I knocked on the large oak doors with the knocker and awaited them opening. The porch was immaculate with numerous embellishments decorating it. There was a rocking chair and lots of red fabric that hung from the sides of the railings. The boards that were painted white below me had no dirt markings on them except for the ones that I had traced up the pathway and onto the stairs.

Time began to tick in my head as I looked out over the large yard that encompassed at least a half an acre in all directions, full of greenway. It was the most beautiful example of the south. This ranch stood as an old testament to times I would never know.

There was a faint smell of juniper and grass that filled me with a sense of euphoria. I watched as a butterfly found its place on a magnolia tree to my left. Its wings fluttered like jewels catching the light. I could only image what life was like in this part of the Americas.

"Hello." Said a shaky voice as the door opened. "You must be Mr. Linister. Please, come in." He must have been a caretaker of sorts. He had to be at least sixty years old. He spoke so slow that I wondered if he was going to be able to finish his sentence.

"Thank you." I tipped my straw hat to him and heard the heels of my shoes begin to click against the white marble flooring. I looked around as I entered the main hall. The floors and ceilings were white and the walls were a sandy color with a dirt colored pinstripe.

There were three halls leading to what looked like very different rooms. To my left was a door opened about twenty feet down the hall. Inside was a kitchen with black and white tiled floors. To my right was a hallway that led to a dining room. Through the crack of the door I could see open windows and a large round table. In front of me was an open hallway that led to a living room or sitting room with large windows and a conservatory on the other end.

The caretaker took me down the large hallway in front of us. "Mister Agaury has been expecting you for some time now. He seemed to think that you would have been here much sooner than this."

I opened my mouth to apologize but before I could say

anything, we had reached the end of the hall. There was a large room before me full of red rugs with a strange swirling pattern on them. There were two couches on opposite sides of the room looking in at one another. This had to be a sitting room. There were supplemental chairs on both ends of the couches and a long, oak table between them all. The room was about thirty or forty feet by fifteen feet with a door to what seemed to be a conservatory to the right of the rightmost couch from where I was standing.

I heard new footsteps from the door to the conservatory. In walked a man wearing a dapper jacket and a smile like an angel. He made eyes at me through the leaves of a large potted rose that he was holding. He placed the pot onto the oak table and closed the gap between us, pulling his hand out before me. "My apologies, Guy, for the dirty hands. I obsess over my plant-work." His voice was singsong-like. It was strangely forced into a Southern accent. For some reason, it sounded familiar to me.

"That's quite alright." I returned his smile in a polite gesture.

"It took you long enough to visit." He began to laugh a forced laugh to ease the tension of the awkward moment.

"Well, to be honest, I'm never too sure about new people anymore." It was true. I went from being socially backwards, to an isolated outcast, back to being socially backwards, only to gain popularity far too quickly. "Which reminds me. What is it you wanted to talk to me about?" I asked, cutting to the chase.

"Wow, you're very blunt." He responded after a long second.

"I get that a lot." I paused as I looked into his edgy, blue eyes. "Before you tell me anything, I want to know how you know about my dealings with Tony."

"Ah, that's a good starting point. Before anything at all," He gestured to his caretaker with an open palm. "Would you like anything to drink, Guy?"

"I'll take gin straight with a bit of the cold stuff." I shot.

"Me as well, then." He nodded. "Thank you, Giles." As Giles walked back down the hallway, he turned to me again. "To be very honest with you, Guy, I've been watching you. Can I confide in you something secret?" He bit his lip in a playful way. I wasn't sure what he was getting at.

"I suppose." I stammered. I was in no position to give him the wrong impression but at the same time, I was a terrible liar. I could tell that the conversation was about to morph into something dour and worrisome.

"You suppose?" His eyes widened as his brows raised his entire hairline. "Well," he began again after a moment. "I do prefer the company of gentlemen and with my money, I have the luxury of traveling. The two happened to make a pleasant meeting when a I saw this posted on a wall outside of my favorite restaurant in New York." He pulled out a large, folded up piece of paper and handed it to me.

I unfolded it to find a poster of me for one of the few shows that wasn't an underground one. It was very rare that I did a show outside of a speakeasy. I remember this particular show. It was my second publicized one.

"You looked like a dream." He made eye contact with me when I looked up. "Forgive me for saying. However, I saw you speaking with Tony at the bar and caught a bit of your conversation." I shot him an angry look. "I wasn't trying to eavesdrop, I swear. I just had terrible flashbacks."

"What do you mean?" There were so many things that he could be alluding to with his statement.

"It's kind of a long story, you see." He drew up a wooden chair and offered me a seat as Giles returned with a pure silver tray and two glasses, clinking to the sound of his steps and the ice, chiming within them, against the sides of the glass.

After he bid Giles out of the room, he turned again to me to toast. "To Guy..." He hesitated, "let him not make the same mistakes as me."

I didn't mean to chuckle but I let it slip a tad as we pressed our glasses to one another. He shot me a wary look. "I'm sorry, I just don't know the full of the story yet and so far, it sounds to me, like you're trying to pick me up!" I chortled into my gin.

There was a moment when I saw a very raw, honest look

painted across his face. Then it turned quickly to a half angry, half strained expression. “I’m trying to save you!” He exclaimed before taking a sip himself. “Listen, you have to listen to me. I mean no disrespect to your life or choices. I surely hope that you do the same with me and mine.” He waited for my reply.

“But of course.” I put my laughing aside and furrowed my brow to show concern. I knew that he was speaking to my gender preferences. I thought that he was beginning to catch the drift that I liked the company of women or at least, that would be all I let slip verbally. “Please go on.” I egged.

“It started almost seven years ago. I was living with my lover, Christopher, in New York. We both were struggling musicians. I did some design work on the side but nothing substantial. We got a gig at a premier event downtown and our singer didn’t show. I was forced to take the spotlight.” He took a drink and cleared his throat. “It wasn’t until we were finished that Anthony approached me with a deal. He wanted to be my manager and get Christopher, me and the band some more gigs and money.

“How could we refuse? It was the deal of a lifetime. Little did I know at the time that Anthony would try and use our fame and popularity to gain money. Enough money to put him on the map. As soon as the anti-booze movement hit, he had enough money to invest in ways to make money off of the law.

“Sure, he covered his ass with us and never made us

suspect a thing. He even bought a couple of run-down joints and had them secretly brought up to standards to create what we know now as the speakeasy. We had a new place to perform and make even more money from the alcohol sales.

"It was the perfect plan, right? That was until he found out about Christopher and I."

"What do you mean?" I interjected.

"As soon as he found out that we were lovers, everything went from an innocent game of using talented artists to... other things." His face went pink and he crossed his legs as he continued. "He..." He choked and his face fell to look into his lap.

"What's a matter?" I tried to lean in from my seat to see if he was crying.

"He used me for sexual exploration. I suppose he didn't know he liked gentlemen in that way until I walked in." He raised his head and his face was a deep red. He looked like he was going to spit. "At first it was subtle. He would make eyes at me in the restroom or smile at me from across the room.

"Then it became insane. He would follow me home when Christopher wasn't around and invite himself in, saying things like, 'Chris doesn't have to know' and 'I can make it quick, you'll see.'" He paused and took a large gulp of his gin. "I finally started to make plans with Christopher to get out once and for all.

"But it was too late..." Tears started to stream from his closed eyes. The room grew angry with his silent sobs. I could tell he was trying to keep it all in. I felt terrible but dared not to utter a single word. I waited in an everlasting silence until his next words broke the silence like a deafening crack. "I arrived home one day to a quiet house. I threw my jacket over our sitting chair and made myself a drink. At this point, I was making so much money that drinking when I got home became a habit." He paused again and tears began to fill his eyes again.

"I walked into the bedroom to find Christopher strangled with his favorite tie." There was a long pause this time. Oliver was sobbing hysterically. "I called the police." He gasped through his sobs after almost a minute. "But I didn't need them to investigate to know what had happened. It was Anthony. I found a note on the bedside table that read, 'now we can be.'" He placed a piece of ragged paper into my fingers.

I stared down at the neatly written scrawl for seconds before he grabbed my hand and made me look him in the eyes again. "I put as much money as I could into a leather-bound case and took off. I didn't even think twice."

"Why are you telling me all of this?" I asked, shaken, already knowing the answer. Suddenly my life had gone from being a ballroom symphony to stark, melancholy ballad. Everything black and white.

He choked. "Because you have to do something about it.

You have to put him in jail where he belongs." His eyes light up and his voice became hoarse. "And you need to get out before the same thing happens to you."

I stared at him in disbelief. "I can't." I muttered.

"What?"

"I can't." I said, more confidently. "I would rather disappear before he knew I was missing than put someone in jail."

"But he killed Christopher." Oliver looked me in the eyes. "There has to be revenge. There needs to be." His eyebrows pulled together and his expression became more desperate.

"That is not for me to decide." I spat. "I understand that he—"

"Not for you to decide!?" His voice was raised. "You don't understand what kind of monster you are dealing with. This man will give you no second chances! Just be lucky that he hasn't tried to…" His eyes swam in all directions.

"Listen, I get that you're upset but—"

Slow, light footsteps clicked and a voice came from the hallway. "What's going on in here gentlemen?" It was Peggy. She had her handgun at the ready.

"Peggy!" I shouted in a voice to advise her to put the gun down.

"What's the meaning of this?" Oliver shouted, standing up from his seat. "Giles!"

"I'm so sorry. This is my… Well, I'm not entirely sure what to call her but she means no harm." I tried to explain in a rushed voice.

"The two of you began to shout. I just wanted to make sure that nothing was going on." Her voice was just as fast as mine.

"Who are you?" He asked.

"I'm Peggy. Peggy Austrait." She went to put the gun in her handbag but it went off and blew a hole in the marble floor. Everyone jumped two feet in the air. My eyes continued to ring as Peggy continued. "I'm so sorry. That was an accident."

There was a long moment before anyone spoke. Oliver was instinctively covering his ears. He pulled them away and glared up at her as Giles entered the room.

"What on God's green Earth is going on in here?" Giles entered and spoke faster than I had ever heard him. He looked like he was on the bridge of a heart attack.

"Nothing Giles. Never the mind. Our guest here just knows how to make an appearance."

Giles looked at the three of us, most likely looking for the source of the gunshot as well as any injuries. He nodded and turned back around.

It was quiet once more.

"Listen," Oliver began, "all I'm asking is for someone to shut Anthony down. You both are victims of his demonstration. Please just—"

"What makes you think that?" Peggy spoke above him.

"I can just tell." He smirked. "Isn't it obvious? You appear while I'm speaking with Guy? With a gun?" He added for emphasis. "I'm willing to guess that he paid both of you to scadoot while he reevaluated his next move."

"Common' Guy, let's get out of here." Peggy shot me a glance. I was already standing at this point. I placed my glass on the tray of the oak table.

"Guy, you'll regret it if you don't do something. He'll never stop hunting you." Oliver said, as I began to leave the room. "By the by, I wouldn't make the mistake of mentioning my name around him. You don't want him thinking that you have dealings with me."

"I think we can handle this." Peggy said to him as I heard her heals clicking with every step towards the front door.

CHAPTER 8: THERE'S NO STOPPING IT

"I get a strange feeling from that man." Peggy opined.

"Why's that? Couldn't you feel his sadness?" I asked her. "You missed the heinous story he told me, moments before you walked in."

"Not by much. I caught the last half." She was speaking fast and began fiddling through my jacket pockets, presumably looking for the key to the vehicle.

"I can't believe you. That man was in all sorts and you had the audacity to show up with a gun!" I yelled at her, procuring the key from my pants pocket and starting up the engine.

"Why are you mad at me? He was the one who was trying to use to you!" She yelled back. "Seriously, Guy, you want to get caught up in someone else's tragedy before you get to fix your own?" She raised her eyebrows as I kicked the car into gear. "Listen to me!" She turned her waist and hoisted up her knees onto the seat, leaving little room between the two of us.

I stopped the vehicle and turned to her. "No! I get that you all have been misled by him and that he's been a terrible person but he hasn't been all that bad to me and I just don't want to ruin someone's life!" I was breathing heavily. "I don't have anything to fix!"

"You don't think you do but you do. I'm not stupid, Guy. You have a lot of unanswered questions and it's making your judgement cloudy. You're not a good judge of character. You don't get it, do you?" Her expression turned wild. "You can't fix everything! There are going to be things that you can't do anything about." She, too, was breathing heavily. "If you're planning on getting out of this with everyone saved, you're wasting your time. You can't try to make up for everyone else's losses. If they can't find their own way to happiness then why should you do it for them?"

I was at a loss for words. Unlike anyone before, she knew me. She understood what I believed without having to say a word. I couldn't just try and drop everything though. I didn't know how to explain it to her. So, I didn't say a word.

I didn't want to talk to her about all of the things that Tony had done when I first met him. That would mean also explaining that part of me didn't have a problem with it. That part of me actually enjoyed it. I enjoyed the attention. Even if it was coming from another man.

"Guy, you have a great heart but I know you have an even greater brain. Don't let this consume you. There's nothing you can do about this Oliver fellow. He's had his chance at revenge. If he wanted to get away and live his life with his money, then he's already done that. What does he need with revenge plotted out by a stranger?" It was a rhetorical question.

"You're right. I feel so foolish. I was ready to jump in with a sword raised and take down Tony for the monster that he is." I started muttering, mostly to myself.

"Let it go." She said. "Let's just focus on each other for now. Maybe find a way to get out of it in the process. We don't have time to make sure everyone else is out of the burning building." She smiled a smile I had never seen before. "Besides, there are two sides to every story and we're not entirely sure we can trust this guy anyways."

"Peggy, you yourself said just a week ago that you think Tony would have Laurel killed off if she tried to leave him." I breathed.

She tossed her head from side to side. "Yes, but that doesn't mean that we can trust him outright. We've got take a little in and keep chugging." She stuck her tongue out.

"You're a saint." I proclaimed, sarcastically, as the engine started up again.

The next morning was bathed in a bright sunlight. I grabbed my leather case and keys and took the car. I didn't wake Peggy as I left.

The ride through the country was exactly what I needed. I swirled through streets I had never seen, making mental note of where I was turning. Once I was out of the town we were staying at, I hit dirt roads and followed a train track to the side of marshlands.

I pulled the car to a stop at a dead end. It was an area that I figured they were trying to make the road pass over the train track but didn't get to it yet. I got out of the car and lit up a cigarette. I didn't smoke but I thought it would help ease my mind.

I had too many things clouding my expectations. I went from having no money, friends or life to now, suddenly being spoiled by some of life's greatest splendors. Everything came easy to me now. Everything except something that I had long forgotten about. Something that was more important to me than anything at one point in my life.

My painting.

I had stopped painting because of all of my sudden fame. How could I be in the right frame to think when I didn't use my painting to clear my mind? After all, it was therapy for me. It was my escape. I never wanted to do music, everyone just thought I was good at it.

I rolled my window down and felt the wind roll through the car. It was one of the most relaxing sensations I had felt all week. The rest of the world melted away and I was swept by a sense of euphoria.

I turned the engine off and stepped out of the car. On the right there were large, thorny bushes with little flowers just beginning to bud and a plain of grass occasionally ebbing and flowing in the breeze. On the left there was a large, wooden gate that was tattered and beaten down by the elements. Behind it looked to be a forgotten farmland. The crops dead and overrun with invasive plants and trees beginning to sprout up in uncontrolled areas.

If I continued down the road I was on, I would have to get out of my car to cross the train tracks and continue forward. I could also take the pathway to the left and try to salvage what little I had left without the safety of my transportation, or to the right, I could run through the open fields, into the unknown, embracing my freedom. I had the possibility of even hopping the next train that went by and leaving everything behind with no safety nets or familiar people to keep me company. The only option that saw me leaving with my car was if I turned around and went back to my life. But then, I wouldn't own me.

A few short weeks had gone by and we were back in New York. It must have been around two months since we first left. Time was irrelevant to me at this point. Life was such a blur. I felt constantly conflicted. Yet, with Peggy, life was a dream. It was like there were two major parts of me fighting at all times.

"I suppose we'll be getting word from the others any day now." Peggy sighed, walking through the door of my kitchen with two mugs of coffee. Her curves were swaying with her step as she halted before me and set one of the cups down on the coffee table. "This is an elegant sitting room, Guy." She pursed her lips and took a sip of her drink as she looked around.

"I had a decorator in before we left. My favorite is the oak table." I told her. "It makes me think of the country. I've never lived there but I've sometimes thought of leaving the city world to get lost in it."

"Sounds lovely." She said dreamily, pulling up a cushioned chair from the other side of the room and sitting in front of me.

"How rude of me. There's room on this couch." I was laying against the back of it with my arms spread. I pulled them in and hopped to my left, patting the cushion on my right.

"That's quite alright, darling." She took a sip. "Sometimes, I wish we never came back." Her lashes batted back her hair, falling in her view.

"Well, you told me that you've always had a secret dream of visiting Paris and I just told you of my secret and we *did* just get back from visiting the country. So, how's about we start our next vacation!?" I proclaimed, slamming my cup down with enthusiasm.

"That sounds heavenly." She beamed at me. "There was something that I wanted to talk to you about before we do anything."

"What's that?" I took a big gulp of my coffee and grabbed the newspaper from the table. I picked one up from the concierge on my way into the building. I figured I had a lot of catching up to do.

"Well now that we're basically an item, I think I should move into this place." She suggested.

My mind blew up. I wasn't expecting something quite like this. "Peggy, we're not married. What will people think?" I asked back, trying to keep my tone from sounding too judgmental.

"I'm starting to get tired of waiting for you to ask." She smiled and batted her eyes once more. Insinuating, of course, to marriage.

"Peggy, we've just started spending time together a few—" but I broke off. "Let's do it."

"Really?" She said, as her eyes began to water.

Just then, I thought of Oliver's story and of his lover getting killed by Tony and a wave of guilt and fear swept over me. "Peggy, what about Tony?" I asked in alarm.

"What about him? He's not going to stop this." She said determinedly.

"It's just that, after Oliver's story, I'm not sure I want to chance anything just yet. Why don't we make plans on leaving him first?"

"Let's just leave then. Now." But even after suggesting it, I could tell that, she too, was having second thoughts about leaving Laurel in this situation.

"I'm afraid that Laurel and Robby are too caught up in their dealings with him. Robby doesn't even know what Tony's capable of." After saying it, I began to wonder if that were true. What if Tony was doing the same thing to Robby as he was doing to me. I don't think that Robby would be one to put up with it, though.

"You're right." She spat. "I think Tony will lose it if he finds out that we're getting married. We could keep it a secret."

"Yeah right, what priest is going to keep his trap shut about that wedding?" I scoffed.

"You're right." Her face fell into a comfortable smile.

"Listen, Peggy, I want you in my life. You're the only thing that has made any sense in a long time. I just don't want to lose you and I'm too scared to do anything about it right now." I paused to look out the window, then back into her eyes. "Let's just meet up with everyone, go to Paris and go from there." My words came out like a jumbled mess. I was afraid she was going to get fed up and walk out the door on me.

"Fine, I get it. It's just, you know that after all of that time together, he's going to find a way to split us up and put me on tour or something." She shrugged.

"And you think our marriage would allow me to follow you? You know that if he's planning something like that, he's going to do it anyway. There's no stopping it." I got up with my newspaper and took my cup to the sink in the kitchen. I heard Peggy light a cigarette behind me. I pulled open the newspaper as I leaned against the counter. *"The ASL's Front Line take up Permanent Residency in New York"* was the headline on the page. I didn't bother reading the article.

We were at her house for barely five minutes before the phone rang. "Oh, honey, let it ring through. I'm not expecting any gentleman callers." She laughed to herself.

I helped her toss a few different garments into a shimmery bag from her sitting room. The entire time, the phone continued to ring. I tossed her a glance about it and she shook me off with a small-lipped expression.

The entire house was glamorous. You could tell that she had been in show business a lot longer than myself. She had two very large chandeliers hanging from the ceiling in her entryway and the floor beneath the long dining room table was a red cashmere. There were white, satin draperies hanging in every open walkway and window fixture.

"Peggy, the ringer!" I shot her another glance after six minutes.

"Oh, alright. Answer it!" She demanded as she tiptoed into the bathroom.

"Peggy's." I answered in a deep voice.

"Guy, thank heavens!" It was Tony. "I've been trying to call my way through to the two of you." He stuttered.

"Why didn't you just show up at my place like you usually do?" I spattered back.

"It's been difficult trying to get out of this joint." His voice sounded tense. "This would be a world easier if you had a ringer at your place, like I suggested."

"What do you mean? Where are you?"

"Home. Listen, no time to chat at the moment, I'm afraid. Could you please do me a favor?" His voice became charming.

"Depends on the favor, I suppose." I tried to keep my voice sarcastic, though I think it was stained in cynicism.

"You're funny, kid." He heaved a dry, fake laugh. "Meet me at my place tomorrow evening around eight. Wear something stunning." I heard his receiver hang up.

"So?" Peggy came back into the room, her voice wrapping around a cigarette as she hooked the back of her bra together. She was wearing nothing but her undergarments.

"Peggy." I tried not to look or smile. "It was Tony. He wants to meet me tomorrow. Listen, I think this will be the perfect opportunity for you to get with Laurel and try to plan her getaway. We can make this work."

"What about Robby?" She asked.

"I'll talk to him after I talk to Tony. Let's see if I can get him on phone. Do you happen to have the number?"

"It should be on the list there." She pointed to a small, circular table next to the telephone with a list of random numbers on it. "He's listed as 'Band Man.'"

I looked at the sheet and began to dial, speaking the numbers aloud, "Seven, eight, eight, three." There was no ring tone that suggested that it worked. "It didn't work." I said flatly.

"Of course not, honey. You didn't dial the exchange name." She laughed.

"The what?" I looked at her with irritation.

"Here." She strode up to me and grabbed the whole phone. She began to dial the number, while making funny faces at me.

I arranged everything with Robby and placed the ringer back onto the side table. "Are you almost ready?" I asked through the open entryway to the bedroom.

She didn't reply right away. I got up from the small, white chair that I was sitting in and walked deeper into the house. There was a room next to the kitchen that had a beautiful, black baby grand piano sitting in the middle of it. There were all sorts of photos lining the walls and another crystal chandelier hanging above everything.

"Peggy!" I called again.

"I'm coming, sugar!" She replied from a room away.

I sat at the piano and twiddled the keys a bit before she entered the room with an awed expression. "I forgot. You play instruments too." She said, bemused.

"Apparently so do you." I raised my eyebrows.

"Scoot." She shuffled next to me and positioned her hands next to mine. "I wrote this when I met you."

Her fingers combed the keys gently, creating a beautiful, glistening sound with her right hand. She was playing in a classical fashion. It was something that I had never learned to play. "You wrote this?" I asked in amazement. "This is beautiful."

"It ain't over yet, sweetie." She smirked and continued to flutter her fingers over the keys.

"It would sound better with words." I told her as she was coming to a close. She looked up and over at me. Her eyes meeting mine. "Your words."

"Is that right?" She asked in sarcasm. "Well, the tricky part would be playing the thing while I'm singing." She made a small smile and looked down at the keys again.

"What do you mean?" I asked.

"I never learned to do both. That's not something you get taught when you're classically trained."

"I could play it if you showed me how it's done. Then you could sing atop it." I made eye contact with her once more. "It could be our duet."

Her face turned a little pink. "I think that would be delightful." Her smiled showed her pearly teeth and the indescribable color of her eyes blazed through the squints of her lids.

I decided to wear my favorite bowtie to my meeting with Tony. I was going to play the part of a listener and barely speak a word. Before I left my building, my concierge stopped me and handed me a piece of paper. "Sir, a dark gentleman in an olive bowler hat dropped this off for you." He said as he put his hands back into his pockets.

It was an address with the words, "New New York" printed below in an untidy hand. I knew in an instant that this was Tony's new address. He was an overly suspicious man who probably thought it best to move once the feds moved in on him.

Sure enough, I was right, as I arrived just shy of thirty minutes later. I drove myself as not to attract any attention. The traffic getting there seemed to be nonexistent. I parked the car and drew up my sleeve to knock on the door. This was, clear as day, a house on the outskirts of the city that I didn't think I'd ever find Mister Reynolds in.

He was the one to answer the door, to make matters even more confusing. "Ah, Guy. I'm so glad that you are here." He beamed as if he had thought I was dead. His hands sprung into the air as he began to embrace me.

"Are we alone?" I asked after a large huge.

"Of course. Laurel is out with a girlfriend." He didn't seem to think that there was anything wrong with this, yet I knew that he was speaking about Peggy. Though, I was unsure if he knew it was.

The place was very honest looking. More honest than I thought was to Tony's standards. It looked like my grandmother's house on Long Island. It had doilies on the tops of every surface and a long-sleeved fabric skirt atop the couch in the sitting room. The kitchen, in the far back had a tiled floor and wooden dining room table sitting up against the back windows. There was a faint smell of something musky in the air.

"Listen, Guy. I wanted to get right into business." He began. "Before I say anything further, I need to make sure. You've been gone for so long. I just need to know that I can trust you."

I gulped and began to sweat. Pulling at the collar of my favorite shirt. He knows that I visited Oliver. It's all over.

CHAPTER 9:
I NEED A SUCCESSOR

“Of course, you can trust me.” I pleaded in a breathless voice. My hands waving in all directions. I probably looked insane.

“Guy, calm down. What’s the matter with you?” Tony asked grabbing a cigar from the sitting room table and lighting it with a quick flash.

Instantly my nerves were calmed. I had suddenly gotten the feeling that he did not know. “Nothing.” I straightened up and fixed my tie.

“I’m glad to hear it.” His lipped were closed around the cigar. He exhaled and continued. “I hope your trip was an easy one. It has not been so easy since you left.” He drew in another deep breath of tobacco.

“Why’s that?” I tried to act calm, my face undoubtedly

turning from red to its normal pallor.

"It's been a trick getting the feds off my bush." He swatted at the air between us as I tried not to cough. "I have to be honest with you. Do you remember how I told you when we had first met that I was in the process of acquiring more speakeasies?"

"Yes. I do." I smiled politely as I chuckled up a small cough.

"Well that was a lie." He said slowly through his wide mouth. He adjusted his spectacles and continued. "I've had close to one hundred operations in the greater New York area for almost four years now. I've also had a few other class-named acts working under my pay roll." He paused, probably thinking of where to go next. I couldn't think of anything to respond with but I opened my mouth to speak anyway. "No, nothing like you and I." He gestured with his arm between the two of us. "Just enough music to keep everyone happy. It's been a bit of hassle, really. I've had to trust so many people in keeping the operation running."

"I know, the New New York operation, right?" I interjected with some knowledge of the subject.

"Yes, however, it's not what you think. I started this operation back in 1919. The government gave us, the people, enough knowledge that this anti-alcohol movement was on the rise." He got up from his seat and walked into the kitchen. "What'll you have?" He asked me behind the refrigerator door.

"Oh, nothing, thank you." I said, being polite.

"Bullshit," He spat, "Ya drinkin'!" He slurred.

"Fine, gin." I said, point blank.

He brought back in two glasses with a dark caramel colored liquid in them and set them down on the sitting room table. "Anyway, I was given enough time to take my money and plan. So, I decided to buy two liquor distilleries in Nashville, one in Chicago and another on the docks of New York. I also bought two wineries in Connecticut and another in Ohio." His words came out in a rush.

"What's the point of this st—" I began but was cut off.

"It was money security. You see, if I bought them all out, pushed production and kept the product, I could use all of it to start a new business, one that I knew the public would go bonanza for!" He exclaimed with excitement. "I would open a place that was like a saloon but operated in complete secrecy. I would charge twice as much for the booze and make my money back in less than a year.

"It was such a success that I made my money back in just four, little months. Before the year had ended, I had to begin investments in the bootlegging trade. I had heard rumors of booze making its way through Canada and others through sea trade." He paused. "I dropped easy cash and brought more alcohol into my business.

"Eventually the money came so easy, that hiring extra help

was needless. The feds were easy to pay off and the company was grand." I was waiting for the point. "The only problem was the increased risk. You see the government has recently invested in private citizens. Making them part of the booze bashing crew. Anyone can become a regulated part of the anti-alcohol league. They've recently hired on around two-hundred thousand civilians as part of a campaign to keep the cops honest."

"Is this why you told us to beat it?"

"Yes." He used his pointer finger and thumb of his right hand to caress his mustache. "It seems to be a problem for New York alone. I needed some time to gather my intellect and keep everyone disconnected from me in the process."

"So, what's the next step?" I asked.

"Could you accompany me to a collection site? I've got a few things to go over with you but I also have some business to attend to." He stood and took down the rest of his gin in a heavy gulp.

"What happened to staying in and playing it safe?" I asked with my brows raised.

"I just received word this morning that I'm safe." He chuckled and walked into his bedroom.

A few short seconds went by when I heard him call my name from behind the semi-closed door.

"What do you need?" I called.

"Could you come here for a moment?"

I took each step slowly, thinking about my next move. It was like I knew what was coming. "Yes?" I asked as I opened the door all the way.

His shirt was unbuttoned and he had a strange look in his eyes. He came towards me with a drunk expression and placed his right hand on the small of my back. I wasn't expecting this. I leaned in as he kissed me softly. His lips were trembling.

He pulled back to look me in the eyes. There was a very human expression waiting in them. "Are you alright?" I asked him. His eyes began to water as he backed up to his bed and collapsed into his hands. "What's the matter?"

"I'm so lost right now." His voice broke as his words uttered outward at me.

I had no idea what to say. There were so many things flicking through my head that I could not come up with the right words. "Tony," was all I could manage.

I walked up to his bed slowly and sat next to him. He was human. How could I have thought that Oliver was right? Clearly there had been a misunderstanding. Tony was undoubtedly a creep but I don't think he would hurt anyone. Not intentionally, that is.

"I'm so sorry. How this must look…" He stopped himself and stood up. "Well at any rate… It's time to go." He dried his face and tore off his shirt, grabbed another off a rack from the closet and began buttoning it up as he left the room.

Was there more going on with Tony than I knew? His attitude was flippant and confusing to me.

He placed a black fedora on his head and then another on mine. "What's this for?" I asked already knowing the answer as he pulled his down over his forehead and opened the front door.

"We shall take my neighbor's wagon." He said, getting into a shabby old vehicle parked to the side of the house.

"Uh, Tony. Don't you think they'll notice and call the cops on you?" I said in a nervous bluster.

"Eh, who cares." He shrugged as he lit up a cigar.

"Tony, we're trying to stay incognito!" I shouted.

"Calm down, kid. I paid them to use it during the day while they're out." He laughed.

We drove through the edge of the city and arrived at a dock that I had never seen before. It had a bluff of land that cushioned the wooden piers to the earth. There were two white boats docked with tall, pale gentlemen, dressed in a light, faded blue, standing on outsides of the ships.

"Friends of yours?" I asked, staring at the three of them.

"I suppose you can say that." He smirked as he pulled the

car to a stop and got out. "You coming?" He asked.

I hopped out of the car, straightened out my wardrobe, and patted my hair flat. "What's happening?"

"Well as the feds start to close their grip in on me, I've begun counter-actions to ensure my business remain unstinted. They're inventing new ways to catch me and after our little fiasco a month ago, they've begun to put two and two together. I think they're just a few short breaks away from understanding the capacity of my plans."

"Which are?" I asked slowly.

"We aren't here to talk about that today. We're here because…" He trailed off as the tallest of the three gentlemen paced over to us and shot his hand out. "Tyler. This is Guy. Guy, this is Tyler. He's my head boatsman."

"Pleasure," was all he spoke and turned to the other two.

"We're here because, I need a successor." Tony turned and gave me a look of mixed expressions. I could make out triumph but also a small sense of fear and indignation.

"What exactly do you mean?" But before I could fully finish my sentence, he began to address the other two men and I watched as business continued as usual before my eyes.

It was hard to watch, knowing that Tony had known something about his fate. Something that he wasn't letting me onto. I knew there was faults to Tony. I knew he wasn't perfect but after everything that I had heard, I wouldn't expect anything to interfere with him. Not any government entity anyway. He had been in the game for over five years after all.

Was he dying? Was he the one planning to make an escape? Part of me was a little excited. If I took over operations for Tony then I could turn the tables around on him and banish him from the New York scene.

I knew as I thought it, that this would be impossible. There was a sense of omniscience to Tony. He would find a way back into power and come looking for revenge. He was a man with connections and somehow used those connections to build the greatest anti-dynasty that the world would ever come to know.

I figured that I could, however, use this new sense of leadership to devise a plan unbeknownst to Tony. A plan that would put the money in a place accessible at just the right moment. The moment that the four of us could escape.

It's strange, though. For some reason, the more I thought about leaving Tony Reynolds, the more I felt a weird feeling in my stomach. He had given me nothing but kindness since I've known him and I've never seen him lose his temper to great degree. There was only one occasion and it wasn't a terrible one. He had walked in on Laurel and Robby making music. That is, if that was what they were doing.

I began to bite the inside of my lip as I heard Tony talking to the others with instructions. Instructions that I probably should be listening to. "There's a lot more than this I will need to go over with you but we'll have to save that for other days. After I drop you back off at your vehicle, I have some plans to set in motion. Plans for Robby."

"What do you mean plans?" I asked.

"A job." He paused. "And that's all I'll say for now."

"Are you meeting him tonight?" I asked, hoping he would say no, because if not, it would interfere with my dealings with him.

"No, no. I'm meeting with my lawyer first, then I'll meet with him tomorrow." He responded quickly.

I drew out a long breath in relief.

I parked a block from where I used to live. I wanted to walk from my old place to Robby's like I always used to. There was a strange feeling in the air. It was summer time and the moisture that surrounded me was suffocating.

The walk took thirty minutes and wove between all of my old haunts. There was the corner café that I used to go with my mother. The barbershop, the confectionary, the museum but none of it compared to Robby's joint. It was a short, brick complex with a flat on the fire escape, that he had inherited from his uncle.

We used to stay at his uncle's place over the weekends to give us a place to smoke. We would pitch our cigarettes off the side of the fire escape. That was back when I smoked for the look of it. Everyone smoked for the look of it.

It had been nearly two years since I've seen the place. Its bricks were more dilapidated than I remembered and looked as if the building was about to collapse at any moment. There were small, square windows lined at the same intervals on every floor and a big, embellished white archway with a small stairway leading to equally big, dark doors.

There was a pair of kids sitting on the steps, asking for money. I tried not to make eye-contact as I opened the front door and walked up the musty stairs to the fourth floor. Robby's place was the last door on the left. The one with the upside down nine that everyone mistook for a six. I rapped three times.

I was surprised when a woman with short, dark hair answered the door. She was holding a large fur coat in her arms and looked as if she was struggling to put her shoes back on. "He's in the back room." Her thin eye brows shot up with her head jerk to the left.

She had a very pronounced jawline and high cheekbones that insisted that she could shout over a crowd. Her curly hair was tucked neatly behind her ears and she was wearing far too much makeup. Not enough to be too noticeable but yet, I noticed. I had the strangest feeling as though, I've seen her somewhere before.

"I'm Guy." I tried to be polite.

"Oh, I know who you are honey, you don't have to be a gentleman." She scoffed as her second heal was secured to her foot. "I'm Ruth, if we must." She stood up straight and examined me from head to foot. "You're a lot more charming up close and in person." She said, bluntly. "And not at the end of a dark stairway. Though, print never does anyone justice, either." She continued to chuckle. "If I ever made anything of myself, I'd rather be painted."

"Excuse me for asking…" I began, not wanting to be rude.

"Why am I here?" She shrugged, again with full honesty. "It's quite alright, darling. We've never officially met." She took a second to think of her words, then continued. "We're not an item if that's what you think."

The room got quiet. It was broken by a familiar, deep voice from behind Ruth. "Guy, what a pleasant surprise." Robby walked into the room wearing a white undershirt and black pants, held up by brown suspenders.

"Robby." I said with a smile.

"I'll leave the two of you to it." She smiled curtly and pushed passed me, pulling on her furry jacket in the process.

"You could not have showed up at a better time." Robby said, passing me a cigar. "Common' big timer. I know you enjoy the beef stick." His words went two ways. I wasn't entirely sure what he was implying.

Instead of being rude, I said, “I have quite a bit to talk to you about.”

“Oh? Is that so?” He said in a whimsical voice. “Well it just so happens that you showed up at just the perfect moment.”

“Why’s that?” I asked, taking the cigar from his hand. He turned to look through drawers in his sitting room kitchen.

“I would hope,” he found a pack of matches from the sink-side drawer and drew a light his lips, “that you would accompany me on a night stroll.”

“A stroll to where?” I asked, waiting for the light.

“I have a few things that need to be taken care of and I think it’s time I told you what has been going on.” He smirked in a way that made my heart skip a beat.

“What’s that?” I tried to keep my voice well composed. “Well, I’ll accompany you if you hear what I have to say on the way.” I offered.

“It’s a deal.” His smile was brighter than ever.

It was a longer walk than I had expected and the summer night air was beginning to nip at my face and hands. “How much farther?” I asked.

“It’s just some little ways left.” He said, a few paces in front of me.

I could tell that we were passing a park of some kind because I could smell the faint scent of flowers. It was roses and lilacs. Both were my mother's favorites. The vague outlines of bushes were coming into view just beyond the street light's grasp. It wasn't late enough for all of the cars to be off the streets. A few still zoomed by in slow wisps.

"Listen Robby, there's something I need to tell you about. It has to do with Tony."

"What about him? Did you just figure out his precious secret?" His voice sounded strange, as if he was mocking me.

"What? What are you—" I shook my head. "No. Listen to me. It's about your..." I didn't know how to phrase it. "Your job."

"What about it? Did he tell you what it is?" He asked without letting me fully finish my sentence.

"Well not exactly but that's not the point. Listen, the point is—"

"The point, Guy, is that this new proposition is going to make me filthy rich. That, along with all of the other schemes that I'm in the middle of."

"What are you talking about?" We had stopped and I was looking at his hard-to-read face.

"We're going to meet a gentleman who is going to

partner up with me and start our own chain of speakeasies. He's got the connections, I've got the money and when the coast is clear, I'm going to steal Laurel right from under Tony's nose."

CHAPTER 10:
MEN & THEIR STEAK

I had no idea what to say after Robby's statement. It seemed like everyone in my life was beginning to work against one another in secret and I was left in the middle, still in confusion. I was beginning to grow angry.

"So, then," I began, trying to stay calm. "What are we up to this evening?" I said it between mostly gritted teeth.

"I've got a few things that I'm planning. It's optional if you would like to join me. I would love if you accompanied me but I understand if you don't want to. After all, you belong to him now, don't you?" It wasn't a question. I knew what he was getting at now.

"Robby, that's not very fair, you don't get—"

"Get what?" He shouted from nearly three feet away. "You're

either very naïve or extremely stupid." His words were sharp. This was the first time the two of us had ever gotten into a fight.

"What exactly are you implying?" I was trying to stop myself from striding away in frustration.

"Oh, come on, Guy. You never get it, do you?" He was looking at me with a new expression. I could tell that he wasn't mad at me. There was a strange sense of pity on his face. It was an expression that enraged me even more.

"I do. You never—" He cut me off again.

"Shhh!" The sound was a blazing one that cut between our words and the silence. "It's business time." As he said it, there was a black figure emerging from the oncoming darkness. It was tall and had some sort of bag hanging from its left hand. The figure wore a deliberately concealing jacket, scarf and hat. It seemed to be the type that was meant to avert the gaze of others as opposed to remaining completely hidden.

"What is—"

"Shhh!" He repeated, quieter than before.

The figure was walking up at a quicker pace, probably realizing that Robby was among the two of us. "Robert Squire." It seemed to be more of a question than just stating his name. His voice sounded as if he was attempting to conceal that as well by speaking into his scarf.

"Sorry about that, James. This is Guy. He's my best pal." Robby sounded collected once more.

A gloved hand bolted out of the darkness and I shook in silence. I was getting a strange yet familiar feeling. After a few quieter seconds, Robby continued, "Do you have the deeds?" His voice was estranged and distant like he was making a business transaction with someone that he did not trust.

"They're right here in the sack." James said like it was obvious, in his accent, which swept the line between Midwest and those born and raised around this side of the country. "Do you have the dough for the next phase?" It took me a few seconds to work out what he had said because his voice was so guttural and mangled that I had to assume parts of his question.

"Yes." Robby replied curtly. He then pulled out a wad of cash and shifted his weight to one side as he handed it to James. James swung the bag in front of him to Robby. "What's this?" His voice was hoarse and exasperated. "Small bills? Look at this bag, James? This isn't discreet, like we talked about."

"S'all I had." James' voice was even more mangled in his anger.

"And they're all here?" Robby replied with his eyebrows raised in uncertainty, grabbing large quantities of money from the sack.

"'Course!"

"Perfect!" Robby continued rifling through the bag. The

sound of paper ruffles was growing louder and louder as he did. "Meet me at the bridge again tomorrow night. I want an update."

James simply nodded and walked back into the night air. "Robby, what in the hell is going on?" I asked quietly, trying to make sure that I couldn't be heard more than ten feet from the two of us.

Robby began to walk in the direction back from where we once came. "I'm in the process of buying more places to open speakeasies."

We walked back to Robby's place in silence. I didn't know what to say. There were so many things that could prove problematic with Robby's plan. On one hand, it was the best course of action against Tony. It could be the perfect avenue to pursue for money and power in the undergrounds of New York. On the other hand, if Tony did find out, it would be a one-way ticket to Death Street.

I couldn't quite come up with the courage to tell him. I knew that he was on a lit fuse tonight. I tried to start subtly. "Robby..." He looked me in the eyes. We had just walked through his door and he was pulling out a large, glass container of whiskey.

"Did you want some?" His eyebrows raised in a social way.

"Not at the moment." I was trying to be polite but he wasn't letting me.

"Now you're too good for my whiskey?" His voice seemed even more estranged than earlier.

"What in the hell is your problem, buddy?" I cut to the chase. "You've been a right old ass all night!"

"You're my problem!" He looked like he was going to smash the bottle over my head. "You have so much swing with Tony and you don't even bother using it to your advantage!"

"Robby, you don't understand. I've been trying to tell you something all night. We agreed that we would exchange stories but you haven't even bothered to listen to me—" I barely finished my rant.

"You always stand in the background, in silence, not wanting to accept things. Well, guess what? You have to and do you want to know why? Because life isn't perfect, your mother died and she's not coming back! You're stuck in the middle of a harsh situation and there's no escaping! You're going to have to accept it at some point and now's a good enough time as any."

He tried to continue his rant but there was a rage growing so fast in me that I couldn't even try to hold it in any longer. I pushed him backwards, almost off of his feet. When he lunged back at me, I clenched my fists and punched him as hard as I could, straight in the face.

There was a loud "pop" and I saw a thick, jet of blood shoot across the room to my right. Robby went to open his mouth, most likely to shout profanities at me, but blood ran from his newly broken nose into his mouth.

He then, tried to lunge again at me with his fists, swinging madly in all directions. I huffed and threw my body in circles in an attempt to avoid his punches. There was a lot of breath between the two of us but neither dared to say a word.

Finally, after almost a minute of his trial, he managed to cuff his hands around my neck. I could barely breathe but I manage to say, "how could you? She was practically your mother." I could feel a sour feeling in my stomach, like he had managed to punch me. I blinked back tears as my eye brows pushed inward.

I could see the look on his face change from a fury to somber expression and then back to fury once more. "Get out," was all he could say. Before I walked out of the house, I turned to see him take a large swig of whiskey through his panted breath.

I stayed in for the past couple of weeks and ignored everyone. Even an angry Peggy had shown up at my door not a week into my solitude. I explained to her what had taken place and she became instantly consoling and understanding. She had told me to give her a ring when I was ready to perform again and she would take to the stage with me.

"What the hell is your problem?" Tony stood with his legs crossed in lazed fashion in the arch of my entryway. "This is the third week in a row that both you and Robby have refused to perform."

"Have you bothered having this conversation with him?" I asked, already knowing the answer.

I was looking out the window, legs crossed over one another. I was wearing my night clothes. My hair was tattered in all directions and in need of a barbershop visit.

"Honestly, Guy," he began, throwing his hands in the air, "There have been quite a few other things taking place as of late that this hasn't exactly been my main focus. I have more business trips to take with you." He studied my expression along with my distance from the conversation. "Listen, if this is about all of those articles from the ASL, you—"

"No, no. It's not that." I had a hard time thinking of what to say. After all, if I told him that Robby and I got into a fight, I didn't know what he would do about it. What if he became violent on my account and went after Robby? That's when a thought came to mind, "Have you seen Robby lately?" If he had, then that would mean he would know something, considering Robby's nose had to be busted up pretty badly.

"No, he's got a ringer… Guy, you're acting funny. What is going on?" His voice became a little worried but mostly somber.

"It's nothing. I'm just in many different places at once."

"Is this because you haven't been painting?" His voice had so much care in it. I was surprised that he had even noticed that. It had been closing on a year since I had met Tony and, in that time, I think I had only painted a few times in the first couple months. I haven't painted since. Yet, he remembered.

"No." My response was distant. "It's complicated."

Tony was a person that I couldn't hide anything from. Whatever I had going on, he would have to know sooner or later. It would just come out. He was too intelligent for it to be ignored.

"Well if there's anything that I can do, please, don't hesitate to ask. I trust you, Guy." He smiled and walked over to where I was sitting. "And I hope that you trust me as well."

It was a half lie but it sounded genuine enough when it escaped my mouth. "I do." I took a moment stand and look down at his eyes. It was always so strange to be standing next to him, I always forgot that he was a few inches shorter than me. It was most likely because of how big of a man he was in action. It made it silly that he was shorter than anyone. "Listen, I'll perform tonight. With Peggy." I added as his eyes lit up.

"Good, because you're not the only one out there who needs some of your gold lighted singing." His white teeth shined in the window way.

After Tony departed, I made arrangements with Peggy after phoning her on the concierge's ringer and started to dress myself up for the night. She was going to meet me around six so we could grab dinner before we headed to Eddie's. I was excited because it had been a long while since I had performed there and I needed that livening atmosphere. I always got a rush from performing there during my starting months and that nostalgia would be exactly what I needed.

I straightened my bowtie and smiled at myself in the mirror. I always hated catching my reflection in mirrors. I had always worn such a serious, standing face, that it scared a lot of people. I think that was why it had always been so difficult for me to make friends growing up. So as often as I would catch my face in the mirror, I always parted with my reflection by making a goofy expression.

There was a faint knocking at the door. It was Peggy. She loves to drive so much that I told her she could meet me here and we'll take a limo out for the night. She disagreed, telling me that she won't have some coachmen preaching nonsense to the public about us the next day. She would drive us. Naturally, I didn't bother arguing.

I straightened my posture and grabbed a bouquet of flowers that I bought her from the corner, floral shop. As I opened the door, her expression became immensely excited. "A few weeks feel more like a month." She said in a half exuberate, half irritated voice.

"These are yours." I handed her the lilac and iris arrangement with a smile and a slight bow.

"They're lovely. What an odd combination." She mused. "I

would have never thought to bring the two together." She took a moment to take them in her hand. "Iris' are my favorite. How ever did you know?"

"I didn't actually." I smiled even wider.

"Where are you taking me for dinner?" She fell into my arms and was drawing my chin closer to hers.

After our lips met, I pulled away and whispered, "Frederick's. It's a new place close to here. It's got steak and lobster."

"Men and their steak." She was shaking her head.

After she had reluctantly valeted the vehicle with the steward at the door, we were seated with my reservation and ordered virgins of our favorite drinks.

"What a shame, they don't have wine." I grimaced, looking at the menu. "I feel like it would pair well with my steak."

She tossed a laugh and pulled a flask from under her dress. She started to pour a liberal amount into her drink.

"Peggy!" I whisper shouted, trying not to attract even more attention to it.

"What?" She smirked.

"Hand me some." I threw her a wild look.

She snorted a chuckle and swung it under the table. We laughed for a solid minute until our waiter arrived. I ordered my steak and she ordered the lobster special. We tried a little bit of each other's meals and continued to laugh through stories we took turns telling.

The conversation took a serious tone when I asked her if she had any siblings. "I used to have a younger sister." She paused and took a second to wait for a gentleman with a bowler hat to pass. "She died of some rare disease. The doctors worked as hard as they could but we lost her in just a few short months. It's was horrendous. My mother has never been quite the same since."

"I'm so sorry. If I would have known, I wouldn't have asked." I choked back another sentence because she looked as though she was trying to say something over me.

"It's quite alright, Guy. Things happen." She paused and settled her expression. "What about you? Do you have any siblings?"

"No. I suppose my parents would have had a few more if my father stayed." I tried to keep my face blank when saying this. It wasn't a sad thing. I was used to it but I didn't want Peggy to worry about it.

"Oh, you poor thing. Your father walked out on your mother?" She looked upset again.

"It's really not a deal." I started.

"But it is. You are parentless." Her face screwed up in a way that I had never seen.

"It's fine. Really. I'm used to it. He left before I could remember him." I recalled many things that my mother had told me as a child. "He just wasn't the right fit for my mother." I explained.

"I'm so, so sorry. If it's any consolation, my father left as well." She explained as her face calmed once more. "I was eleven. My mother kicked him out because he was a drunk. Kind of ironic, really."

"Why is that?"

"Because my mother has fallen down a similar boat recently. I gave up months ago. I can't fix her. She seems to be skipping more times than an old phonograph." She seemed introspective. "Listen, let's leave the country this month." She said, instantly changing the topic. "Let's go to Paris, like we talked about."

"Alright, I'll start making the arrangements."

"Look into air travel!" She said exuberantly.

"What?" My voice was shrilly with surprise.

"Yes, I read something a week ago about a man named Charles who flew from New York to Paris and I think the whole idea is very lavish." She was wearing a dreamy expression.

"Peggy, I doubt there are aero planes that are willing to take two celebrities across an ocean." I laughed at her gumption.

"I just think that the whole thing was rather coincidental, don't you? A man flying from here to Paris. It's a sign." She huffed. "Well, what exactly did you have in mind then?" She laughed along with me.

"I could look into small cruise ship tickets tomorrow morning." I explained, setting our plans in motion.

The rest of the dinner, we explored other topics and took our time getting to know one another. "Look at the time." I turned my wrist back into my sleeve and got up from the chair. I walked over and pulled her chair from the table and helped her up with one hand. "We'll be late if we dally any longer."

We made it there earlier than expected. The place was lit up more than I had ever seen it. It was fixed up in a way that rivaled that of the Palace Hotel. Tony paced up to Peggy and I and clasped his hand on my right shoulder. "Guy! For a minute I didn't think you were coming." He smiled between the two of us. "Peggy, it's good to see you after so long."

She returned his smile, made a small curtsy and said, "Marvelous evening, Mister Reynolds. What are we singing?" She separated her words in a humorous tone that only I could catch.

"I figured you can start with a shaking duet. Then a ballad. Followed by some of Guy's solo, off-head singing!" He was beaming now, folding his hands over one another and walking back to the bar.

I could tell there were a few negative things on Peggy's mind. So, I tried to lighten the mood. "I don't see Laurel. Do you think she's even here?" I asked.

"No, I don't suppose so." She too, began to look amongst the crowd. Just as I stopped looking, I saw Robby enter. His nose was still pretty battered. "Guy." Peggy gasped.

"What?" I was alarmed.

"His nose. You really did a number on him, honey."

"I know. I don't think he's here to forgive me…" I trailed off. "I don't suppose Tony even tried to get a replacement horn player for the evening."

As we spoke, Robby zoomed to our left and sat at the bar. "What do you think Tony's gonna do once he sees that and finds out what happened?" Peggy asked in a suspicious tone.

"I don't know. To be honest, I've been dreading that, myself." I shot her warning glances and tried to find Tony, who was on the other side of the bar.

"They're literally sitting directly across from one another." She pointed out.

"Let's just get this show on the road. You tell Robby. I'll grab Tony." I told her and we split.

We started the show without the two of them meeting, but I could tell from Tony's expression in the audience, that he was wary of something. We sang through the heel stomping beat and into the swimming, dreaming ballad to arrive on my solo performance. I helped Peggy off the side of the stage and sang through a couple numbers that the crowd ate up.

After the music died for an intermission, I too, hoped down from the stage and shimmied over to Peggy and Tony. They looked a little uncomfortable standing near one another. "How's the night?" I shot Tony an excited look.

"It's going quite alright..." Tony said through a half-opened mouth. He seemed irate.

"Like the performance?" I asked through a forced smile.

"Everything but the band leader's gang mug." He said, grumbling.

"What do you mean?" I asked, as Robby was approaching from the front of the stage.

"What do I mean, Guy?" He shot out a hand in Robby's direction. "He looked like he was jumped. I don't want a man performing on my stage with that busted up chunk of watermelon he calls a nose." There may have been more irritation from Tony towards Robby that wasn't on the surface. I could tell this much from the way he said his words.

"Then why don't you ask this little, piece of—" Robby began in a shout.

"Hey, there is a lady present!" I retorted, pointing with my thumb to Peggy.

"Ask him what?" Tony looked grave.

"What happened to my face!" Robby yelled.

Tony turned to look at me and I knew that trouble was about to break loose. So, I told the truth. "We got into it a few weeks back."

"That's why!" Tony yelled. "This is an outrage!" He grabbed Robby by the collar of his shirt and backed him onto the surface of the closest table. "You touch even a hair on his head and I'll have you in your grave quicker than you can blink!" His voice was so severe that I would have thought his words were coming from someone else.

"Hey, hey. The two of you need to knock it off." Peggy tried to interject.

"You get out of here, you trollop!" Tony looked red in the face as he turned to glower at Peggy.

She turned around and bolted for the door. I was torn in two places. Tony and Robby or an upset Peggy. I chose Peggy and peeled through the people, looking for the doorway.

"Peggy!" I called down the empty street.

"Guy, just leave me alone." She said as I neared her pace. "You didn't seem keen on leaving anyway."

"What's that supposed to mean?" I was bewildered.

"What do you think?" Her face was hard to read.

"Peggy, don't let Tony get to you... He doesn't mean it." I tried to calm her.

"Doesn't mean it?" She looked angry. "The queer's a creep!" She shot.

"Peggy," I repeated, "he's a good guy deep down." I had felt some sort of semblance of this after I had my last conversation with him. That didn't make him any less of monster if he did commit murder.

"What!?" Her wild eyes traced all of me at once. "You've got to be kidding? You better not be his cat!"

"His what?"

"Cat. It means that you're offering up sex for money and protection. Oh God, Guy, if that's so I can't bear to think it." She was clutching her chest, dramatically. I could still see the color of her eyes in the darkness. The way that they captivated me the first time was lingering over me. Before those eyes, I didn't know color.

"No." I said, flatly. "That would never—"

"I just don't think I can believe you anymore!" She

shouted and hopped into her car, leaving me standing on the street. Alone with the faint smell of her perfume, lingering like a ghost.

CHAPTER 11:
STOP LYING

I took twenty minutes to get back to Eddie's. I sat on the side of the road for a long while and tried to convince myself that everything that had happened wasn't a big deal. It didn't help.

I passed the man at the door and saw Tony and Robby standing by the bar once more with glasses in their hands. Everything seemed to be normal again. "Is everything alright?" I directed my question to Tony but Robby was the one to answer.

"Yes. Everything's fine." He was staring through me like he had drunk too much already.

Tony was wearing a strange, distant expression and Robby looked as though he was on the verge of laughter. Neither one of them looked as though they were speaking to one another before my entrance but there was a very social appearance to their stances.

I looked between the two of them as two gunshots rang out from behind me. I turned in circles so fast that I almost knocked Tony's drink out of his hand. By the door, there was a woman with long brown hair and a tight, buttoned uniform that looked uncomfortable. It was undoubtedly Ella Hastings from the ASL. There was a very large man standing behind her with a gun in his left hand as well as the lady who stood behind her in the alleyway the day that we had met.

"We have blocked off all exits and entryways!" She yelled to the handfuls of people rushing to every open doorway.

"Not to worry, Guy. I'll handle this." Tony was turned to me with an eased expression, as though he had everything under control.

"No, Tony. I don't think you know who that is—"

I barely finished my sentence when Tony strutted over to her. "Ma'am. I don't think you know what you're doing here." He said in a plain voice.

"Robby." I said, in a hushed voice to my left.

"What's that?" Robby whispered loudly back.

"We have to do something. I don't think Tony knows that this is the lady who's been doing all of the club raids. It's been all over the newspapers lately. I even met the woman before I left

New York." My voice was rushed, as I tried to overhear what Ella was saying back to Tony.

"I don't think you know what you are doing here, sir!" Her voice was loud and shrilly, ringing with dramatic enthusiasm. "This is the puddles of sin! You are taking up congregation on the gates of hell!"

It felt as though she was awaiting everyone in the club to turn and listen to her like she was performing some sermon but all anyone could do was cower under their tables and behind the bar. No doubt afraid to be detained and taken in.

"Everyone will have to follow me, single file, to the entrance. The police will be here any moment to assess your crimes!" Her hollering echoed throughout the halls in a horror-like fashion.

"Quick, Guy, this way!" There was a whispered yell, shouting from twelve feet behind me, wrapping around the side of the stage.

I turned to find the top of Cyril's head, peering out from the darkness. Tony was already a step ahead of me, probably knowing that a secret exit was in that direction because he stopped to distract Ella. I could just barely see him blocking her view from us. As I made my way through the dark, I could hear a clutter of footsteps behind me.

I heard Ella shout after us, "Quick, stop them!" There was

another bang of a gun and as I turned to see behind me, I noticed a few people trying to follow Tony and Cyril as Robby got tackled to the ground by the large gunman. It had all taken place within a few blinking seconds.

In rapid flashes of light, I saw Cyril shoot his hand out for mine, I grabbed it without thinking. I almost fell trying to keep up with him. There were random sets of stairs that I clamored up and down, my hands desperately searching for a railing to grab hold of.

We reached what was most likely a backroom. There was faint light breaking through the two small windows on the far end of the room. "The right one opens easier." Tony whispered as our footsteps died in the entryway.

The two of them hurried over to the window and opened it in a matter of ten seconds. I remained at the door to keep watch. "Guy." I heard Cyril's accent say, egging me forward.

I ran up from my post and went to grab each side of the window. As I did, both Tony and Cyril began to pick me up and help me through. "You'll have to be next," Cyril began to explain, "or you will have to lunge yourself through it without help from either of us."

"Alright." Tony grimaced as he too, pulled through the window. "Come on." He said to me as he straightened his footing. "Let's go."

"Wait, Cyril." Was all I could say as Tony grabbed my

shirt.

"Who cares, kid? We have to get out of here!"

"Cyril, hurry. We're in an alleyway." And if Ella was telling the truth, that would mean that the police would be surrounding the place any minute.

He had a little difficulty trying to prop himself into the frame without any help. I turned to see Tony's face, pale with a fear that I had never seen flood it before. Once Cyril was on our side of the window, the three of us took off into the darkness.

The alley seemed to be closing in on us in both directions as the brick buildings drew in closer. I heard Tony exclaim in a whisper as he stepped in some sort of liquid. It sounded like a swear word.

"Do either of you know where we are heading?" I asked the two of them.

No one replied. The three of us continued to walk in silence with our hands in our pockets. We made sure to head in the opposite direction of the front of the building and the alley spit us out next to a theater. Its lights were still shining. All of its bright bulbs were going in and out in a fashion that made them draw a line around the sign. There were a few people walking down the street. A few of them were running. I assumed it was because they had just escaped Eddie's.

Tony hailed a cab and let me in first. "Listen, fella, no

offense. I just don't know you." Which had answered the question that I failed to ask Tony a long time back.

Tony continued to halt Cyril when he replied. "I can hide the two of you easier than you probably can."

Tony replied, "I don't think you can." I couldn't see the look on his face but I could tell that it was a stern one.

"Tony, you'd be surprised. Just let him in." He did save us after all. "We need to hurry." I urged.

"Absolutely not." Tony said and slid into the cab next to me and closed the door. "Drive." He said to the cabby.

The drive was quiet as the driver wove through empty streets. We went from cityscapes and tall buildings to more residential dwellings. You were always able to find one or two people walking up and down the road at this hour but in the neighborhoods that we were driving through, I didn't see a single person.

We had arrived at Tony's house on the outskirts of town some time later. As we got out of the cab, Tony handed the man a large wad of money. "You didn't see either of us tonight, buddy." His voice was bold and grim.

We walked up to the house and Tony pulled out a key and opened the door. There was a pounding in my head from everything that had happened. Now at least I knew that Tony and Cyril did not know each other.

"There's going to be quite a few changes over the next couple months. I wanted to at least warn you in case you see very little of me." Tony's voice seemed distant and marked by the knowledge of things that I knew he would not tell me about.

I wanted to ask what he meant. Instead, I asked, "What do you think will happen to Robby?"

"Many things. The first of them being an interrogation." Tony began pacing his sitting room, flicking on lights as he passed them. The room glowed greener than I remembered in the lamp light.

"What do you mean?"

"That lady knows that there's some sort of operation taking place in New York and I'd bet she's trying to narrow the search and pinpoint the kingpin." He spoke fast as he undid his tie and buttoned shirt, walking into the kitchen and swinging open the refrigerator. "Whatcha' drinking?" He called in a point-blank manner.

"Gin." I hollered back, thinking about all of the things that Robby must be experiencing at this very moment. Was he held in some sort of cell? Was he intoxicated enough for them to blame the whole gathering on him? I felt a singe of guilt. The last time we had talked, we had the worst argument that I had ever had with any human being and I had broken his nose.

"Are you alright?" Tony asked me as he handed me the whole

cold, glass bottle of gin.

"I'm fine. I just feel like an ass." I wasn't so sure if I could tell Tony things, especially tonight. He might fly into a ranting rage but I spoke the truth anyway, as I usually did.

"Why do you feel like an ass?" Tony sat across me at the circular table that sat by the back of the couch that faced the front door. We were under the archway of the kitchen.

"The last time Robby and I spoke, we had a fight. A literal fight." I took a large swig of gin and coughed as it made its burning way down my throat.

"Yeah, that son of a bitch. I oughta beat the living pulp out of him for that." Tony set his glass container down and looked as though he was going to continue pacing around the room again.

"Tony, listen, you have to let me fight my own battles. Robby and I are friends. We've been friends for over twenty years." I tried to calm him.

"You're right. I trust your judgment." He took a moment and squinted as though he was thinking of what to say next. "I just don't like him."

This wasn't the first time I had heard it. It was really strange to me because my entire life, Robby was always the handsomer of the two of us. He had always found a way to wow the ladies. At this particular part of my life, anyone who had feelings for me didn't like him.

There was a pressing quiet that began to fill the room as Tony polished off his bottle. My mind began to become intoxicated. I could feel it working its way into my brain. It was a funny tingling that made the pressures of the night simmer and die a little.

Thinking about it; I had more than one person mad at me. I had started a conflict with Robby as well as Peggy. I couldn't imagine Cyril being alright with the events of the evening either. My drunken mind wandered into places that made me feel alien to my current state.

It was depressing to think that it took a little liquor to unlock hidden thoughts inside me. I took another gulp and tried to think of what I would do tomorrow. I wanted to patch things up with Peggy but I thought it would have to wait until Robby was out of the slammer.

I got up from the table. Tony's eyes traced my movements for a moment. I turned and watched his mouth open. "I'm going to the pisser." I told him before he could ask.

There was a long running carpet that led down the hallway to the bathroom. It was on top of the already existing carpet of the off-white floor. A few paintings hung on the walls but what really struck out to me was a portrait photo of a tall black man, standing with his wife and son. It was Morgan. He didn't look much younger than he was now. The only thing that set apart from the real Morgan was the bright smile on his face.

I opened the bathroom door and switched the light on. The

room illuminated in a yellow glow. I splashed my face with water, coming to realizations in my head that took me longer than the sober me would have taken. I had to wonder about the photo. About the house we were in. About Tony.

I switched the light off after I was done and walked slowly back to the sitting room. I sat in the wooden chair and peered into Tony's drunken eyes. "I have a few questions for you." I said with a slight slur.

"What's that?" He asked, his eyelids drooping slightly.

"Is this—" I stammered. "Is this Morgan's house?"

"Yes. One of them." He said with a hiccup.

"Where is he now?"

"I can't talk about that just yet." His response was curt but seemingly honest.

I had a million questions. I thought back to the day that Peggy and I left for the south. Laurel had said something about Tony and Morgan being alleged poker buddies. She had also called Tony a vampire of sorts. Now that I was seeing photos of Morgan with a family, it began to make a little more sense to me.

"So, is Morgan another one of you play toys?" I asked, my voice filtered with indignation.

"I don't know exactly what you mean." Tony's voice became quizzical as he straightened up in his chair. His expression began to wake up.

"Just like me, Tony, think!" I sputtered.

"Guy, I don't think you understand." Tony's voice became a little confused.

"I had a suspicion that day that Peggy and I left town. The two of you—"

"The two of us don't have what you and I have if that's what you think. Morgan has a very complicated past." He sounded more put together and reasonable than before.

"What do you mean?" I said, ignorantly, spilling gin on myself. "I hope for your sake, you're telling me the truth, Tony. He's got a family. A child." I exclaimed. My drunken mind was putting pieces together immaturely.

"He *had* a family." Tony held his hand to his goatee.

"What? What do you mean had?"

"Guy, the year that I met Morgan, his wife and son were killed in a car accident." His voice was rational but quavering.

"What?" I thought about the smiling facing in the portrait, now starring back at me in my mind with a haunting effect that made me wince.

Suddenly, it brought me to many conclusions. Had Tony had them rubbed off so that he could move in on Morgan? I thought of Oliver's story and my assumptions became even more dramatic. I had to stop myself.

"It was terrible." Tony's voice was convincing enough but I still didn't feel as though I was getting the full story.

"Tony, can I ask you something?"

"Of course." There was no denying his response.

"What really happened to them?" My drunken words sputtered out of me like an accident.

"I don't get what you're implying, Guy." His tone was crowded with the understanding of knowing exactly what I meant. I could hear it in every syllable.

"Don't play stupid. Did you have them killed so that you could encroach?" My voice didn't sound like me when I had said it.

"What?" His brows furrowed into an expression that I had never seen on his face.

"There *is* something going on with the two of you. Everyone knows about it. Even Laurel mentioned it." I began to accuse him in a manner that I didn't understand the cause of.

"That's nobody's business but ours." His voice drew back a bit. He bit the insides of his lip as he stood up and began pulling his hair.

"What's the real story, Tony. Stop lying!" I enraged.

There was another long moment, in which, he grabbed another bottle from the fridge and slammed it in an instant. The bottle came crashing to the surface of the table with a loud bang.

"I came after his wife. What we had was secondary. I'm still secondary. He's still in love with her." He looked like he was going to cry. He slowly unraveled into a drunken mess that I couldn't believe. He wasn't lying.

"Tony." I tried to sound somber and caressing with my words. I was being a drunken asshole. I placed my hand on his shoulder.

He pulled away and looked me in the eyes. "You wouldn't understand. You're lucky to be a naïve mess. Not understanding your feelings for people. You get to wander into other people's personal lives and do what you please. You don't get what it's like on the inside."

His words crashed over me like a wave. I wandered about the living room before plopping into an armchair by the door to the sitting room. The alcohol was spinning like a drain in my mind. The pieces of things that made so much sense to me moments ago were lost in a blur of confusion that fed me false explanations now. "I am sorry." I said slowly, trying to keep my breath. "I just assumed."

"What an assumption to make." Tony said through gritted teeth. "For your information, Morgan has always been just a good friend. We had an on and off thing that I don't consider anything special. We are there for each other in a way that our wives were and are never there." He looked through me with his words. I don't think either of us were sober enough to continue this conversation.

"Let's go to bed." I said, simply. "Before other stupid words are uttered." I said it in such a drunken spill that I saw a smile crack on Tony's face. "What's so funny?"

"That's got to be the most expressive thing I've ever heard you say."

"What? Let's go to bed?" I repeated.

"No… All of that. You really are dramatic when you drink too much." He continued to chuckle. "Well, there's only one bed in this house and it's in the master bedroom. I hope that doesn't make you think I'm trying to… What's the word you used." He was being humorous now. "Encroach upon you." He smiled devilishly.

"No, it's quite alright." I smiled back, grabbing the empty glass containers from the table and setting them next to the trash in the kitchen. "Let's hit the hay."

There was a different energy about Tony that began to make its presence known. I started being less concerned about what damage he could do to others and more concerned about myself and what I would do with this other side of Tony. He had always been an enigma to me. Always balanced along the line of the extraordinary. Carelessly throwing caution and money to the wind.

My drunken mind was pulling him apart. He was more than just a gentleman with money and power. He was a human being. He had always fascinated me from day one. I never wanted anything from him in those days. I just found myself in an interesting dilemma. For some reason or another, there were parts of him that I couldn't help but wonder about now.

I followed him to the bedroom. There was a single light shining on the left side of the bed. I watched as Tony pulled his unbuttoned shirt off and toss it on the floor, followed by his pants and socks. "Don't worry. I'm not going to try anything that will make you uncomfortable." His words sounded comical. Part of me had wished that he didn't say that.

I pulled off my outer-garments and got into bed. The silky warmth engulphed me as Tony got into bed and clicked his bedside light off. I felt a strange sensation as what seemed to be Tony's body ebbed closer to mine. There was a new warmth that enveloped me.

I felt his hands begin to pull my under-trousers down and I didn't fight to pull them back up. I was too tired and feeling too careless.

"This is nice." Tony whispered in my ear. I could almost hear the smile in his voice.

I couldn't complain. I had never had another human being snuggle up to me, like this in bed, before. I didn't fight him off as my mind swam into unconsciousness.

I awoke the next morning to the smell of bacon and eggs wafting into the bedroom. There was a dim light seeping through the window behind my head. I sprung forward and pulled the covers off of me, swung my body to the side of the bed and pulled my pants on. There was a faint humming sound coming from outside of the room.

The room I was in had a wooden closet to my right and a dark wood dresser by the door. The head of the bed frame was made of mirror shelving with two lamps on both sides. It was a large, two-person bed that took over two thirds of the room.

There was a painting of a beautiful, dark skinned woman by the door. She was smiling a bright smile and holding a bouquet of flowers. The walls were a dark rose color and the crowd molding was a deep, mossy green. I thought the contrast was a little sickening.

It took me a second to get my head working again. I thought perhaps I had dreamed the night before but trying to remember it was becoming more bothersome than trying to collect myself in the here and now.

I pulled on my shirt and walked to the door. Pulling it open, I looked down the hallway. There wasn't a sign of Tony besides the breakfast smell in the distance. So, I used the restroom and entered the kitchen minutes later.

Tony was wearing a pair of boxers and his glasses as he flipped pancakes with a faint smile. "G'morning sunshine." His smile grew wider. "Did you sleep alright?"

I scratched my nose and sat at the kitchen table. "Fine, thank you." I thought about the events of the night before and shuddered. To think, I almost gave too much away. "I'm sorry about last night. I think we drank too much." I wanted to make my wording sound mutual.

"It's quite alright, Guy. Truly not a problem." He waved his hands as he prepared two plates and brought them over to the table. "I hope you like your eggs sunny side up. That's the only way I know how to make them."

"Nice and gooey. Can't complain." I scarfed down the two eggs and poked at the bacon. "This looked amazing." I prodded at the pancakes with maple syrup.

"I was thinking a big breakfast would cheer both of us up." He paused to eat a bit before saying, "you feeling any better?"

"Yeah. The only thing is…" I finished my bacon. "Robby. I still feel terrible. I just don't know what to do." My mind raced through the raid from last night with shockingly close detail. "We'll have to call around and figure out where he is. That way, we can go bail him out."

"That is something you'll have to do on your own." Tony said, finishing his plate and giving me a wary expression.

"Fine. I just can't leave him in jail like that. He's my best friend."

"Well, if this is how you're taking the news of Robby being incarcerated, then I'm glad I didn't tell you—" He broke off like he was about to say something he'd regret.

"Tell me what, Tony? What happened?" I hiccupped.

CHAPTER 12:
ANOTHER WAY

"It's nothing, Guy. We'll talk about it some other time." He tried to wave it off.

"Tony." I insisted, my eyes meeting his with venom swimming through my expression.

"It's really nothing." He continued to act unabashed by the disturbance in our conversation. "Come on, let's get you home." He stood and cleared his plate in the sink.

"Is this about Robby or Laurel?" I asked trying to spark the argument back into life. His eyes met mine again and he made a slight shake with his head. "Tony, you can't avoid it forever. What's going on?"

"I think I messed up." He sounded slightly guilty but there was an edge of confusion lingering in the air.

"What do you mean, exactly?"

"I may have accidently locked up a friend of yours." He said it so casual that I didn't react immediately.

"Who?" I said sharply.

"His name is Markel. He's a short, German fellow." He tried to continue to explain but I cut him off.

"Markel!?" I was outraged. "Why? What did he do?"

"It's nothing that he did on purpose. It was merely an unlucky coincidence, really."

"Tony, you had better explain everything before I shoot you."

"Well, do you remember how I had told you that I had a plan to set things in order before you came back to New York with Peggy?"

"Yes, actually." I replied, curtly.

"Well, for a few weeks, I watched this fellow coming in and out of our speakeasies. I decided to build up a case against him. I was going to pin the whole ordeal on him while you were away to throw the feds off our path for a while…"

"Uh, huh." I said, egging him on.

"Well, it sort of backfired." He said tersely.

"How so?" My enraged voice rang.

"I had heard from a friend on the inside that he had started telling the feds at his holding cell that he knows you." He spoke fast, probably in an attempt to downplay the whole scenario.

"Of course, he would. What happened?"

"It only made the whole case worse." He took a brief second, then continued. "He probably thought by telling them this, that they would let him go. Not knowing that to know you would implicate him even further into suspicions."

"We have to get him out!" I shouted at Tony. I was more pissed than I had ever been in my life. Especially with what I had let Tony do last night. I couldn't believe him. The fact that he was trying to play this off like a happy coincidence was probably the worst part. Maybe everything that I thought about him being a sensitive human being was a bunch of Bushwa.

"It's a bit more complicated than that, kid. If we bail him out, it will look even more suspicious and after last night, I wouldn't be surprised if there was warrant for our arrests. We were caught by one of the highest-ranking members of the Anti-Saloon League. They're—"

"I know what they are, Tony. I tried to warn you not to get in her face last night. She knows us. Well, at least, she knows me." I sighed. "This is such a mess. All of this and on top of it, Peggy's mad at me too. Everyone who comes into contact with me ends up miserable." I huffed and slumped back into my chair.

"What exactly is going on between the two of you?" He asked for the first time, most likely because I finally gave him an in to do so.

"What's going on between you and Laurel?" I responded cockily. "I don't think you're in a position to be asking those questions, Tony. I'm so mad at you right now." I didn't try to elaborate. I had to think of a clever way to get Markel out of jail. By now, he was probably so mad at me that I wouldn't be surprised if he never wanted to speak to me again. Even if I did break him out.

After a long bout of silence, I suggested, "Why don't we give the bail money to someone disconnected from this whole thing?"

"It's even more complicated than that, kid." He did look a bit guilty, leaning against the counter by the sink and the kitchen window, light pouring in from the morning sun behind him.

"How so?" I began to bite my lip, fighting the hangover that ebbed back into my head after eating my breakfast.

"If anyone tries to go in with the bail money for Markel, specifically, they're going to try and interrogate them as well." He shrugged. "That's where this whole thing gets messy. We either have to break him out or find a way on the inside."

"What do you mean on the inside?"

"Well, we have to try and find a policeman who can work a little legal magic to get him out. I don't have someone with a high enough clearance to make a dent in the case. Trust me, I've been trying since the day it spilled that he was in league with you. I felt terrible." He traced his eyes up and down the length of my body and back to my eyes. "How do you know him?" His jaw settled in a jealous way.

"I met him shortly after I met you. He works for a bank. We're just friends." It didn't look as though Tony believed me. "He seemed like a nice guy. That's why I'm really upset about all of this. I didn't know him close enough for this to happen to him and for him to understand it, either. He's probably so confused."

"Give him a break, kid. People read the newspaper. He's got to know that in some swimming social circles, you're a wanted man. The feds have been trying to gather enough information to connect you to every illicit action in this city for months."

"You're right." I nodded slowly, thinking about four or five things at once. "But it doesn't make it any less terrible." I said defiantly.

"You're right. We just need a head on the inside." Tony said again.

I couldn't believe that it didn't hit me the first time he had said it. Cyril. He said to me after I met him that if things got too hard to bear that I would need his helping hand. "We do have someone." I said, a slight smile breaking across my face.

"Who?" Tony had that jealous look again.

"I don't think that's any of your business, honestly." I wanted to make him feel even more guilty. "Every time it comes to be that I have a connection with anyone, you get jealous. Lay off me for a minute. You've messed things up enough." I said in a tone that advised him against his usual, heinous course of action. "Let me try and patch a few things up before you jump in again." I paused. "I'm not stupid. I've learned a lot from you."

That last part must have sweetened things up a tad because he didn't continue to argue, instead he said, "Well, if you do need me. Let me know." He took a second, then paced to the door, where his keys were sitting on the drawer of the sitting room. "Need a ride home?"

"Yes." I said, putting my plate into the sink and drawing on my overcoat.

"You know, the only reason I ask so many questions are because I care about you and I don't want to see you hurt or in jail." He said somberly.

"Well, sometimes your questions lead to things that make me feel as though you're trying to control me and my life and I don't like it. No one should have that kind of power over someone else and I would think that after all you've experienced in the last decade, you would let loose a tad. Not just for your sake but for—"

"What's that?" His eyebrows drew together, confused.

"What do you mean? Everything that I've experienced in the last decade?"

"I just know that you've been through a ton since starting this Speakeasy thing and you're in a position to change so much." I began to explain, trying to avert the direction of the conversation away from Oliver.

"Who told you about my past?" His eyebrows let go and raised. "I'd like to know if they are worth the information that they falsely planted in you. 'Cause I'd be willing to wager that their information is wrong." I opened my mouth to counter his argument. "I'll tell you, right now, Guy, that most of the crap that comes out of everyone else's mouth is a boldface lie. I only open up to a small pocket of people."

"Tony, you say that, and you say that you care about me but there's a large chunk of your life that I don't know anything about. Hardly anything about you ever even comes up in conversation and the few attempts at learning more about you have been refuted." I said, flatly.

"This conversation's over, Guy. Let me take you home." He said, simply, stuffing the keys into the pocket of his lapel.

The ride back to my place was silent. At one point, five minutes into our journey, Tony had cranked the window down to fill the noise gap. I glanced a few looks at him from my side of the cab and noticed an unreadable expression on his face. We had reached a new avenue: mad at one another.

I had arrived a place that I couldn't have thought possible. Peggy mad at me. Robby incarcerated. Cyril probably miffed with me. Markel locked up as well. Laurel not really speaking with me and now Tony mad at me too. I have successfully alienated myself from my own circle. I couldn't say that it wasn't a strange scenario.

I hopped out of the car and grabbed my copy of the newspaper from my mail cubby in the lobby. The concierge shot me a glance that seemed to drain the color from his face. He looked like a ghost.

My face instinctively scrunched up in reply to his pale look. "Monsieur Linister? I'm surprised to see you." His French accent was broken a little by shock.

"Why's that?" I asked dubiously.

"Well..." His voice turned wry. "You may want to take a look at that newspaper." He pulled back his words at the end of his sentence.

I looked down at the mangle of papers to find the newspaper, wrapped in a rubber bundle. On the front page was a photo of Tony, Peggy and myself with the caption, "WANTED," stamped across the bottom of each of our mugs, made to look like wanted ads.

"Excuse me, Jefferey, could I use the ringer, please?" I asked politely. My voice cracking slightly at the end of my question.

"But of course, sir." He handed me the receiver and dialed upon my command. I didn't expect him to answer, considering he had just dropped me off but I let it ring for seven minutes anyway, hoping to catch him as he entered his home. I couldn't count, in my mind, the time it took for him to get to me.

I then, hung up and dialed Peggy's number. Another dead response. I wondered where she could be. "Do you mind if I come back down in a few minutes and use this tele again?" I asked with the same voice from minutes earlier.

"But of course." He repeated, then added, "but I would advise you to wear something more concealing."

I didn't reply with pleasantries. I understood what he was saying. That was one of the reasons why I like Jefferey so much. He liked me. Therefore, he felt a particular affinity to me when confiding certain social knowledge. I trusted him. Something that Tony would probably tell me is a naïve thing for me to do. I didn't care.

I raced up the stairs to my penthouse and sprung the door open. I began to look for a piece of paper and any writing utensils laying around. After placing both on the table in my sitting room, I began to pack a giant bag with clothes and anything else that I would be using over the course of the next week.

I finished, zipping everything up in the bag, and sat down

at the table. I wrote down everyone's names on the paper, an equal distance apart from one another and drew a line to myself. I then added everyone's current place and disposition with me under their names.

Cyril was the only clear one on the page and I knew that I needed to get into contact with him in order to get Markel out of the slammer. I just didn't know how to get ahold of him. It took me a few minutes to remember that he once presented me with a card that, I believed had his phone number on it.

I ransacked my house, looking even closer through pants pockets and drawers. It had to be here. I didn't just throw things away without looking at them first. After a good ten minutes, I gave up and decided to disguise myself for another series of phone calls in the lobby.

I pinched my shoes back on, refusing to untie them first and swung the door open. Cyril stood before me, dressed in a policeman uniform. "God, I'm glad to see you." I smiled.

"Would you believe me, if I said the same?" His voice was clear but stained with worry. "Guy, you are officially a wanted man. We're going to have to get you in hiding."

His words combed over my brain for a moment. "That will have to wait. There are two men in jail that we need to bust out." I exclaimed.

"Let's not talk out here." Cyril gestured to the hallway and pressed his way into my house. "We're not in a position of luxury anymore." He scanned my frame up and down. "You're also going to have to find a better disguise than that one. I can easily tell it's you!"

"I had five minutes!" I bellowed back. "I have to warn Peggy and Tony about what's going on." I explained in a rush.

"There's no time for that and I don't think it wise of you to break anyone out of jail at this time. Not even legally by means of bail, Guy. They are waiting for you to come and bail Robert out of jail."

I wasn't used to anyone calling him by his full name. "I can't just let him sit in the slammer."

"You don't have a choice. You're lucky that I took the responsibility of coming here to lookout for you or you would have iron clasps around your wrists!" He emphasized by wringing his hands up in front of me in an arrested gesture.

"Cyril!" I shouted back. "Can't we have a stranger bail him out?"

"Yeah, sure... And have that same stranger locked up and questioned as to why they came to bail him out?"

"They can't just lock someone up for bailing another person out of jail, can they?" I was bewildered with an array of plans, swimming in and out of my consciousness.

"Yes, I'm afraid at this point, they can do many things. I believe that with the ASL, having the control that they have now, we will be seeing a dirtier form of vigilante justice. Straight from the local leader of the league." His words came out so clear, they sounded practiced. Like he had thought about a counter argument to my guilty conscious.

"That's disgusting." I spat. "There has to be another way." I retorted.

"Guy, if I offer up another way to get your friend—"

"Friends!" I corrected.

"Friends out. Can you please promise me that you won't do anything risky and you'll listen to every word I tell you? And if at any moment we have to pull the plug, we do so?"

"Yes." I said easily.

"I mean it. Because it's not just your life on the line now. It's also mine as a policeman."

A thought occurred to me before I answered. "But you're not just a policeman, are you, Cyril?" It was a bold question.

"I don't know what you're implying but I can tell you that thoughts like that will not help us right now. We shall discuss those matters on another day, sweeter than the present." His voice was singsong on the final count of syllables.

"Alright. Yes. I promise. What's the plan?" I let go of

everything else, dedicated on getting Robby and Markel out.

"There is a gentleman named Alvah. He's new to the force but he's part of a private citizen sect of the police."

"A private citizen sect? What do you mean?" I heard the words twice more in my brain.

"They're private citizens hired by the police force as well as the ASL to bring other private citizens to justice. They are the reason why your gathering last night was crashed. Someone blabbed." He explained brusquely.

I gave him a look in reply to his sudden change in attitude but didn't reply right away. I took a moment to let the information settle, then asked, "How does this connect with talking to Alvah?"

"We will be able to get Robert out on a technicality and blame it on Alvah being green." He spoke the words like I should have assumed the plan already.

"What do I need to do?" I asked.

"Nothing at the moment. We can't have you running around doing anything. You'll give yourself away and get arrested as well. I wouldn't be surprised if Tony or Peggy were arrested by now."

My stomach did a flipflop like I was turning a pancake in it. After a few more thoughts, it lurched and I gave Cyril a worried glance. "I have to call them."

"No. We need to get you somewhere safe right away. You seemed to have packed before my arrival. Did you need anything else here before we go?" He twiddled his fingers around as he gestured to the rest of the room.

"No. I should have everything."

We decided to take the fire escape, which wove in and out of the main stairway in a way that gave me a perfect glance at the main lobby area. I caught a glimpse of what appeared to be Ella standing there, checking her watch every couple of seconds, like she was waiting for Cyril to come and deliver her news. I realized my luck that he caught up with me before I wandered down to make another phone call.

On our way to my new safe-haven, I came to a conclusion. "I'm not letting you do this without me. Disguise me if you must but I'm going with you." I made sure he understood my position. Though, it wasn't without argument.

"I'm sorry, Guy, but this is whole matter is more arduous than you can comprehend." He turned to look at me from the driver's seat. "At this point, you're lucky to be where you are now."

A slew of things passed back and forth from my mind. "I'm not giving you a choice."

"Then, I suppose your safety doesn't mean much to you, does it?" Cyril sounded cynical.

"Cyril, please. He's my best friend." I pleaded.

“Fine but you will not say a word.” He replied sternly.

“Alright.” I smirked.

We arrived a few short minutes afterward. “This will be your home until I can work out a way to negate your charges and lead the ASL in an alternate direction. Though, to be honest, I doubt it will be plausible at all. Considering the head of the New York chapter caught you at Eddie’s. This is going to be tough. I think I can do it but you really, truly have to do everything I say.”

His words were softer than Tony’s had been in the past. There seemed to be a sense of nurturing to them. A sense of sensitivity that I had not heard in situations like these. I felt a strange sense of comfort in them. Though, the whole of me was disagreeing with my easy trusting nature. Only from past experiences. I awaited a reason behind Cyril’s behavior.

He helped me with my bag, unloading it from the backseat on the street of a seemingly residential neighborhood. The house we headed for was like the side-house Tony had acquired from Morgan. It was a one-story, blue house with white shutters and a long, gravel pathway that led from the street to the front door.

“It’s extremely humble compared to what you’re used to.” He made a modest smile, then continued, “And for that, I’m sorry.” He turned the doorknob and swung the door open to reveal a beautiful interior with furniture that my mother would have adored.

The entryway was a long hallway that led to a large living room with a single couch against the wall and an open area with a rug to the left. There were two main hallways that led out of the room and large windows to the right. Everything had lace draperies atop it and the room smelled faintly sweet and inviting. The walls were a dark blue with white crowned lining and a large oak door stood at the far end of the room from where we stood.

I sat the small bag, that I had clutched to my side, down next to the drawing table against the right window and looked at all of the shelves that lined the walls next to each hallway. I wasn't used to seeing so many books. "What is this place?" I asked in wonderment.

"This is my main house." He responded even more modestly than before.

"I love it," was all I could manage to say as I peered down the hallways, looking for more to the house that didn't exist in this room.

"You really think so?" He asked, surprised.

"Yes. I love the mini-library that you have here." I smiled a little too jokingly.

"You do?"

"Yes. I've always wished to read more." My reply seemed distant still. I was lost in my surroundings.

"You never really struck me as the bookish type." He wondered aloud.

"I'm not. I've always been more fascinated in painted works and music." I ran my finger along a few titles that stood out to me.

"That makes sense." He continued to smile, standing in the main archway. "Maybe when this whole mess is over, I'll take you to my favorite gallery."

"You have a favorite gallery?" I turned to look at him again, then shook my head. I shouldn't be getting wrapped up in pleasantries while there was work to do. Maybe I was a tad hungover still.

I thought that Cyril could tell this change of tone because he then said, "I'll show you your room and then we'll go over the plan."

I followed him down the closest hallway to the front door. The door at the end of the hall was oak as well. It creaked slightly as it opened. It was a room with the same colored walls at the main rooms but with a small bed and shelf with more books to its left. There was a closet to the left and a window behind the bed.

"I hope this is alright."

"It's fine." I replied. "So, what's the plan?" I asked with immense anticipation.

CHAPTER 13: THE MAN IS INNOCENT

We looked at one another for a few minutes in the doorway before he said, "I'll go over everything in the living room." He said it like it was something we couldn't tarnish the bedroom with.

I walked ahead of him and sat, crossed legged on the couch, a wide grin splashed my face to give him the air that I wouldn't take no for an answer when we addressed the topic. "So?" I edged.

"A witty disguise, first of all." He barely sat before beginning to pace the room for odds and ends of wearables. "I've got an old pair of glasses we could use, but then you wouldn't be able to see well." His voice was precise, cold, distant. He was digging deep into his mind.

"Alright, I can deal with that." I added. "We could mess with my hair, add a hat and I'll keep from talking."

I wanted the plan to move on without a hitch. I was tired of waiting and I could tell from the way that he was acting that this could be an all-day thought process. I didn't think I had time for that.

He sat for hardly a second, when I said, "Get up! What are we waiting for?" My voice sounded slightly strained.

"Guy, if they've been locked up for a day now, I hardly expect the minutes to make a chunk of difference." His words were drawn back, calculated.

"My friend Markel has been in for months. I can't stand the thought of him being locked away for something of my fault." I said, not holding anything back.

"Markel?"

I explained everything without conviction. I wasn't sure if I could trust Cyril yet, but it did not matter. I could tell from everything that he was saying that he was going out on a limb for me. He nodded and sighed in places. Then put his hand on my leg. "Well, I promise that we will succeed in getting them both out of jail. However, Guy, I want to stress that from now on, this road will not be an easy one to journey down."

We discussed and debated five or six more costume ideas for me before settling in on a solid idea. I was to play the part of a close family member while making our way into the joint. Then, once we could get his correspondent one on one, we would break character and strike a deal.

Surely, my appearance within the civilian world and the underground scene is the topic that Cyril was banking on during this meeting. I couldn't argue with him. He had seemed to know that side of things quite well and took in quite a number of things in the proper measure to ensure the outcome.

That was one of the things I liked most about him. He was very analytical, in ways that I could never be. I had always thought of myself as a person of control. I contemplated everything to the last drop but the problem with that was that it left me in a belated position of things. With Cyril, he was quick and seemed to meet those deadlines in a very proper manner.

I reveled in our plans and his perfect certainty with them for minutes before putting on my jacket and getting into his car. He didn't take a long time getting there and parked the car around the corner. "I would normally park in a space designated for the authorities but in this case, I'll have to go in and pretend to get to work for a minute before you come in. I'll be your main point of contact. Try not to say a word to anyone else. We don't want you to give yourself away at the start of things. I'll handle all of the uncertainty in the office."

The words of the plan spun in my head many times before getting out of the car. We had decided to get Markel out first, for many reasons, but the main two were that he had been in the longest and I wasn't on perfect terms with Robby at the moment.

Sure, I wasn't still bitter about what he had said about my mother, but he had never apologized and neither of us had any time to talk about our argument since.

I adjusted my suit and fake facial hair as I began counting in my head. "Remember," Cyril began, "wait five minutes, then come in."

"I know, I know. I remember." I waved him off.

He flew from the car to the side of the building and out of sight. I kept thinking that if this went wrong, I could be locked up as well. The thought swirled inside me like the echo of a bad dream. However, I didn't care. It was practically my fault that they were in there. Well, at least in Markel's case. Robby wrote his own anguish for the most part.

I tapped my leg with my hand and finished my count, sighing heavily. I took each step like I was awaiting my turn at the guillotine. I picked up my pace after turning the corner of the building. Grabbing the front door, I could feel the immense pressure waving over me like the rush of the ocean, threatening to engulf me in its enormous power. This was the most important thing I had ever done in my life.

I swallowed hard as I approached the front desk. It was Cyril. He was scrambling around, pretending to look for a form from the receptionist desk. This meant that phase one was working. He must have sent the front desk cop on an errand while he covered for them. "Excuse me." I said in a strange voice that I practiced on the way there.

"That's perfect." Cyril whispered, winked and gave me an okaying hand gesture. He continued to whisper. "Everyone is upstairs. So, no need to go through the complete speech." We had one prepared for this moment. "Just follow me and don't say a word from now on. I think we'll be just fine." His white teeth shined through his smile.

He placed a "BE RIGHT BACK" sign on the desk and led me up the semi-circular, stone stairway and into another desked area full of cubicles and sectioned off rooms. It was very organized and had five people visible from the top of the stairs.

"George." Cyril address a man at a desk on the left side of the cubicles. "This is Henry Hamburg. He's Markel Hamburg's cousin. He's here to bail him out." His words seemed natural enough.

But that didn't stop George from standing slightly and eyeing me up and down and whispering to Cyril. "Do you think this cat's legit, then? You know what'll happen if the chief comes back and you'll legged him out?" His tone seemed distant like he was in on the chase but I knew that Cyril didn't have enough time to coordinate that.

"I checked his ID. Everything seems to line up, my friend." Cyril said in his usual charismatic manner.

"Well, you'll have to out-process with Alvah. He's back in the civil office. He's the agent assigned to Mister Hamburg." George sat back down and took a large bite of a sandwich.

"Thank you." Cyril tipped his hat and began to lead me down a hallway behind the desk.

There wasn't anyone down the hallway and I felt Cyril's hand grab mine. I looked up from watching my steps to find his face turned to see mine. He had an odd expression on his face. One that I had never seen him use before. I wanted to say something but bit my lip as he turned back around and let go of my hand.

The room we entered was very bright. There were two men sitting at a table with files littering the top. "Gabe, can I borrow Mister Abadi for a moment, please?"

Gabe was a slightly chubby, pale man with thinning brown hair and a wide nose. He was wearing a similar black suit to the other man in the room. He nodded with a suspicious expression, then said, "I'm heading to lunch anyways. They don't pay me over time." I could hear him continue to scoff as he walked down the hallway behind me.

Cyril shut the door a moment later. "Am I in trouble?" The other man asked.

"No." Cyril said. "Alvah, this is Guy Linister." He gestured to me and I removed my hat and glasses.

It seemed to take a few minutes for Alvah to make the

connection between the two of us but after a few minutes, he said, "What does this mean?" His voice had a slight accent that I had never heard before.

"It means that there are things going on that are larger than either of us. Can you help us get an innocent man out of jail?" Cyril importuned. His words were deviating script slightly.

"He's a wanted man, Cyril." His face became worried and his posture grew a tad resistant to our presence.

I could instantly tell what angle Cyril was taking with him. Alvah was obviously a virtuous man, who believed in justice. I just hoped for our sake, that Cyril knew what he was doing.

"Alvah, you've heard his own words. The man is innocent." Cyril pleaded.

"Then why is he here?" Alvah pointed at me with conviction.

"Markel happens to be a friend of his who was in the wrong place at the wrong time." Cyril replied.

The two seemed to look at one another for a long while, when, Alvah finally replied. "I'll help as long as my name doesn't get thrown into the mix. You will do all of the paperwork." He ran back to a cabinet and pulled out a large file and handed it to Cyril. "I have to stop by Johnson's desk to get the keys." He paused. "This is going to raise some eyebrows, Cyril. I hope you're prepared for the gossip."

"You know I'm a fan of gossip." Cyril jousted and the two of them left the room.

I wasn't sure if I was to follow. So, I stood were I was and waited several minutes. Anything could happen on their way to get the keys and then on the way to the cell. I wondered if it was going to be this easy to break Robby out. After all, this trickery might not work on Alvah, considering Robby was actually caught at a Speakeasy.

But then again, I didn't know entirely how Markel was framed. Maybe, he too, was caught at a Speakeasy. Probably invited by Tony himself. I slapped a hand to my face. I made a vow to make sure Tony didn't have this much power in the future.

It seemed like forever passed before I watched Cyril appear again in the doorframe, followed by Alvah and Markel. "Guy!" Markel exclaimed.

"Not now." I said back, in a hushed voice. "We will have to wait on the pleasantries for the time being."

I waited in the silence for Cyril to say something about Robby but he didn't. Instead he and Alvah left shortly after sitting the two of us down at the table that sat in the middle of the room. Markel was making eye contact with me. A slight smile breaking from his face. I felt guilt shroud my stomach.

There were a few thoughts beating me up at this point in time. What if Cyril left because he was in the process of getting me locked up as well. It was a fleeting thought because I reminded myself that he had arrested me once before and didn't bother actually bringing me to jail but let me loose, only to find a million articles about me the next day. So, this had certainly not been his intention.

Was he talking Alvah into letting Robby go as well? I swam through thoughts, trying to pick out the most logical as Markel continued to stare at me. "I'm so sorry." I mouthed in a silent whisper.

"For what?" Markel said in a funny tone.

Did he not know? Maybe being locked up for all this time, he hadn't read the papers. No, that couldn't be it. They had to have questioned him. He would have to know at this point.

"Markel, you got arrested because you were framed by someone in league with me." I knew that what I said was going to implicate me more than I wanted it to but I had not been the one to commit the iniquity in this situation. It wasn't I who put him in this place. It was Tony. I was guilty by association and if he was going to be mad at me for that, then I deserved every bit of it.

"I know that." Markel said, his voice still light. "I was waiting for you to come and get me out. I spent a lot of time being mad when I was first brought in but now, I'm ready to get into it."

"Into it?" I swung my head to the side in confusion.

"Yes. I want in. If you're really in league, as you say, with the men behind the anti-anti-alcohol movement, then I want in." His voice seemed lighter still.

"Hasn't being in here taught you anything?" I proclaimed. "I would want out."

"There's so much more money in the underground. I'm tired of working at a bank. You're famous and you have connections. I won't take no for an answer." His voice took on a serious tone.

So, this was his game. He could tell that I was guilty and he wanted to use that guilt as a device to get in on the alcohol business. I wish I could express how much more trouble he could be putting himself into but I felt my grief wall over me.

"Alright, you're in, but I'm telling you, it's no picnic." I kept shooting looks to the door, pleading with the heavens in my head that Cyril would hurry up and come back. I was beginning to become more unnerved than ever before.

"Anything is better than the shit I've been through in here." Markel said, rolling his eyes. "When are we leaving?" He asked, innocently.

"We're working on that, Markel. Just relax for now." I hushed him as I stood to pace, nervously.

Cyril popped his head in. "Just ten more minutes and we'll have Robby as well." He winked again, making a flattering face, then pulled his head from the doorway.

Markel peered at me with a look I couldn't define. Then, after a minute, he said, "You guys close?" It sounded more like a statement.

He continued to gaze at me, leerily for another few, silent moments. I broke the silence with, "Not entirely. We've just been working on this escape plan for a while now." I tried to bluff a smile but failed.

"Ah." He nodded slightly, trying to break the awkwardness, I was sure. "He seems nice."

"He's all we've got at the moment." I said as Cyril reentered the room with an impatient look.

"We need to go."

"What's going on?" I asked.

"Follow me. I'll explain in the car."

We followed him through the hallway, back into the main office area where all of the cubicles were. The man at the desk raised his hand to try and speak to Cyril. "Not now, George." Cyril waved him off and led our way down the stairs.

I heard fast footsteps coming from the hallway we just came from. "Quickly now." Cyril said in a hushed voice.

We picked up speed and got to the front door. "Stop! Wait a moment!" I heard a familiar woman's voice call from the top of the stairs.

"I messed up, Guy." Cyril's voice was riddled with contrition.

"We'll talk later." I said, nearing the corner of the building.

Cyril got there before either of us. There were already two men in the car. I piled into the back seat with Markel. Robby was already pressed up against the window and Alvah was sitting cross-armed in the front seat.

The vehicle roared to life and Cyril spun us off the side of the street and barreled us down the road as quick as the thing would go. "Who're your new friends?" Robby asked, confused about what was going on. He still smelled like alcohol from the night before. He must have drank quite a bit.

"It's hard to explain. I'm guessing that we'll get to that any minute now." I didn't want to have to repeat myself.

We arrived at Cyril's second, hidden home shortly. Robby practically kicked his door open and Markel opened his as well and held it as I tailed him. The two slammed their doors closed at the exact same time. Cyril was already ahead of us, unlocking the door to his place and ushering everyone inside.

"We can't go back." Alvah said to Cyril with a miserable look as he took a seat and buried his head in his hands.

Cyril sat next to him on the couch and put a hand on his shoulder. "It's alright. I can have you protected if you stay here."

"My wife's going to kill me. I don't know what I'm going to do. I shouldn't have listened to you!" He shrugged Cyril off and looked him in the eyes.

"Would someone please explain what is going on?" Robby looked at everyone in the room one by one until he met my eyes.

"It's a long story." I replied, wishing that Robby would be at least a little grateful for being sprung from jail.

"Well, apparently, we have a few minutes." Robby raised his eyebrows. "Anyone have a cigar?" He gestured for a light from the other men.

"Robby, sit down and stop being rude. These men risked their lives to get you out of jail." I grabbed at his coat tail and tried to get him to sit at one of the chairs against the window.

"But I didn't do a thing wrong!" He sounded like a child, caught playing with fire by his mother.

"Oh, shut up, Robby. Everyone here knows everything."

"Actually, I could use some enlightening." Markel piped up from the entranceway.

"I'm not entirely sure of things either." Alvah said in an exasperated tone.

I caught everyone up to speed in small bluffs with each person. By the time I had finished, we were all drinking and a few of us had a smoke or two. Everything seemed normal when I looked around the room, littered with shelves and shelves of books, each taunting me with their little perfect escapes.

"None of this changes the fact that my wife is going to kill me once she finds out." Alvah said again when the dust cleared in the room.

"Why though?" I asked.

"I joined the civil side of the police force to help the ASL bring down alcoholism in this country." He stood with a sense of pride.

"I take it, your wife is part of the ASL?" Markel was the one to ask.

"Yes. She happens to be Ella Hastings' right hand woman." He sat and buried his head again. "She probably wishes I was dead. There's no doubt that Ella told her exactly what happened."

"What did happen?" I asked Cyril, who was grabbing Alvah another glass of water. He was the only one not drinking.

"I screwed up." He set the glass on the small wood table in front of the couch. "The man guarding Robby was a little too curious and I said a few wrong words to him." His explanation told me what I needed to hear but it didn't tell me everything and I craved to know the full story; however, I didn't press out of respect for Alvah's silent grieving.

"Regardless of being loose or not, you have to continue

thinking of yourselves as wanted men… All of us, actually." Cyril's voice was calm and composed, though I could tell there was a faint hint of uncertainty to it. He wanted to sound strong to the rest of us, though, and that's all that mattered.

"We can't all stay here." Robby said, after a moment of wild eyes looking in all directions.

"Don't worry about that." I said back. "Before I left my house, I grabbed a ton of cash. I can set everyone up with a safe house for now. Just don't enter or leave it without making sure that you don't look like yourself." I looked specifically at Robby. "And make sure you're not being tailed."

The next step on my list would be contacting Peggy somehow and making sure she was safe and aware of everything happening. I couldn't lose her now. I wouldn't be able to bear it.

As much as I hated the idea, I also had to find Tony. He would be the only one who could manage this congregation in an organized manner. I thought that this particular part of my list could wait a little while longer. I needed to track down Peggy first.

"Cyril, any luck getting a message from my old building without giving away our location?" I asked.

"If you made the call at a random location, I don't see them having any way of figuring out where we are." He furrowed his brow. "What are you planning now?" He sounded worried.

"I have to find Peggy. Maybe she tried calling the front

desk at my penthouse. I'm going to take a walk." I threw on a coat as Cyril shouted more warnings at me. I decided that using the fake facial hair and large hat would be within my best interests now.

The air was hotter and wetter now, and I licked my sweaty lips every minute or so trying to keep my mustache in place. I found a little ice cream parlor in the neighborhood that I thought would be the perfect place to call from. I knew that Cyril would think that I would need to be farther away before doing anything of the sort but I didn't care. It was one call.

I asked the lady at the counter if I could use her ringer and she obliged without argument. It rang five times before a familiar French voice answered.

"Jefferey. Has a Miss Peggy Austrait tried to contact me lately?" I tried to keep my voice quiet.

"Monsieur? Guy?" In his shock, he forgot to address me by my surname like he usually did. "I thought they got you!" His voice sounded a tad worried now.

I felt a strange feeling in my stomach, realizing that he cared so much. "No. I need to find Peggy. Has she called?" There was panic in my voice now.

"Yessir. Many times, Monsieur. She's in trouble. She said that she'd be at the docks in the marina until four today. She said that she had little time. They're onto her."

CHAPTER 14:
A MAN WEARING HEELS

"Thank you, so much. You are my favorite concierge." I smiled through the phone and hung up in a rush.

I had originally planned to go back and check on the others before looking for Peggy but that was when I had thought that I wasn't going to be able to find her. I flattened my hat onto my hair so hard that I could feel it along the top of my head. I tucked my hair into the sides and strutted out of the joint as fast as I could. I heard the lady at the counter yell a polite, "have a nice day!"

The marina was a forty-minute walk from where I was but I worried about catching a cab in leu of getting noticed. Instead, I ran with my head down, watching my feet as they blurred beneath me. The summer air was making my clothes stick to me and I poked my head up occasionally to see the hustle and bustle of the city pressing in around me. I was getting closer now.

As the people of the city began to move faster and faster as the marina grew into vision, I too, clicked my heels so quickly that I was afraid of breaking a shoe. I passed the gateway of the entrance and found myself at a dock that ran perpendicular with the coast. That way, I could see all of the launch docks shooting out into the harbor.

I couldn't see a woman amongst any of the persons wheeling and dealing in and out of the boats. Peering in all directions like a madman off his medication, I began to move, keeping rhythm with my feet. My neck crooned left and right, down docks that I may have missed.

I almost gave up, when I saw a lumped over figure of a man, sitting with his legs crossed at the end of one of the docks that didn't have a boat fastened to one of its boards. Though, it wasn't a man after a minute of careful evaluation. It was Peggy with a very large, black coat draped around her small frame.

She continued to sit as I approached. "Isn't that outfit a little hot?" I asked, sitting next to her and placing my left hand on her thigh.

"It's a man's jacket." She turned and softened her smug look. Where her defined eyebrows usually stood strong, were two brows furrowed in a worried fashion.

"Peggy." I flashed sympathetic eyes back. "Come here." I

pulled her into a hug. "What's the matter?"

"I was hassled in my own home." She almost began to sob.

"What?" I struck. "By who?"

"The landlord of the fancy schmancy pants penthouses!" Her words pitter-pattered out like rain.

"What happened?" I asked as her head sunk deeper into my shoulder. This was a side of Peggy that I had never seen before.

"He knocked at my door at six o'clock in the morning and told me that, if I didn't want the police to be called on me, I'd better get out." Her voice was calmer now.

"At least he warned you." I lightly combed her leg with my fingertips. "It's going to be alright."

"That's not what I'm upset about." She pulled away from me and stared into my eyes. "If I had gotten locked up, I would have never gotten the opportunity to say that I'm sorry." Her amber brown eyes gazed into mine.

"For what?" I asked, trying not to break eye contact.

"I said some pretty disgusting things to you last night and I feel like a beef stick." Her eyes started to water slightly.

"Peggy, it's quite alright. I didn't care. I understood what you were going through… What we were all going through, actually." I thought about it again. I couldn't believe that it was just last night that everything unraveled. It had seemed like days ago now. "We have to make an even harder effort now. More than ever before. Things are getting serious."

"You're telling me!" She shouted. "We're wanted!"

I covered her mouth. "Peggy." I yelled in a hushed voice. "Try not to run around shouting that."

I released my hands and found a slight smile spreading across her face. She wasn't wearing her usual array of makeup and her hair was disheveled.

"Come on. Let's get you cleaned up." I helped her up. "But first, let's get you a hat."

"Why?" Her voice was incredulous.

"Because, sweetheart, your red hair gives you away. You're like a star in the night sky." I smiled and took her hand in mine.

"Well if I'm a star in the night sky, then I'll blend in just fine." She smirked.

"Not in the New York sky. You're practically the only star!" I laughed.

We played with the idea of dressing her up like a man but that idea didn't go over very well with her. Mostly because that would require removing what little makeup she was wearing and she didn't feel comfortable with me seeing her that way.

I bought her a top hat and some pins and she hid her hair well. We walked the hour back to the safehouse. I explained everything on the way there. "So, where's Tony, then?" She asked, wanting to get the full scope of things.

"I'm not entirely sure. He wasn't on my radar at the time. Did you have any luck with Laurel recently?" It was a thought that reoccurred in my head.

"No." She was wearing a bunched expression that I couldn't read. "Where is this place? I feel like we've been walking forever." I couldn't tell if she was changing the subject or if she was actually annoyed with the situation.

"I told you twenty minutes ago that waving a cab down would be risky." I retorted.

"I know. I'm not arguing. I'm just wondering how much longer do we have to walk? I look like a man wearing heels!" She said, playfully.

"Good!" I chuckled.

"It's not good. I'm causing more of a spectacle than being me." She laughed as well. "It makes it even stranger that you're holding my hand."

I gave it a little squeeze and we continued onto the property of the safehouse. I rapped at the door three times. There was no response. I did it a second time, before calling, "Gentlemen!? It's me."

Cyril was the one to answer. "We need to develop a code for the door. I didn't open it instinctively."

The way that he had said it made me think that there were previous knocks. "Who else came by?" I raised one eyebrow.

"Robert's lady friend." His voice was fluttery and goofy.

"Robert?" I continued to raise my eyebrow.

"I'm sorry, Guy. I'm used to his name on paper." He opened the door and ushered us inside. "You must be Peggy."

"Yes sir!" Peggy made a curtsy in her usual sarcastic manner.

"I've heard and seen so much about you. It's a great pleasure to actually meet you in person." Cyril's posture straightened and his palm opened in her direction. She took it and he placed a kiss upon it.

"I'm overcome!" Peggy said, even more sarcastically than before.

Robby and Ruth came walking towards us from the left hallway. "Guy, any word from Tony?" Robby asked.

I knew that he was really wanting to know about Laurel, not Tony. "No."

"What about Laurel?" His voice played innocent but had tones of harshness to it.

I shot him a look of indignation. My expression gave me

away. “No.” I said in a voice that tried to sound just as innocent as his but was stained with worry. Our entire past with the topic somehow came out in four words.

Peggy made eyes between the two of us. I was afraid that she could see the sibling rivalry that was sparking in our eyes. I felt instantly guilty and my face turned red. Peggy wasn’t a stupid girl.

Ruth gave Robby a foreboding expression with her hands on her hips. I could tell that this was a touchy subject with the two of them. I wondered if she knew everything as she tapped her foot on the floor, looking between the two of us.

The silence grew in the room until Cyril broke it with the words, “Refreshments!” He turned and raced into the kitchen, grabbing the serving tray from the coffee table and giving me a wink as he did so.

“I’m sure we’ll find them.” I said, after a few more moments. I led Peggy to the couch, pulled off her hat for her and took a seat. She swung her overcoat onto the back of the couch and huffed out a large breath as she fell to my left.

“That jacket was heavy!” She exclaimed.

The other two were still silently making faces and mouthing words by the hallway. “One moment.” Robby said, raising a finger and pulling Ruth into the nearest bedroom.

“What’s with them?” Peggy asked me in a whisper.

"You didn't catch all that?" I whispered back.

"Sort of. You sure were passing some faces back and forth." Her eyes fluttered around the room.

"Well, it's complicated."

"Let me guess." My nerves shot to my stomach. "He has a thing for Laurel." Her head shook slightly and a small smile struck her face.

"That's a big part of it."

"And his chickey-poo doesn't like that." Her smile widened.

"Actually, I'm not entirely sure." My eyebrows furrowed as I looked down the hallway and then to my left as Cyril reentered the room. We could hear mottled voices from the bedroom now, like an argument was beginning.

"Is everything alright?" Cyril said, whimsically.

"Yes." I looked up and smiled. "What do you have?" I looked at the tray he was placing on the coffee table. It was littered with seven tea cups.

"Tea. I figured we all needed a little pick-me-up." He smiled solemnly and sat on the chair opposite us.

"This is delightful!" Peggy picked up the little porcelain cup and simpered as it reached her lips.

"Sorry, it hasn't cooled down yet." Cyril looked abashed.

"It's alright, darling." She smiled back at him.

This was a sight to see. I was used to the "not taking a liking to any man" Peggy. She was quite the picky gal. Though, it was hard not to like Cyril. He was polite, charming and had an even more bedazzling accent.

"Guy, can we talk?" Robby busted out of the bedroom and headed toward the front door, wrapping his coat around him.

"Sure." I said, slightly confused.

"Boys, you might want to use the backyard." Cyril suggested as he grabbed two cups and started walking down the hall, most likely to offer Alvah, Ruth or Markel.

We walked through the kitchen and a small laundry area to a ratty door with a mat. He opened it and led me onto a small porched area with a rocking chair, stool and a small wooden table. The backyard was fenced and surrounded by three other yards from other houses.

There wasn't anything in the grass and it didn't look like any of the neighbors had anything in their yards either, though, it was hard to tell through the wooden fences.

"What's going on?" I asked before I could let him yell at me.

"It's Ruth." I couldn't read his voice. It was somewhat angered but also a little exasperated.

"What about her?" I crossed my arms as he took a seat on the stool.

"She's driving me bananas." He shrugged, got up from the chair and leaned against the side of the house, placing his hands in his pockets.

"Then ask her to leave. You invited her." I reminded him.

"It's not that. Guy, I invited her over to discuss business plans. It's going to be hard for me to make appearances and I've been steadily planning having her take the reins in certain scenarios. I just never thought—"

"Never thought what?" I cut him off. "That she'd like you?" I scoffed. "Robby, everyone likes you." I wanted to laugh in a teasing manner but his face told me not to.

"It's worse than that." He said through pursed lips.

"What?" I opened my palms and raised my raised my shoulders.

"She knows about my plans to run away with Laurel and I think she's trying to blackmail me." His voice was more cautious now.

"How so?"

"I think she's using the fact that I'm wanted to make me choose her instead."

"Like she's going to turn you in?" I asked as he was already nodding in response. "Robby, this is silly. You couldn't choose Laurel, even if you wanted to. She's married."

"Guy, there's more to it." His face turned a dark red.

I didn't even ask. I simply looked at him incredulously, slightly aware of the answer already.

"We've slept together." He said, point blank.

Of course they have. Why would I ever have thought otherwise? It was Robby after all. He was the heartthrob. The lady's man. The cat-eater. I would have never had a chance with Laurel to begin with.

Suddenly, there was so much running through me that I felt dizzy. I would have walked back into the house if he hadn't followed up with, "It was right after you and I had our fight. She was the whole reason for the fight to begin with." His words were rushed and forced. "I'm so sorry for that, by the way. I was being a complete ass." He grabbed my shoulders and made me face him. "But I need you now. You're my best friend."

"Robby…" I began slowly, thinking about everything that he had just said, along with the last time I had seen him and our fight. "I still haven't forgiven you. I don't think I will anytime soon. What you said was really mean. You were being worse than an ass that night. What's a matter with you?"

"Well, I always thought that you had some secret affair with Laurel this whole time and it made me angry. I don't generally like to talk about my feelings and instead of telling you straight forward, I pussyfooted around the topic and started to pent things up."

This was more a word than I had ever heard out of Robby, besides the other night. He was beginning to talk about things and understand himself. It was shocking because he has never been the self-aware type. It was probably the reason why he didn't speak so much.

I didn't know what so say. So, I stayed silent, looking him in the eyes and waiting for him to say something. I still didn't feel like talking.

All of the suspicions that I had about the two of them had just been confirmed. A part of me felt betrayed but the other side of me was telling me that I had never told Robby of my feelings for Laurel. It was fair, especially now that I had Peggy, but things were more complicated than that. I felt like a boat in a sea with nets to catch fish in too many directions.

"I had been working the bill for Tony Reynolds for four months before you showed up. I was trying to cozy my way in on Laurel for quite a time. Then, you show up and get invited to all of their secret gatherings and have a chemistry with her that I couldn't have even dreamed of." His words felt like a stranger was speaking through him.

"But Robby, you can literally have any woman you want. You know that, right?" I replied, angrily. "You've always been that way. Ever since we were children. I was the invisible one." I looked him in the eyes. "It doesn't feel pleasant, does it?" I asked bitterly.

"No." He dropped his head and looked at the ground. "I guess I never really thought about that." He paused. "I guess, I never really cared." He looked up at me and placed his hand on my left collarbone. "You know, you weren't the only one who spent a lot of time reflecting when your mother passed away. I didn't have my best pal to get along with anymore. You were a ghost.

"I had to find myself and put myself out into the world. It wasn't easy at first. I did odd jobs for years until I got lucky with this gig. I never thought those days spent playing horn at my uncle's place with you would ever do anything for me."

"Are you kidding? We played great music together…" I began to smile. "I miss those days. I feel like I haven't played piano in a long time, thinking about it." I mused.

"Maybe we'll write more." He suggested. "Once we're in the clear to perform music again."

"Do you think that day will ever come?" I grimaced slightly.

"Of course. You don't know the pickles we were in when you left New York. Things got crazy. Tony almost shut the whole operation down."

"Oh, I know. He told me." I thought back at Tony telling me that he had my friend Markel arrested.

"Where did the two of you go? I was reading in the papers that you had run off to Mexico or something. Until Tony had the whole thing sorted, the papers were making it seem like you were trying to make a getaway." He looked like he was on the verge of laughter.

"We went to New Orleans." I smiled and explained the whole story, leaving out some of the more personal notes but explained that the music there had a different feel and since we were on the topic of writing, we should try and develop our new material to suit it.

"That's incredible." He beamed.

"Gentlemen." Peggy came out of the back door and crossed her arms. "Looks like the two of you made up." She raised an eyebrow at Robby. "Cyril needs a word with you, Guy. He said it's important."

"Alright." I looked between the two of them and passed Peggy to open the door. "You going to play nice?" I asked her.

"No promises." She said curtly.

I met Cyril in the living room. He was sitting on the couch, stirring his tea and had a baleful look about him. "Everything okay?" I startled him as I entered the room.

“Everything’s fine. I just wanted to tell you that I believe we’ve found Anthony Reynolds.” His words sounded a tad worried.

“And? Is everything okay?” I asked again, sitting next to him. The plush couch consumed me as I sank into it. “You sound a little strange.”

“Oh, it’s quite fine. It’s just… I’m afraid you’re going to try and go talk to him.” This response seemed even more cautious than the first.

“Well, he’s not in jail, is he?” I asked.

CHAPTER 15: A FEW LOOSE ENDS...

Cyril sat there for a second with a debating face. "No. He isn't. However, Guy, it was one thing to run around the city looking for your girlfriend. It's another to go looking for the most wanted man among us."

"I never said that I was going to." My words came out in a flutter.

He looked at me for a few moments, thinking of what to say. I didn't know Cyril to the degree that I was reading him well. From the expression he was giving me it seemed that he wanted to be nice but thought I was being stupid. "You say that, but Guy, I know you pretty well now." He was wearing a cheeky smile. "You care too much about people."

"So, what if I do?" I fronted.

"It's not a bad thing, Guy." He said surreptitiously. "But it's not exactly a good thing either." He was beginning to sound like

Peggy. "Trust me. I know how you feel. I give most people the benefit of the doubt. It's gotten me into quite a stammer." He was talking about how he couldn't return to his job as a policeman. All because of me.

"I'm sorry." I felt guilty.

"Stop. That would make two of us." I watched his facial expression falter but I did not ask him to elaborate.

"That's not going to stop me, Cyril."

He drew out a long breath. "I know that. I just wanted to make sure you watch your back and give us a ring if you encounter trouble." His smile was slowly beginning to pronounce itself again. It was a manipulating smile. Even if he didn't intend it to be so. It was telling me that he would feel terrible if I got caught. "Although, I don't recommend bringing Peggy along. It's one thing to be one person on the run but being two is another thing. They'll be looking for everyone together."

"I don't understand how she's wanted as well. She left before the raid." My eyes swam about the room in wonderment, trying to think back to the raid. I came to the conclusion that I needed to stop drinking as much when I go out. Though, I felt like I came to that conclusion often and it probably wouldn't change a thing.

"She's already been suspected of being involved in the past. The raid only put everything into perspective for the ASL and the police operation."

"But she wasn't caught in the act." I rebutted.

"They have the power to say anything now. They're going to use it. It's not like they have recording devices to solidify their claims. Besides, I read something this morning about how she was seen fleeing the scene in tears by many passersby."

"Of course." I grunted.

"Everything alright?" Peggy walked into the room, tapping the back of her hand, at the knuckles, to the wall to announce her entry.

"Yes, ma'am." Cyril said back to her as Robby entered the room and began to walk down the hallway.

"Cyril, could I have a moment with Peggy?" I asked him.

"Of course. I was going to check on Alvah anyway." He smiled and bowed slightly as he walked backwards down the hallway.

"What's going on?" Peggy asked as she took Cyril's place next to me on the couch.

"We're going to Paris. Just like we planned. I'm leaving now to get the tickets." I explained.

"That's great." The impossible hue of her eyes lit up.

"There's just one thing." I added.

Her face fell. "What's that?"

"I just have a few loose ends to tie up with Tony first." I tried to keep my voice light.

"That's actually perfect."

"What do you mean?" I glanced up at her face, confused.

"Well, he most likely has us tailed." She said like it was nothing. "Laurel said in the first two years of their marriage that he knew absolutely everything that she was up to. He most likely has the same men following you. You'll have to tell him that you're going on a vacation and that you will return soon. Otherwise, he'll do some investigative work and have us eliminated." Her face was defiant and cold.

"Peggy, that's absurd. I doubt he—"

"Guy, you really don't get it, do you?" She gave a dark chuckle. "He's not who you think he is. He's definitely been checking up on you. I just know it."

"Peggy, if you were right, he would have known about the fight between Robby and me." I explained. "I just don't think that that is the case." My voice was calculated and stern.

"Fine, have it your way. Don't tell him." She gave me a grave expression. "But if you don't, I'll be looking over my shoulder every chance I get when we're overseas."

I took a minute to wrestle with the idea. "Fine." I huffed. "Just trust me. I'll be back in a few hours. Please stay here and—"

"Play nice?" She raised her eyebrows sarcastically.

"Exactly." I stuck my tongue out in retort.

I grabbed the address from Cyril before I left and asked to use the car this time. I knew based off the address, that he was in the same safehouse as before and that it was not far from where we were. Still, I hated the idea of having to walk even more in one day.

The drive was quick and easy. I took a large breath before getting out of the car. I knew that this was going to be a challenging endeavor. I had a lot to spill out before I felt comfortable with leaving the country.

I could already feel the anxiety of the situation hitting me. Tony wasn't always the easiest person to speak to. I knew that I never gave him a reason to be upset with me, though, I would be within minutes. Thinking about those who disappointed him and how Tony become caused me to shudder.

I walked slowly up to the door, looking in all directions for even the slightest glimpse of a cop. The coast seemed clear as I knocked my usual three knock salute. Anticipation made it feel like five minutes for the door to crack open. "Are you nuts?" It was Tony's usual disgruntled voice. The one he usually saved for making people feel stupid. "You could have been tailed!"

"Relax. I'll explain everything when you let me in." I said in a hurry.

"Go around back!" He shouted. "And keep your head down!" He added before I tucked off the steps and hugged the bushes next to the gate.

Before I could even reach the door, it swung open and Tony grappled me into a suffocating hug. "God, I was worried you were in the slammer!" His voice boomed.

"Me? Nah. You taught me too well." I snickered and hugged back, glad that our previous tension had been eliminated by shear fear of the other's safety.

"Well? Where is everyone?" He asked, leading me into the house and sitting at the kitchen table.

"We're at a safehouse not far from here." I said, sitting down. "That's not why I'm here."

"Then, what's the word?" He still had a delighted look on his face. Like he had been without friends for days.

"Tony… Where's Laurel?" I asked, changing the subject.

"She's positioned somewhere safe." His words seemed practiced and edgy.

"Why isn't she here with you, then?" I asked, thinking about what Robby had told me just an hour ago. Did Tony know?

"We're in the middle of a… marriage quarrel." His face turned blank.

"Is she okay?" I asked, instead of asking if everything was okay in general.

"She's fine. I don't want to talk about it right now." He looked me up and down. "What's going on?"

"I'm leaving the country for a little while." I said.

His face looked drained of color after a moment. "What's that?"

"Yeah. I wanted to get out for a minute. Everything in New York has been so—"

"You're leaving town!?" His voice sounded angry in a way that I had never experienced firsthand.

"Tony, it's no big deal, I'm just tryin—"

"Trying to get rid of me, huh??" He yelled, sounding paranoid.

"Tony, please!" I pleaded. "That's not it!" I yelled back. "If that was the case, I wouldn't even tell you!"

"Then where are you going?" His voice sounded even more paranoid.

"Paris." I looked him in the eyes with a wild expression. "With Peggy."

"Paris with Peggy, huh?" He asked sardonically. "Then go have fun, Guy! Get the hell out of here!"

"What the hell is your problem, Tony?" My temper was starting to grow in response.

"Are you fucking?" He asked, standing and looking around the room, half-delusional.

"What?" I replied, shocked at the question.

"Are you fucking!?" He said even louder.

"Why the hell does that matter!?"

"Because you're mine!" His voice was shrilly and lacked his Italian accent. He took heavy footsteps to the fridge and grabbed a large bottle from it. He pressed the glass to his lips and started chugging down the alcohol.

I began to pry the bottle from his mouth. "What is your problem, Tony? You're being ridiculous!"

He threw me off of him, pushing me to the floor. "You're my problem, Guy! You just let me into your life and play me and now you're going to do this!?"

"Do what? Tony, I never meant to mislead you." I shouted from the floor. I could feel my face beginning to screw up and my eyes growing progressively wetter.

"That's a joke." He fake-laughed and took another big swig.

"Can you stop drinking? It's making you crazy." I started

pushing myself off of the floor.

"You're making me crazy, Guy. You're a harlot!" I had never heard anyone use that word on a man before but it still stung as he said it.

"Can you stop this!? You're acting like a child!" I didn't dare to walk towards him. "I came here to tell you that I was leaving. I didn't have to, Tony. I could have just gone on my merry way and come back weeks later."

"Weeks? You're going to be gone for weeks?" His voice broke.

"Yes. It takes around ten days to get there and another ten back. I figured we'd be staying about a week there." I explained.

"That's a month, Guy. Not weeks." He choked down another gulp.

I didn't plan on staying much longer. Soon, he would be intoxicated and my experience with drunk individuals, especially Tony, told me that this was going to be quite a spectacle if I stayed. I forced myself to think of ways to get out of the place.

"Then, I suppose, you have two options. You can either accept the fact that I'm leaving and coming back or you can be mad and continue pushing me around and run the risk of me never coming back into your life." It was a bold move but I was running out of viable options.

"How could you do this? I made you!" He shrieked.

"Tony! Stop!" I shouted. "Let's just talk calmly. It's not like I'm leaving forever. I tried to tell you the last time we talked that you can't do this to me. You have to let me go about my business and live my life. You don't own me, Tony." I forced my voice to be calmer.

"You're right." Tony gave me a piercing look. I could tell that the idea was beginning to sink in and he knew that there wasn't much he could do about it. Maybe the reality was beginning to settle into his mind.

"It won't be long and I'll be back." I continued to convince him.

It took a long minute for him to respond. His face grew calmer. "This may be good." Tony started to add. "If you leave, they won't be able to throw you behind bars." He starting musing aloud. "You'll need my help getting out of the country. They'll be making sure you don't try to give them the slip. You'll need disguises and fake passports."

I tried not to look excited at the fact that our argument had ended. Instead, I said, "That would be great!"

We continued to talk for another hour or so. I could tell that part of him was trying to make sure we were alright. He knew that if he pushed too hard, I would disappear. I think that scared him. Maybe after everything that had happened with him and

Oliver, he finally learned that his power isn't enough to keep people in his life.

I gambled on the fact that it may take time for that to sink in but I knew that he would have to succumb to it eventually. He couldn't go through his life thinking that this behavior was acceptable.

We parted with a large hug. "What? No kiss?" He asked me as I began to open the door.

"Tony... I—"

But before I could finish my sentence, he pulled me into an unwanted kiss that sent a chill down my whole body. "I know that I don't talk about it much," he said, with a saddened expression growing on his face. "But I really do love you, Guy."

I looked him in the eyes and tried to muster my feelings to reply. After I had been in so many emotional fiascos over the course of the month, that I couldn't quite place myself in his shoes. "Tony." I said, simply. "You know that I love you." I said it like I was going to continue with a "but".

"But?" His voice was suggestive.

"You only get this way when you've been drinking." I reminded him. "I don't think that I've had one sober encounter, like this, with you." I gave him an awed expression back, trying to keep the mood light.

"I swear the feeling is there." He dug into his pocket like he was going to pull the emotions from his pants.

"I know it is, Tony." My voice was wishy-washy. "But you're married."

"I would leave her for you. If the world was ready for something like that." He stared more fiercely into my eyes. "I know that you feel the same sometimes."

The atmosphere had changed. The whole room felt like a cage and I felt like a lion tamer, stuck inside with my lion. Trying to confront the wild natures in him that made me feel more and more compelled to break them.

I couldn't deny his words but I knew that it wasn't right. I knew that I couldn't let my heart be in multiple places at once anymore. I knew that I loved Peggy and nothing would stop that. I almost slipped up and let him have me the last time we were together but I swore to myself that I wouldn't do it again and that was that. I knew that I was becoming something that I never wanted. Who knew leaving my four-year solitude would implicate me in ways that I never deemed possible?

Even Cyril gave my stomach reasons to invite butterflies. I didn't want to let myself give into a feeling that I knew would cause me more pain. I couldn't quite place it. No one bothered to ask me to stand on one side or another. I could tell that this confused and frustrated the ones closest to me and they probably would want to make me choose.

I had encounters with Laurel, Robby, Oliver, Peggy, and after our argument the other night, now Tony. Everyone knew. Everyone, that is, but me. I spent a long time ignoring all of the facts. Until just this moment, with Tony looking through me. Reading things about me that even I refuse to acknowledge.

I waved it off. I repeated his name aloud and continued to stare into his eyes, wondering what he was looking to find in mine. "We could run away." His voice had a hopeful sense to it, that I had never heard before. He was revealing a vulnerable side that I had only seen once before. This time it was begging.

"I can't." I turned to look out the window, wishing that I had never decided to come. I should have just listened to Cyril. It was easier to deny the truth. Easier to ignore the signs. Better to walk away. "I'm sorry, Tony. I have to go now."

He didn't bother trying to stop me. He stood there in a dazed longing that I wished I could have stopped. His face looked like it was going to break at any moment. I don't think he was expecting himself to say what he did and for me to reject those words so easily. It wasn't easy. It was complicated. It was messy. I hated myself for disappointing him. I couldn't truly be his and he couldn't truly be mine.

He didn't know the side of me that longed to be free. Free of obligation. Free of complication. Free of the social situations that chained me to these emotions that I couldn't explain. I couldn't express. I never wanted this. I never wanted to open myself up to all of this pain.

I closed the door quietly behind me and walked to the car with each step feeling like mini earthquakes below my feet. There was something in the air that reminded me of my place. It was not here.

I turned the key and kicked the vehicle to life. The feel of the wind passing in and out of the car slapped my head back to reality. I had someone waiting for me. I felt a sense of bliss take over for a moment. Until I realized that I was being followed.

CHAPTER 16:
NEW YORK'S CLASSIER SISTER

I had no idea what to do to evade the car behind me. I only just noticed it a block back. I took two completely different turns, which indicated to me that they must have been following me. Was I becoming paranoid for no reason?

It definitely wasn't a copper, or least a policeman in a normal squad buggy. I revved my engine and sped up five-miles-an-hour. It didn't do much, except confirm my suspicions. This wasn't good. This whole trip was a disaster.

If I headed back to the others it would expose us. I drove around the same block multiple times, hoping to lose them but it didn't work. I made strange turns, trying to make sure I didn't get lost in the process. I kept thinking of my location versus the location I was heading toward.

I found a sand alley in the middle of a block of houses. I peeled into it and caught sight of a spot between large shrubs. Without thinking, I parked in it and jumped out of the car. I didn't have time to turn to see my pursuer. I jumped the wooden fence of the nearby house and crossed their yard in seconds, jumping the other side of the gate.

It was a two-block run to the safehouse from there. I couldn't see a wagon in any directions. I slowed my pace as I neared the door. I was lucky to find it unlocked. I slammed the door behind me and sank to the floor.

"What in God's name!?" Alvah jumped from the couch, his eyes baring down at mine. "You scared the living ghost right out of me."

"I'm sorry." I huffed. "I was being followed.

"What?" Cyril asked, entering from the kitchen with another pot of tea.

"Yes. I'm sorry." I repeated, clutching my chest, attempting to catch my breath.

"What's going on?" Peggy came from a door down the hallway, followed by Robby, Ruth and Markel.

"Guy was apparently followed here." Cyril said, panicked. "Were you seen entering?"

"No. There weren't any vehicles on the road as I rounded the block." I explained. "I left the buggy in an alleyway two blocks away." I turned towards the door and pointed in the direction of the car.

"Good. Then I'm less worried about them knowing where we are and more worried about who they are." Cyril put his hand to his chin.

"I sure am worried about them knowing where we are. If he got out and ran here from a few blocks away, that could narrow their search down." Peggy said, rushing next to me defensively. "Are you alright?" She placed her hand on my shoulder.

"Well now that there's no car outside, it will look like there's no one home." Robby pipped up. "Let's just not answer the door for anyone. No one leave."

"My Tin Lizzie is out front!" Ruth said to his left.

"Yes, honey, but you parked it down the street. That could be anyone's ottomobile." He smirked, disregarding her.

We all talked for hours, speculating on the driver of the other car and their intentions. Some drank, some sang. It was a surprise to me that everyone seemed to be getting along. It was even more peculiar that Peggy didn't seem to have an attitude towards Robby. They weren't necessarily socializing but they weren't making scowling faces or ignoring each other either.

It grew dark outside and it became time to prepare the sleeping arrangements. I could tell that this was something that

Cyril was putting off. He knew that there wasn't enough sleeping space for everyone. Which most likely meant that he would have to take the couch.

He paired the women to one room, Robby and I to another, and the third room to Markel and Alvah. He offered to make tea for a third time, which everyone declined, and went about the house, turning all of the lights off. Everything fell silent and dark.

A large banging made me spring out of bed. Sunlight filtering in the blinds caused me to shield my eyes for the first moment. I slowly crept down the hallway to find Cyril getting up from the couch and looking over at me, jumping slightly out of shock.

"What's going on?" Robby came from behind me, rubbing his eyes.

Sure enough, after a few seconds, everyone was awake and in the living room once again. "It's got to be seven in the morning!" Ruth complained, loudly.

"Shush!" Cyril replied in a whisper. "We don't know who's out there."

"Look out the window." Peggy said, splitting herself between the crowd and pulling a large bathrobe around her chest.

"I'll do it. I have a steady hand." I said.

Cyril stopped me for a second, then whispered, "be

careful," as he drew back behind me.

I used the back of my hand to part the curtain next to the front door and peered out onto the porchway. "There's no one there." I whispered to the others.

"No one?" Peggy asked, in shock.

"Yeah." I said, slowly. "It looks like there's a pad of paper on the ground." I squinted, trying to get a better look.

We sat there in the silence for a minute. "Should we open the door?" Markel asked.

"I'm not sure." Cyril said. "You really can't see anything?"

"I can see everything." I said back with an obvious tone. "I can't see anyone."

"Not on the streets or sidewalks?" He asked.

"No one." I replied.

"Let me take a look." Cyril pushed me aside slowly and gazed out the window. "Hmm. I'll open it." He moved everyone back with his hands and opened the door slowly, as if he was awaiting a bomb on the other side. He grabbed the package of papers and closed the door again. "They're addressed to you and Peggy." He said, looking me in the eyes and handing them over.

"What could they be?" I began to open the large, white envelope.

"Well, it's not an explosive. That's for sure." Cyril said.

"How can you tell?" I could hear the worry in Peggy's voice.

"Too small." Alvah said from behind her.

As I unraveled the inner papers and pulled them up to have a better look at them, I asked, "Lights, anyone?"

Robby flipped the switch next to the hallway and lights poured around the room. The four separate pieces of paper looked like tickets. There was also a folded note inside another envelope, that upon opening appeared to have hand writing on it. "They're boat tickets to France." I said aloud. "With a note." I added, slowly, looking at the envelope's front, that read, "*For Guy's Eyes Only,*" In a familiar hand.

"Read it." Peggy said, moving closer.

I skimmed over it with my eyes, realizing that parts were private but decided to skip over it and read the necessary parts out loud.

"Dear Guy,

I apologize for our argument and wanted to do something for you. Lord knows you have done so much for me. That is why I have enclosed two tickets to your desired location. You can go with my blessing.

You will be delighted to know that you were not being followed yesterday. I had a gentleman tail you, so that way, I could send along this package as soon as I was able to secure your tickets. I used connections to get them. Please board disguised and under the names provided on the tickets themselves.

I wish you both the best of luck overseas. I gave you three weeks there. Please find the return tickets enclosed as well. If you wish to stay or return sooner, please purchase those tickets on your own dime."

I skipped a large chunk of the letter and continued with,

"Yours forever truly,

Anthony Marlon Reynolds"

I looked up to find every eye in the room looking at me. "Well, that was nice." Cyril said, after a long bout of silence.

"Yeah right." Peggy scoffed. "He only did it because he wanted to control our time and place. He wanted to keep tabs on if we use the tickets, that way, he'll know that we really are in Paris and not trying to run away." After she said it, I could tell that she would have rather have told me privately.

"Why is that?" Markel asked confused.

"It's a long story." I said. "Anyway, that's not the point. The point is; we're safe." I smiled.

"So, when were you thinking of ditching us for Paris, big boy?" Robby asked with a sour expression.

"Peggy and I are leaving tomorrow morning." I said, looking at the tickets again.

"That doesn't give us a whole lot of time. I have to get my car from the docks. It has all of my clothes in it." Peggy said in a fluster, as Robby continued to make eyes at us.

"You guys are coming back, right?" Robby asked rudely.

"Yes, Robby." I replied, annoyed.

"Good." He said it like there was something he wasn't telling me.

We used the day to get both vehicles from their hiding spots, pack, and be ready for the following morning. It wasn't an easy feat but luckily, our disguises were becoming easier to get into and harder to discern. Most of the disguise was acting a certain way. So, we tried our hardest to blend in.

We were boarding the boat as Phillip and Elizabeth Sherman. "Elizabeth?" Peggy said, aghast. "I guess it's still better than Margaret." She laughed as we walked up the ramp.

"Margaret?" I said, shocked. "Your name's Margaret?"

She nodded. "I thought everyone knew my name." She giggled.

We passed the man at the door, checking tickets, and walked through the threshold into a long hallway. We took the main stairs to get to the deck of the ship. I had never been on a boat this large before. "Isn't this the bee's knees?" She smiled into the fresh air. "We did it! We got away!" She chuckled.

"Peggy." I laughed along with her. "Aren't we heading back in a few weeks?" I continued to smile but felt worried on the inside.

"No, silly. We're done with this place!" Her expression turned a little malicious.

"Peggy!" I shouted, as she covered my mouth.

"Shut up, stupid! Do you want everyone to be looking our way?"

She let go of my mouth and I began to whisper, loudly. "Peggy, we left everyone in a pickle. We have to go back!"

"That's their problem." She smiled again. "We're the ones that matter most, after all."

"Peggy, that's not how I wanted everything tied up. We're

literally in the middle of so many things."

"Guy, do you really want to go back? You're a wanted man. You're basically being hunted at all times." Her voice changed pitch.

"Yes. I'm not leaving everyone to fend for themselves. I feel responsible for quite a bit of it."

"When are you going to stop worrying about other people? They're grownup men and women. They can make their own decisions." She was so careless. I envied her for it.

I knew I couldn't make everything perfect. Robby wouldn't give up the business because I was worried about him and I knew that I couldn't fix Tony's loveless marriage. Still, I wanted to try and get everyone to see the light.

"I have to prove our innocence." I said after a moment.

"What?" Her voice changed again.

"Yeah. When we get back, I'm going to try and put it all right again, so that everyone can continue on with their normal lives."

"Guy, you know that I was just teasing about getting away, right?" Her voice grew concerned. "I would never just jump out like that but this… this is just reckless. I thought the plan was always to grab the ones in need of a way out and leave the ones that won't cooperate. You realize that you've tried to get Robby to listen to you and I have no idea how to even reach Laurel anymore. Our best bet is to use this trip to plan our getaway. Solidify our placement in Paris and plan the rest when we get home."

"Peggy," I began, trying to get her to see my point.

"No, Guy. You have a big heart. I love you for that but I want out. I can't do it anymore." She said.

"I know. I want you out as well." I replied with a slight smile curving the right side of my mouth. "I couldn't stand to think of anything happening to you. When I thought you may have been arrested, it killed me."

"Then let's please just do what I say from now on. I know what I'm talking about." Her voice pleaded with reasoning.

"No. I'm sorry. I agree with what you're saying but I can't."

"Fine Guy, but you'll regret it. Maybe not any time soon, but one day when this whole mess gets even more complicated and we're stuck in a cycle, you're going to wish you took me up on my offer."

Her words were knives. There had to be another way. I couldn't just leave everyone for Paris. I loved Peggy and I needed them in my life as well. There had to be a way to have both.

I knew what she thought of Tony and I knew what Oliver wanted from me as well but I still felt compelled to Tony in a way that I didn't want to admit out loud. There had to be a way for everyone to come together for one another. If there was one thing I learned from my mother, it was that family is everything and they were my family now.

The boat trip took longer than I wanted it to. After the third day, I was over the feeling that crept up on me when I thought about being on water. It made me feel dizzy. I hated it.

The food was incredible and our room was a suite with three separate spaces, including a kitchenette and a small parlor room space. Peggy loved it for the closet. "Gosh, I could have brought my entire wardrobe!" She said at least three times.

I didn't personally like the olive colored carpet in the room. It was a weird pair to the pearl colored walls. All of the furniture was a Venetian finish with swirls and patterns that my mother would have probably owned if we'd had the money.

After what felt like an eternity, we arrived in Paris. The trip had too many pit-stops for me to deem it a pleasant one but I was glad with the outcome. It wasn't until we arrived that I realized how Paris was a dazzling lady of many colors and sights. Too many to really keep in my brain all at once.

We saw the most beautiful Opera house, tons of brick buildings and squares and thousands of people parading up and down the streets. "This is like New York's classier sister." I said, one afternoon during lunch.

"And isn't the food to die for?" She said, pressing her fork to her lips.

I could have stayed, like Peggy wanted. The magic that seemed to emanate from the city was sheer gold. We attended a few shows at the Opera and saw some jazz acts. Some of our music was prevalent in their stylings and a few bands even played music that was relevant in New York. Most of the music that we witnessed there, though, were ballads.

One day, we found a jewelry store that Peggy had to go into because a diamond ring caught her eye. I could tell that this was her subtle way in asking me to propose to her. The moment would be perfect in Paris but I didn't know how to gain the strength to ask.

Peggy and I talked about plans to move into town in the future and joked about the possibility of staying even now. I had to pull back from the latter because I could tell Peggy grew hopeful of that outcome. I couldn't help but humor her, however. She had a way about her that I couldn't help but give in to.

We spent every night dancing our hearts out and doing things that we probably would have been arrested for in New York. I couldn't believe how open and real Paris was. Everyone was so interesting, even if they didn't speak English. The art scene was alive and I was happy to find my style of painting flourishing on the streets.

"I think when I get back, I'm going to paint." I smiled as we passed a beautiful park full of trees and greenery.

"Paint?" Peggy asked, shocked. "Paris is inspiring you to paint?" She laughed.

My face fell from my smile. I thought back to when Peggy and I began talking. At that point, I wasn't painting at all. I had stopped. That resulted in me never telling her that I could paint. No wonder she was laughing. "Peggy, I used to paint all of the time." I turned like I was telling her something serious.

"You did?" Her voice flattened from her laughter. "I'm sorry. I didn't mean to patronize you." She gave me a furtive look.

"It's quite alright. I guess I never realized that I had never told you about it before. I used to aspire to be a painter before I got into this whole music thing."

"Wow." I couldn't read her face. "But music is where you really belong, honey. You've got a knack."

"I've heard." I gave her a solemn smile. "Listen, do you want to get painted?"

"Do I what?" She shrieked.

"Painted! Like a caricature." Her reply was in her impossibly colored eyes as they lit up like a thousand stars.

I pulled her over to a vendor on the street who was painting another couple in front of the Eiffel Tower. We waited our turn and handed the man a ton of money. "Make sure she's pretty." I said, winking to the man.

He gave us a look. "Rends-moi belle." Peggy said in a perfect accent. The man kissed the ends of his right hand and tossed it above it his head.

"You know French?" I asked, flabbergasted.

"Haven't you been paying attention this whole trip? I know quite a bit. My mother made me start finishing school. French was the only thing that I couldn't get enough of. Though, I—"

"Dropped out." I finished her sentence, thinking back to our conversation in Georgia. "I remember."

She nodded, her face turning slightly red. "I tried to immerse myself in the culture after I left school. I used extra money, that I had from my first shows for Tony, to take private lessons. I didn't learn what I wanted to, but then, shortly after that, I had lost the time to do so."

We enjoyed the rest of our day outside and decided to retire early. My feet were beginning to blister from all of the dancing we had done the past five days. We headed back to our hotel and barely passed the front desk before the concierge called for us to come over to him. I was worried for split second, until he held out an envelope.

"It's Tony." I shrugged, grabbing the letter from the man and thanking him.

"Boy, he is good." Peggy looked down at the envelope and rolled her eyes. "He has probably been checking in with us through all sorts of individuals this whole time." She huffed as the bellhop called the elevator for us.

When we got back to the room, I pulled the paper open and saw two small paragraphs in his usual scrawl. I stared in shock at the letter.

"What's the matter?" Peggy shook my shoulder.

"It's Laurel. She's gone missing." My mouth hung open.

Her voice quaked. "Do you think he's killed her?"

CHAPTER 17: ON THE RIGHT SIDE

The trip home seemed to take twice as long as the one to get to Paris. Different, constant pangs of worry drove the two of us to fear for Laurel's safety. It created an obvious rift in time that caused our heads to circle unhealthy thoughts.

Everything seemed to be fine while we were on dry land but the second we got on the boat, Peggy asked me every hour, "Do you think he did it?" or, "He had to have had her rubbed off." Sometimes, she would add, "She probably tried to get away from him once and for all. Maybe she thought that we weren't coming back."

I could tell that she felt guilty because we had been back from the South with the plan to grab our friends and get out before it was too late but she failed to do so. She even failed to get Laurel's attention at all. We were both distracted, beautifully, by one another.

I felt guilty because I tried harder and harder, each time Tony did something a little too edgy or harsh, to humble and anthropomorphize him. It was my way of coping with his inhuman approach to objectives in his everyday life. It was this very nonhuman characteristic that I fell for. It was probably the same thing that everyone had found charming in him. His godlike nature.

The worst part about all of it was the fact that I couldn't tell Peggy a word of it. It would only spark her suspicion about me and confirm that she was right all along. That feeling would loom over our entire relationship. I couldn't let that happen. Not when I had plans on marrying her one day, when this mess ceased to exist.

I placed my hand on hers as the skyline of our home began to seep into our vision from the dockside of the boat. A strange feeling entered my stomach. It was a mixed excitement and worry that made me feel a little nauseous. I glanced over to find a mix of emotions plaguing Peggy's face. It shouldn't have, but it made me feel a little bit better to know that, she, too, was worried.

We grappled the side of the boat harder with our hands as the ship docked. It ebbed back and forth in the sway of the current before tittering into a standstill. A line was forming to our right, where the exit stairs were. We steadily pushed our way through the crowd and took our first steps onto solid ground in over a week.

"Marvelous trip, honey. I wish it would have lasted longer." Peggy said as we passed the usher at the door. Her voice was pressed into an accent that I had never heard before. I assumed she did it to add to our disguises, which weren't any different from the day that we took off.

We hailed a cab and made it back to the safehouse by dusk. The houses on the block had dim lights shining through the windows which added to the beauty of the twilight hour. The darkness of the sky was pressing down on the air and there was a light fog drifting in from the east.

I rapped three times and called, "Boys! It's Guy and Peggy!" Peggy and I shot glances at one another and waited in the silence. There were crickets chirping a chorus in the distance.

"Thank god!" Cyril opened the door and ushered us inside quickly. "After all of the news, I thought something terrible had happened to the two of you as well." His face was painted with a daunting expression that balled my stomach into twists.

"Cyril, what the hell is going on?" I shut the door behind me and followed him into the kitchen, where he waited eagerly by the telephone.

"We're not entirely sure, actually." He took a second to look at us in the kitchen light, then said, "Guy, your hair." He smiled. "It's gotten so long since you left. I like it."

"Thank you. It was difficult to find a barber shop that had

English speaking employees." I tucked my hair behind my right ear as my face reddened. "Well, what do you know?" I asked, trying to press the conversation back into urgency.

"Is Laurel alright?" Peggy asked.

"When the two of you left, Robby and Ruth got into a colossal argument and went separate ways. Tony showed up the next day, looking for Robby. He had suspected that the two of them had run off together. It was a very awkward interaction, actually. I don't know Tony that well and he already doesn't like me. I suspected he thought I was lying about everything." Cyril's words flew by as he made multiple gestures with his hands.

"What did you tell him?" Peggy asked.

"I just told him the truth. That I didn't know anything. I just knew that he and Ruth got into an argument and the two stormed out of here." He paused. "Listen, Guy. As it turns out. You have a few people waiting to talk to you about some matters that arose while you were away."

"Who?" I asked.

"Well—" The door sprung open and Robby busted through the threshold, carrying a large bag.

"Robby!" I jumped almost a foot in the air. "What in the world—"

"I don't have time for chitchat!" Robby shouted, looking in all directions.

"What are you looking for?" I asked, watching his eyes.

"Where are Markel and Alvah?" Robby asked Cyril.

"In the backroom, I suppose." Cyril shot me a confused expression. "They've become quite the pair." He added in the silence before Robby began to walk down the hallway.

"Robby, what's going on?" I tried to ask as I followed him down the hall.

"Your little boyfriend tried to have me offed!" He said loudly.

The door at the end of the hall blew open and two bewildered faces stared back at us. "What on— " Markel began.

"Boys, do you remember our little talk before I left?" Robby asked the two of them.

Alvah shook his head and Markel replied, "Yes. What about it?"

"Let's go. We don't have time." Robby nodded back to them and turned past me to edge to the front door.

I watched as the other two grabbed bags and followed behind me to the sitting room. "Robby, could you please explain what's going on?" I tried to keep my emotions out of my voice. It wasn't easy.

"Can I trust you?" Robby's eyes looked gravely into mine.

"Yes. I'm your best mate." I continued making eye contact without blinking.

"Can I, though? Guy, you've been working with Tony for a long time now and I need to know that our friendship is still more valuable than your relations with that man?" His voice retained the urgency, but his volume decreased. I could tell he would have rather have had this conversation in private.

"Choose us, Guy. We're on the right side." Markel said, pointing to his chest.

"What? What's going on?" It was one thing that Robby was talking in codes but what could he have said to have Markel and Alvah leaving on a dime with him?

"It's a long story." Robby said, looking at all the curious faces in the room. "When you left, I didn't think you were coming back. My mind went through a couple of quick scenarios. One of which was fighting Tony's plans to take over New York with my own plans. I talked to the two of them," he nodded in their direction, "and decided I needed more men I could trust. We're leaving this safehouse because, if I'm not mistaken, Tony wants me dead."

"That's ridiculous." I replied without thinking.

"Exactly what I thought you'd say. Hasta La Vista." He waved his hand in gesture and the three of them began to exit.

"Wait." I grabbed Robby's shoulder.

"I told you guys that this would happen." Robby said as he smirked to Markel and Alvah.

"Guy. When I got put away, I lost any chance of getting my job back." Markel said, looking through me. "I need to be able to live again. Robby offered this opportunity and I didn't think you were coming back either. Now that you are, we can all be in on it."

"I'm not saying it's a bad idea because I'm on Tony's side." I explained, standing in between everyone. Peggy's face was hard to read but I could tell she knew what I was going to say. She always did. "I'm saying it because it's going to be tough operating around Tony. He's a megalith. If he finds out, he'll have us all rubbed out."

"I'm glad you see it that way." Robby said, placing his hand on my collarbone. "Because that's exactly where you come in." His smile curved around the sides of his face in a creepy fashion. "Tony will never cease trusting you." He paused and waited for my response.

"Uh huh." I nodded, raising my eyebrows.

"You will have to play him. You'll be on our side and get the scoop from him as well."

"No, Robby, it'll never work." I shrugged him off. "Tony will see through it all. I'm a terrible liar. Everyone knows that." I began to ramble.

"Relax. You can do this." Robby said.

"No. He can't." Peggy interjected. "Listen, what Guy is trying to say is—"

"I'm sure that if he wanted to say it, he would." Robby got in her face.

She placed her hands on her hips and vehemently stared into his eyes. I could tell that she was about to say something terrible. So, I interrupted them both. "Listen, I just don't want anyone hurt. I think our best course of action is to get out before it's too late."

"It is too late, Guy! What do you think he's doing with Laurel right now? Do you think she's going to get out of this alive?" Robby's voice shook out of him and his strained expression thickened.

The room began to look strange to me. I tried to focus on Robby with my eyes wide open. I knew that if I broke away from his gaze, I would lose my composure. I swallowed hard. "What happened?"

"It was Ruth." His voice seemed even more mangled. "She had me fooled from the beginning."

I could tell that he was nervous about talking in front of a group of people. So, I shook his arm and made him look me in the eyes. "Tell me everything."

"I met Ruth a week before you began to cover for our singer." He gulped. "Tony took the band to a joint that had... extravagant pleasures." His voice took on a dreamy quality. "He was trying to schmooze us into continuing to do shows with him. He didn't need all the glitz and glamor. His very presence and music in the underground attracted us. He may have thought that we were thinking of leaving because of the scene. It was appropriately considered dirty dough. We didn't care. Any money was good money.

"At this place, there was a cute brunette, who had an obvious interest in me. I didn't know how to carry myself around her. My heart was in other places, but she piqued my interests and could dance unlike anything I had ever seen before.

"Little did I know that Tony was making moves with her behind my back. I kept in contact with her because I began my plans to do what he does but in a different fashion." He paused and pointed at his chest with his thumb. "I want to call the shots." He grabbed the glass bottle from the coffee table and began to chug it. "And she had the energy and interest in me that I needed.

"I made connections and was finally in a position to get things rolling. The only problem was Ruth. Tony must have had her following me. She found Laurel and I leaving town. She came with Morgan and another man that I've never seen. They took Laurel and I'm sure that if I didn't think about it in the split second that I saw them arrive, I'd be dead."

His face rotated between three expression and he looked over at me again. "I can't believe I never noticed what was going on. That must have been how Tony found out about Laurel and I." Robby's words were spoken mostly to himself.

Cyril pushed his way between Peggy and I and stood next to Robby. "Do you think they're on their way here?" He asked him.

"It's been a whole day." Robby said. "I would think that they are still here."

Cyril ran to the window and pulled back the blinds frantically. "Did they follow you?"

"I have been in a number of places since they discovered us. I don't think anyone has been following me." Robby said.

"She's here." Cyril said, dauntingly.

"Ruth?" Robby jumped, set the glass container down and picked up his bags again. There were loud poundings on the front door. Robby then dashed past everyone and headed for the back door. "Lock her out!" He called from the kitchen. "Boys!?"

Markel and Alvah followed. "Robby!" Cyril called from the window. Within a few seconds the back door flew open and a dark-haired figure stood in the doorway.

"Hello, boys." Ruth said in a sultry voice. Peggy snorted. "Trying to run away, are you?" She grabbed Robby's tie with both of her hands and traced them up to his collar.

"Ruth." Robby's voice quivered as his hands grabbed hers. I could see him trying to regain his confidence in the situation. "How long have you been working with Tony?"

"For quite a while but that's not what's important now." She smiled a forced smile as she slid her hands from his and peered into his eyes. "You know what's at stake now. If you don't want anything to happen to anyone else. You should just come with me."

"You don't even know what you did, do you?" Peggy said, walking into the kitchen. "An innocent woman may have just lost her life because of you. Does that mean anything to you? In this day and age where women should stick together, you sold one of us out!"

"Why do I care!? It's every woman for herself, isn't it? He was mine. She knew that!" Ruth's voice was maniacal and crazed.

"You stupid girl." Peggy said before turning and heading down the hallway.

"Listen, I'm sure we can fix all of this." I tried to keep everyone calm. I was afraid of things getting out of hand.

Before anything else could be said, Peggy came back into the room, brandishing a pistol. "Peggy! What in the world!?" I was surprised to hear my words escape Cyril's mouth.

"Get out!" She screamed at Ruth, whose face broke in fear.

"You're going to regret that!" Ruth spat as she slammed the door behind her.

"Where the hell did you get that piece?" Robby asked with a smile across his face.

"I hid it in a bookcase before I left. I wasn't sure if I needed it or not." She couldn't help but smile back.

"I was wrong about you." Robby replied. "Thank you for that. You may have just saved my life… She's a little—"

"Lost?" Peggy asked.

"To say the least." Robby looked down.

"I get why Markel is following Robby but Alvah, I thought you were against the whole booze thing?" Cyril said, looking over at him from across the room.

"I am." Alvah said, defiantly.

"I'm sorry, sir, that just doesn't make any logical sense." Cyril replied.

"It does to me." Alvah's tone didn't change. "If I go along with Robby's plans, I'll get a chance to run into my wife. I can explain everything and—"

"And what, Alvah? Do you honestly think that your wife is going to believe you? You've been gone for weeks." Cyril's voice sounded reasoning.

"I don't know." Alvah's tan face grew a little flush. "I'm just hoping that things will work out and I'm tired of sitting here, doing nothing."

"I'm in." Peggy's voice broke next to me.

"What?" I asked, shocked.

"Yeah." She nodded in my direction. "Give us the address and we'll meet up with the lot of you later on."

"You're not trying to double cross us, right?" Robby asked her.

"Of course not. I was friends with Laurel. I want to see that monster fall just as much as the rest of us."

"Alright. That just leaves Cyril." Robby said.

"What? I never said that I agreed." I told him.

"Yeah but your little chickadee did. Which means that you're in as well, buddy." Robby's voice took on a careless nature.

"I'm sorry. I just can't condone this behavior." Cyril said in response to Robby's words. "I don't want any part of bringing anyone down."

"Guilty conscience?" Robby asked.

"Guess you could call it that." Cyril looked at the carpet.

"Alright." Robby said, grabbing a piece of paper from the

side table by the window and scratching something on it. "Here's the address. Eight o'clock work?"

Peggy nodded and took the paper from him. The three of them left through the back door. Markel came back in a few seconds later and took parallel to me. "This is going to work. Trust me." He smiled a bright smile and clasped his hand to my left shoulder.

I forced a smile and patted his shoulder in a return gesture. After which, he left, closing the door slowly. The room grew quiet for a few minutes. Cyril was pacing around, most likely in the thought process of making tea. Peggy kept looking at me, waiting for me to make eye contact with her.

After Cyril left the room, I asked, "Why did you agree to join them?"

"Guy, I know you. I know that you're going to have trouble leaving this whole thing if Robby isn't wanting to leave. Besides, I need to know what's going on with Laurel."

"You think she could still be alive?" I asked.

"Of course. There's something about this whole thing that has me thinking."

"About what?"

"We need to go talk to Tony." Her words were slow and calculated. "I think if we tell him what's going on with Robby, he'll give us the information we're looking for about Laurel."

"Wow… ten seconds and you've already committed insubordination." I scoffed. "That's a stupid idea."

"Really?" Peggy asked with a wild look in her eyes. "When was the last time Tony gave you information without a little kickback first?" She gave me another look of eagerness. "Because I can't think of any, Guy."

"Peggy." I said, trying to think.

"We don't have time to sit around. We have to play both sides. You want Robby out of this whole mess? Well I want Laurel out! We're not going to get any of that done if we're just sitting around picking at wounds!"

"Where are the two of you going?" Cyril reentered the room with a tray of tea. He was probably assuming that if he made us tea, we wouldn't go anywhere.

"We have to figure out what happened to Laurel." I replied, putting my coat back on.

"Not even here an hour and you're already headed out." Cyril's voice was worried. "Do you ever stop playing the hero?"

"Trust me, he doesn't." Peggy rolled her eyes as she followed my lead.

"We'll be back." I reassured him.

The drive to Tony's was quiet, though I felt as though she could read my mind. What was a typical handful of neighborhood blocks felt like an eternity away.

Tony opened the door with the biggest grin I had ever seen. That is, before he saw Peggy behind me. "I didn't think I'd see you this soon." His voice was surprised but carried an innocent tone to it. Like he was guilty of something.

"Tony." I returned his smile and gave him a hug.

His hands fell a little south. I shook out of his grasp and looked between the two of them with obvious irritation. Was he playing a game to show his dominance with Peggy?

"Mister Reynolds." Peggy nodded instead of her usual curtsy.

"Ah, Peggy." Tony returned the nod and looked at me. "Why the two of you?"

"It's a bit of a business proposition." Peggy said without candor.

"Hmm. Come in." He sighed and waved his hand toward the living room, politely.

We walked in and sat at the couch. Tony closed the door and walked slowly over to us with a blank expression. "I don't suppose you have anything dry?" Peggy asked bluntly.

"But of course." Tony said, passing us and entering the kitchen behind the couch.

Peggy made a circle of expressions at me. None of which I could make heads or tails of. Tony came back into the room with crystal glasses filled with caramel colored liquid.

"Before we toast, I'd like to know what business proposition we're toasting to." Tony's voice was composed and well-mannered as he took a seat on the opposite side of the couch from us.

"Robby." Peggy said with a mechanized grin. "He's trying to uproot our operation by starting his own. We're still behind you."

"You are?" Tony raised his eyebrows. "What makes you think I'd trust you, darling? I know you don't like me and if you don't like me, who's to say you can trust me?"

"It's a matter of whom I dislike more." Peggy's voice became calculative. "I don't like the band leader. I'd rather follow the shark. You gave me my big break and I think his head is full of mush." She faked a laugh so perfectly that the hairs on my arms stood on end.

"Do you follow her sentiments, Guy?" He turned to ask me. "Because I know he was your best friend."

Peggy gave me a look. I felt the pressure of the situation fall on me. "After everything he did?" I asked no one in particular. "He and I got into a fight. I'm not necessarily a fan of his anymore." I tossed words around nonchalantly.

"But you broke him out of jail." Tony said.

"Yes. That's because I'm a good person. That has nothing to do with which side I'm on." I tried, convincingly, to keep my composure.

"If that's the case, then welcome back aboard." Tony raised his glass in a toast.

We followed suit and clicked the three crystal cups above our heads, slamming the liquid down afterward. I turned to see Peggy's face, not changing. I felt a betraying squirm in my stomach as the alcohol hit.

"Is Laurel here?" I asked in a bold move.

"Not at the moment, no." Tony's voice was slower and quieter now.

"Is she alive?" I asked, standing up.

"What kind of a fucking question is that?" Tony asked, enraged, standing to match my stance.

CHAPTER 18: IT JUST BACKFIRED

"That's not what he's meaning to say." Peggy said, getting up and waving her hands in his face to try and get him to sit back down.

"No, I think he means exactly what he says." Tony said, not removing his gaze from my face. "What are you implying? That I've killed my wife?" The other side of Tony was making an appearance now.

"Or had her killed." I said, trying to match his attitude.

"Guy!" Peggy shouted between us. Her uncharacteristic expression pressed like waves upon me.

I stifled for a moment, continuing to look at Tony. "Why the hell would you think that I had her killed?" Tony asked.

"Well, all things considered." I replied with a shrug.

"All things considered, I'm hurt!" He shouted. "I don't have the stomach to kill someone I love and I can't believe you would ever think that!"

"Then where is she, Tony?" I asked, banging my fist to my chest and gritting my teeth.

"She's with Morgan for now." He paused. "But I don't see how that's any of your business. There are situations presenting themselves and I'm in a messy one at the moment." He took a large swig of alcohol. "Ya know, for someone claiming to be on my side, you sure are doing a lousy job of it."

"I'm sorry." I took a few, short breaths. "It's been a long day. I'm just confused and disgruntled."

"We all are. Imagine if your wife was running around on you." Tony's words didn't quite hit me the way they were intended to do so. I knew that if Peggy was aware of Tony's constant advances on me, she would agree.

"I get that Tony. I still don't get the full story." I said. I was trying to make it seem like Robby didn't tell me a thing.

"What's there to get? Laurel was sleeping with that bandmate of yours and then they tried to run off together." Tony took another sip and cleared his throat.

"I know that but how did you catch them?" I tried to keep my voice emotionless but interested at the same time.

"That poor sap, Ruth. She has always had a thing for Robby.

I've been having her keep tabs on them since the day I suspected them having an affair. You remember, don't you? That day on the boat?" His words weren't real questions. "Well, did you think I was going to just let it continue without my knowledge?" Another rhetorical question.

"That's right! She was there that day!" I said, finally realizing where I had seen her before. "She saw our little argument on the stairs, behind the stage… come to think of it, there have been quite a few times that I've seen her."

"All on my watch, that is." Tony's face turned smug and proud. "Listen, I don't want this whole mess to take over my marriage. Laurel is a free woman. She can do whatever she pleases to do. I'm sure the two of you will see her out and about. Possibly at your next performance." He drew his hand out before him in a good faith gesture.

I looked to see Peggy's face cracking slightly from his words. I could tell she was beginning to grow angry with his lies. "Tony, how can that be? We're wanted. You want the most wanted musicians and singers to continue performing in the speakeasies?" She asked him.

"Why, yes! It's part of my new master plan. We're going to start an even more private, even more illicit club. These speakeasies will tower over New York's underground scene in a way that this city has never seen before!" He was smiling. I didn't want to say anything to break his thunder. "Trust me, you'll be protected. You both are my ace in the hole with this whole Robby thing, you know."

"How do you mean?" Peggy asked.

"Well, what gimmick does he have? A washed-up musician who hardly anyone knows, putting on speakeasies in the normal fashion." He laughed to himself, rolling his eyes. "Just wait until the world sees that you are both wanted and still performing! It's going to blow their minds out!

"It'll be revolutionary. You'll be the first to evade, not only the eighteenth amendment, or the cops, but also the ASL and even incarceration. You'll be showing people that you're not afraid to fight for the right thing! It stirs the imagination! Creates empowerment!"

"Tony, it sounds like you're starting a movement." I thought aloud. I never really thought of Tony as a political person. I always knew that he used his power and money to accumulate business and to make more money. I wondered what Peggy was thinking.

"It's a beautiful idea." She said. Peggy, with her radical views on rights, would think that this idea was best. I was just surprised that she would come outright with her positivity to it. She and Tony had never gotten along in the past and I was thinking she wouldn't want to stir the pot of something so dangerous.

"Great. Then it really is a deal." Tony beamed. "Another toast!"

. . .

We were barely back at the safehouse for ten minutes when we heard a knocking at the door. "What a busy day." Cyril exclaimed, coming back into the living with his infamous tray of tea.

"It's Robby." Peggy said between a cigarette, while glancing through the window curtains.

I opened it to find Robby wearing an anxious look on his face. His pocket watch was dangling on the outside of his lapel like he was running from the car to the door. "Is it all set?" Robby asked us. "You two never showed at my place!"

"Is what all set?" Peggy asked him with a frantic appearance.

"Did you guys make your peace with Tony?" He was smiling.

"Why is this so exciting to you?" I asked.

"Because I got to see her." Robby's face was blazing.

"Laurel?" Peggy asked.

"Yes."

"How on Earth did you manage that?" I asked, coughing through the smoke from Peggy's cigarette.

The two exchanged a look of annoyance and Robby continued. "I followed Ruth to Morgan's safe place. After she left, I knocked on the door." He tucked his watch into his suit pocket. "After a brief talk with Morgan, he let me see her."

"Just like that?" Peggy put her cigarette out in a dish on the table. "Some guard dog." She scoffed.

"That would make sense." I said aloud, thinking about the story that Tony had told me and the night that he and I spent with Morgan at that bar in Harlem. "He's actually a nice person."

"He is." Robby agreed. "He thinks that Tony is being unreasonable with keeping her there but he doesn't want anything bad to happen to himself either. So, he's complying with Tony's word."

There was a very prominent change in the atmosphere of the room. With the news of Laurel not only being alive but being with a person whom did not agree with Tony, everything felt somewhat easier.

"Do you want to see her?" Robby asked us.

"Of course." I could see the gears cranking in Peggy's head. She was probably thinking of an escape plan for the four of us.

"Robby…" I said with an ease to my tone. "I have an idea. Now that you're listening to me, I have to ask that you, please, wait until I'm finished before interjecting." I looked him squarely in the eyes.

"Sure." Robby nodded.

"Peggy and I have been working on an exit plan since we got back into New York earlier this year. We made some arrangements in Paris and we're going to get Laurel in on those plans. We think it's best. There's going to be no fighting Tony forever and it's getting to a point where things are becoming impossible here in New York. Would you be open to the possibility of leaving town with the three of us?" My words sounded forced at first but, as I continued talking, they came easier and easier.

He looked between the two of us for a long moment, before Peggy said, "Before you answer, remember that this isn't just about you. Yes, you may have a booming business now but you have to think about Laurel. She's basically a prisoner. You can do what you do elsewhere."

We were all quiet for another minute. Robby paced around the room, rubbing his chin and changing expressions until he found one that matched his next words. "I think you're right."

I wanted to make a joke about the fact that the most stubborn person I knew was being lenient for once. "Robby, we're going to make this all right."

"I think you're right. If Laurel agrees to go along with the plan, then I will too... We don't have much time, though." His words were cautious.

"What do you mean?" Peggy asked him.

"We have until Friday to prepare." He replied slowly.

"Why Friday?" I asked.

"Because that's the day I solidified a performance for the two of you. I spoke with Morgan and got him to accompany Laurel to my latest joint off Park Avenue. It's going to be a grand spectacle." His eyes lit up.

"Friday? When were you going to tell us about this?" I asked.

"Before we got into this conversation. I need the two of you to perform. At first, it was just a way to kick off the opening of the event but now it makes sense because it's my last tail effort in getting some monetary backing for this trip of ours." He was pacing again. "There's more to this Friday than just your performance, you see."

"Why do I have a bad feeling about all of this?" I couldn't help but ask.

"Just relax. It's going to be a doozey." He smiled.

Peggy and I got ready for the night by making sure everything was packed. We had already worked out the solid plan of coming back to the safehouse to grab all of our bags. We would be staying in a hotel close to the waterfront. We would get our tickets in the morning and leave as soon as the earliest boat was available.

"I have a question for you." Peggy said, coming in from talking to Cyril in the living room. They have been talking a lot this week. I watched them get closer and closer each day.

"What's that?"

"If they don't agree to leave, are you going to stay here?" I couldn't read any emotion in her question but I could tell what answer she wanted from me.

"I'm not sure." I replied.

"Guy." Her voice was sympathetic. "We've had this conversation before. Staying isn't doing anything for us. We've been going in circles since we got back from New Orleans. The best part of the last year was leaving for Paris. I really hope you agree with me."

"I do, Peggy. I just wish there was something I could say to really convince Robby. He's a bit rough around the edges and likes to do everything his way. I wish he'd just listen to reason."

"You have to show him." She forced a smile. "Once we leave, it will set an example. There's only so much time that will go by before he realizes that leaving is the best and practically only option."

"Maybe you're right." I looked down into the sink at the flecks of hair I just shaved off my face.

"Hey, how's about we play our duet tonight? The one we've been working on. You can play piano and harmonize with me."

She was referring to the song that we had been working on since our night back in New York some months back. We titled it,

"I Could be Looking at the Stars." The other title idea was, "But I'd Rather be Looking at You." Both titles referred to the lyrics in the chorus. It was talking about how we felt for one another.

"Let's do it. I think this is the perfect time." I smirked into the mirror at myself, Peggy's face swimming in smiles behind me. Her face was holding back words that she refused to say. There was a secret in her expression. One I wished I could unlock.

We were picked up by Markel and Alvah. The two had become quite the friends since we had busted Markel and Robby out. We sat in the backseat, listening to their conversation. I kept wondering why Alvah thought it would be a good idea to run into his booze hating wife at a speakeasy of all places and how that would translate into the reconciling their marriage.

Peggy looked over at me from the left side of the cab. The street lights were running across her face in flashes. She was an angel with a devilish smile, always knowing things that I didn't know.

We parked the car in a place that wasn't designated for parking. "You sure this is okay?" Markel asked Alvah, who had told him to take the spot in the first place.

"Yup. Come on. We can't be late. This is our big night." Alvah had a determined look on his face as he opened the front door of the place.

It was arrogantly named, "Robby's." I laughed on the inside. We were seemingly the first ones there. Robby wanted us there early to set things up.

It was a quaint place with head spinning furniture. The bar was lined with gold embellishments and there were separate rooms dividing the place. Each room was designed with a theme in mind to suite anyone going out. There was a sitting room with elegant chairs and a simple, yet noticeable chandelier swinging slightly overhead. Through the first door was the bar area with a small seating section. Beyond that room was a dancehall with spotlights centering the room. And the final room was a showroom with a stage.

"What is she doing here?" Peggy's voice was agitated as Ruth walked out of the final room, towards us.

"Relax." Robby said, point-blank, walking up behind her with a glass in his hand. "She's part of the entertainment." He smiled and cupped his arm around her waist.

"Didn't she turn you in to Tony?" Peggy asked him.

"Yes, but we've had a little talk since then. I guess she's not a fan of what Tony was doing with Laurel. So, she's agreed to join up with us." Robby explained.

"You're raving!" Peggy said.

"Possibly." Robby laughed.

"Just deal with it, chickadee." Ruth flashed her teeth and threw her scarf around her neck as she pushed past us.

"Robby, I don't think this is a good idea." I said.

"Don't worry about it. We'll be gone tomorrow anyways." He smiled and took a generous drink out of his glass. "Besides, I've got many surprises in store for this night."

"You keep saying that but I have yet to see anything good." I said through gritted teeth.

"This whole place is good, fella." Robby laughed and walked out to the bar area.

"I have a bad feeling about this, Guy." Peggy drew her coat tighter around her waist and laced the band into a bow.

"That's why I came." A voice called from the bar.

Before I could even blink, I watched Cyril take a seat in one of the chairs by the door. "But Cyril, you haven't wanted to leave the house in weeks." I said without thinking.

"Yes, and it's about time I do something about that. I'm tired of playing it safe... Besides, no one was listening to my advice anyway." He smiled, looking at Peggy.

"That's not true." Peggy returned his smile.

"Darling, you are the exception."

In a few hours, things were shaking. There were more people there than I had ever seen at one of Tony's speakeasies. Everyone gathered in the dance hall area to a performance by Robby's band. They played very quick paced music while Ruth danced with a glowing smile. She was the centerpiece of the performance, dancing with a shimmering, sequin outfit.

When her dance ended, Laurel walked into the room with a bruised eye. Her dress and hair suggested that she took a long time to prepare herself before leaving. Morgan was on her arm with a solemn face and an all-black suit, like he was attending a funeral. The two looked unusual staying in contrast to rest of the guests in the room.

I watched as Peggy embraced Laurel for what felt like minutes. "I've missed you." Laurel's voice was strange to hear after so long. She turned and gave me a look that I couldn't describe. It was layered in so much history between the two of us. I hadn't seen her since the day I left New York for the first time. It felt surreal.

"Hiya stranger." I said, mimicking something that she would have said to me.

"Hey there." She smiled, looking down at her feet before looking back up at me and pulling me into a hug.

"Listen, Laurel, we have to talk to about something." Peggy called into her ear. "We're planning a getaway. Robby, Guy and I. We can leave this city and escape Tony."

Laurel's face changed from a smile to worry. She looked between the two of us as Robby came up from the side of the stage and put his arm around her. "No." Laurel said, looking at Robby. "It will never work." She looked panic-stricken. "He'll find us and kill us. There's no escape."

"What's this?" Robby asked the three of us.

"They think we can get away from Tony." Laurel's voice was shaking.

"We can. I think we have a chance if it's the four of us." Robby placed his fingers under Laurel's chin and made her look him in the eyes. "You trust me, right?" Even his voice was unsure.

"I trust you but you're all being fools." She broke away and darted across the dancefloor in tears.

"I knew she wouldn't go for it." Peggy said, grinding her teeth and looking at Robby.

"I'm going to have to do this the hard way." Robby said, shaking his head in exasperation.

"What do you mean?" I asked him.

"I'll have to rub him off." He turned, unperturbed and hopped onto the stage where he grabbed the mic. "Everyone, Guy and Peggy!" Robby's voice boomed. The spotlight found us and guided us through the doors to the room with the stage. I helped her onto it and sat at the piano on stage right.

We spent a good minute looking into each other's eyes, trying to process the whole situation. I felt a terrible feeling in my stomach. I had to ignore what just happened to put on a good performance. I planned to try and convince Laurel after our song was over.

"This is an original song that Guy and I composed." Peggy said into the mic, her voice amplifying one hundred times its usual volume.

I twinkled the keys and watched as Peggy swept the stage, back and forth, watching all of the eyes in the audience. Her face told stories before she even began to sing. Her thick eyebrows raised as she sang the first couple of words, while bending her neck back to look at me. The whole room could tell that we were in love.

When the song ended, I pulled away from the piano, during the cheering of the audience, got down on one knee and pulled out the ring that she had her eye on in Paris. "Margaret Pamela Austrait, would you marry me?" I asked over the heavy cheers and jeers from the hundreds of people packed in the tiny room.

Her eyes creased into tears and her face bore an expression that any man would empty their checkbooks to have for their own. I could tell that she wasn't expecting this from me. She was choking back her tears, fighting to reply to me. "Of course, I will, Guy Leon Linister." She smiled and cried at the same, crouching down to my height and peering into my eyes.

The crowd went wild as I placed the ring on her finger. Robby came up from behind me and patted my back as I straightened up, pulling Peggy up with one hand. "Oh, boy! This night keeps getting better!" Robby exclaimed in my ear. "Congratulations, pal!"

Before I could settle myself into the comfort of the situation, I saw Tony's face parting the crowd at the doorway. My heart dropped into my stomach. His face was contorted into a jealous fury.

I turned to see Robby catching a glimpse of Tony's arrival as well. "Men, women. I would like to make an announcement." Robby's voice boomed over the speakers. "Tonight, I retire. My business partner Ruth will be taking over for me. She will continue to offer exciting nightlife in the form of future speakeasies from now on, as my successor."

"Nice try!" A voice broke from the audience. Two women broke their way through the crowd and helped themselves onto the stage. Ella and Kamila stood in front of us with tyrannical features written on their faces. "Just because you denounce your actions of ill deeds, you are not innocent and will still be placed under arrest!" She was riling the crowd into a frenzy.

"You'll have to take me, first!" Ruth pulled herself onto the stage and stood between the two of them.

"You're insane!" Robby pulled a gun from his pants pocket and aimed it at the three women. Peggy and I pulled back behind the piano. I watched as, without a word, Robby let off a shot at Ella.

At least, I thought it was Ella. Ruth tumbled to the floor as Robby readied another bullet as Kamila pulled out her pistol. Alvah jumped onto the stage behind them and threw his arm around Ella. "You don't want to do this, Kamila." Alvah's voice was slow and deep as he held Ella into a locked hold.

"You call yourself a husband?" Kamila's accent mirrored Alvah's. She had a venom in her eyes as she stared into her husband's face. "You've got some nerve trying to talk to me at a place like this. Trying to tell me what to do. I'm not your slave anymore. I don't take orders from you."

"That's not what I'm saying. I'm saying that there's a different way." Alvah's voice became pleading.

"The man you want is here!" Robby yelled between the two, at Ella. "He's in the audience. He's the man you want. He started this whole thing!"

I tried to comb the crowd, looking for Tony but I couldn't see him anywhere. "I want all of you!" Ella choked out from Alvah's grasp. "The second the police get here, you're all getting locked away for good."

The crowd scattered and ran towards the door. Kamila raised her hand in the air and shot. Alvah let go of Ella and everyone seemed to freeze. "No one is leaving here. We have ASL members stationed at the door with guns. Anyone trying to leave with be shot at sight. We're not playing games anymore. This ends tonight."

"I messed everything up." Robby whispered to me from the other end of the piano. He was crouching down now, with his gun securely in his palm.

"What do you mean?"

"I tried to use this event to get Tony and Ruth locked up. I think it just backfired."

"You invited the ASL?" I asked, in horror.

"Yeah, I'm just now realizing how stupid that was." He said, quickly.

"Lady, gentlemen." Cyril's whispering shout came from the side of the stage. "I believe there's an exit this way. Come on!"

The three of us bolted for the stairs on the side of the stage. "Oh, no you don't!" Kamila shouted, shooting her gun in our direction. I watched as Robby fell in slow motion to my left.

"Come on, we have to keep moving!" Cyril said, turning around to look at us as he ran into the shadows.

I grabbed Peggy's hand and we followed into the backroom, footsteps clicking behind us, quickly. I turned only once to see Ella and Kamila followed by Alvah in the distance.

We entered a room with a large door. "On the other side is an alleyway. It's dark, so you'll have to guide your hand along the brick wall in order to get safely to the main street." Cyril explained, as we neared the door.

"Stop right there." It was Ella, entering the room. "Where do you think you're going?" She was directing her question to Peggy. "You think you have any kind of say around all of these men?" Her face was hardening as she spoke.

"What on Earth are you talking about?" Peggy asked back, fiercely as Tony entered the room with Alvah and Markel.

"I'm saying that if you wish to have any opinions that are actually yours, ditch these men." Ella said, even more angered than before. "You look like a smart girl. You would make a beautiful addition to the ASL. We're fighting for you. Your words, your ability to have a place in this world. You want to throw that away for this man?" She pointed to me and laughed. "He's hardly a man. He doesn't love you. I've seen him take the sides of other women in the past. You're just another shake in the dance to him" She tried to work her Christian woman angle that she's used to win over so many in the past.

I watched Peggy's eyes as she looked between her and me multiple times. "You're wrong. You're doing it all wrong. If you can't fight for love, then you shouldn't fight at all." She turned and ran through the doorway.

Cyril and I followed, listening to the footsteps as we

continued into the alleyway. We were through the door. We were safe. The darkness engulphed us as we ran into the nothing. I could see the light from the main road in the distance.

The footsteps behind us quickened in pace, which made me run faster and faster. As I neared the light, I heard a gunshot behind me. There was a faint spray of blood coming from the blackened alleyway. Cyril entered the light and gave me an expression of true horror. We turned to find a body lumped over in a pile on the pavement.

"It's Peggy." Cyril's face broke into tears.

CHAPTER 19: I'M JUST NOT READY

"No. It can't be." I turned to run back for her but Cyril beat me there. I could hear whispers coming from Cyril in the dark.

"Guy!" I heard a shout from the alley and two more gunshots were fired. Markel's face emerged from the shadows. "We have to go back for Robby."

"Don't worry!" Alvah called. "We've knocked Kamila and Ella out!"

"Go!" Cyril yelled, passing me with Peggy in his arms. Her eyes were closed and her head bobbed as he walked. "I'll take her to the hospital." I couldn't take my eyes off of her as he came to a halt in front of me. "Guy, Robby was shot. Go grab him and meet us at the hospital." I continued to look at her face. Refusing to break my concentration. Afraid if I did, I'd lose her for good.

"She's still alive, Guy, go!" He swung his back seat open and put Peggy inside. "You're the only one who can help him. I've got Peggy. You can trust me! She's going to be okay."

I felt the world slowly going out of focus as I followed Markel and Alvah down the alley and back into the building. My vision unfocused by the panes of the situation. This was all happening because I refused to leave with Peggy. If anything happened to her, I would never forgive myself.

"Through here, Guy." Markel said in a sensitive voice. "We got him to this corner here." They led me to a small kitchen area in the back hallway. "We couldn't lift him with our guns out. So, we made sure to clear a path for escape."

"Here. Markel's a better shot than me. Help me lift him." Alvah gestured his hand to Robby, who was collapsed on a dining room chair, blood leaking from his mouth.

"Where was he shot?" I asked as I grabbed his right side.

"Next to his left shoulder." Markel said.

"Kamila was aiming to kill." Alvah's words were cold and sounded like they echoed from one hundred miles away.

"Are you alright, buddy?" I whispered in Robby's ear.

"Peachy." He coughed.

"Guy, let's not encourage him to waste his energy just yet. We may need him to walk in a moment." Markel said as he led us through the doorframe and back into the last room with the escape door. "They could be waiting for us out there. Are you both ready?"

I nodded as Alvah said, "right," and Markel kicked the door open, pulling out his pistol and darting into the darkness.

"Come on. We have to move as one now." Alvah said to me as he tucked Robby's head above his arm and clasped mine with his palm.

We moved through the darkness like a ship in the ocean, cutting a path to the light to our right. "Almost there. Looks like we're clear." Markel's voice stayed calm and steady as I watched his body enter the side street's light.

Before Alvah and I could get Robby to the street, Markel jolted to the left and as we neared the corner, I watched car lights flash on and heard the rumble of the engine. "Throw him in the back!" Markel shouted from the driver's seat.

We heaved him into the back area and Alvah got in next to him. "Get the front." He nodded to me.

"I can sit with him." I told him.

"Not this time!" I heard a female voice piercing through the darkness behind me.

"There's no time for that. Get in the front!" Alvah yelled.

I threw myself into the vehicle and Markel kicked the

engine to life as we sprawled away from the curb. Bullets grazed the side of the vehicle. I turned and caught one last look of the street where it had all happened. Ella was pulling her hair out of her red face and still brandishing a gun in her palms.

We arrived at the hospital in record speed. Markel was a daring driver who ran street signs and dodged pedestrians with ease. We pulled Robby from the car and hobbled up to the lobby doors. As they swung open, a surprise guest was waiting for us.

"I saw everything from the curb and had to get here first. You haven't been in a situation like this one to know how to take care of it with the proper delicacy." Tony stood by the front desk with a foreboding expression on his face.

"Thank you, Tony. I'm glad you're here." I said.

"It's all been arranged by me and Fredrick here." He patted a tall gentleman's shoulder. He had dark hair and green eyes. He and two other men came closer to us, helped pull Robby onto a gurney and wheeled him down the long hallway behind them.

I turned to the counter. "Ma'am, what room is Margaret Austrait in? Has there been any word? Is she okay?" I asked in a fluster.

"Oh dear." The woman behind the counter looked through her paperwork, frantically. "I believe she's been cleared to leave, sir. Let me see if I can find her out-process paperwork." She thumbed through files in a black divider and turned back to me. "I'm having trouble young man but you'll find her in room twenty-seven if she's still there." Her face stayed blank as she finished her sentence. Then she pointed down the same hallway that Robby was taken down.

"Thank you." I said quickly, turned and bolted past people striding up and down the halls.

I arrived at room twenty-seven. Without knocking, I pulled the door open and found Cyril sitting on the only bed in the room. His face was buried in his hands.

"Cyril, where's Peggy?" I asked with a lump in my throat.

"They couldn't save her." His voice broke as he forced himself to finish his sentence. He refused to look up at me. "She was taken into surgery when we arrived. I just got the news from the doctor." He finally looked into my eyes. His face was wet and his eyes were bloodshot red. "I hate that I have to be the one to tell you. I'm so, so sorry, Guy. I wish there was something I could have done."

Before he finished his words, I turned to run down the halls. "Where are you going?" He asked me, getting up from the bed.

"Where did they take her?"

"Downstairs." He said slowly. "Guy, please."

"I have to find her. She's not gone!" I yelled, feeling a part of me slipping away as I spoke. "Where is she!?"

"The morgue. Guy, listen to me!"

I threw the door open and ran as fast as I could for the stairs. I could hear footsteps behind me but didn't bother stopping. I spiraled down steps and steps of concrete. With every step I could feel pieces of me letting go. I was losing myself as I ran. My head was spinning and the world around me was beginning to feel like an illusion.

I found myself on the bottommost step. I ripped the door open, feeling the hinges bounce at the mere strength of my forceful throw. My pace slowed as I found the blackened words on the gold plaque reading "Morgue" next to a large, steel door.

"Guy, stop!" It was a different voice than that one I was expecting.

"I just need to see her." I said, feeling the tears finally make their way down my face.

"Come here. I don't want you to go in that room. You don't need to see her." Tony wrapped his arms around me as I fell to the floor, feeling my knees crack under my weight.

"He's right. You can't bring her back." Cyril's broken voice caressed the other side of me and the three of us were huddled in a mass on the floor of the basement.

"She can't be gone." I whispered to nothing.

. . .

Days went by.

More days passed.

Every bit of the world felt like it was drained of any color.

I could count each heartbeat in my chest like it was the only thing that made any sense to me now.

I secretly hoped, every morning, that the sun wouldn't rise in protest to the disaster that had befallen me.

Some nights, I would stay awake, waiting for the silence to settle in but my mind refused to let that happen. I repeated the events of that night over and over in my head. Trying to find all of the mistakes that I made. Wishing that I could find some sort of conclusion to it all. Wishing that I could go back in time and rewrite what had happened. So that I wouldn't have to lose her. I would do anything. There was no way this was real.

I waited months for the darkness to cease and for the color to return only for it to be in vain. Everyone seemed able to go back to their business as usual. Robby returned to head his underground operations in a treaty from Tony. I assumed it was because Tony felt bad about everything that had happened with me and did not want to add to the whole thing by making Robby's life complicated too.

Alvah became Robby's righthand man. He swore off his

connections to his wife and the ASL because he believed that it was Kamila's fault Peggy lost her life. He dedicated his life to hunting them down and ending their need for justice.

Markel showed up at Cyril's place twice a week with cigars, booze and other charming artifacts to try and cheer me up. I never said a word but I could tell that he felt just as guilty as anyone else. Each time he visited, his outfits became more and more lavish. Apparently, business was booming even more so now.

Cyril was a gift from the heavens. He stayed by my side for most of it. He refused to leave the house when he knew I was going through a particularly troubling time. He constantly made tea and demanded that I stay sober through the whole ordeal, which was a challenging endeavor, considering my need for numbness. I wanted everything to end.

Tony called a few times and showed up with flowers every Friday, begging me to come back and perform for him. "This will save you. You'll see. Your music is what should bring light to you." That side of Tony that seemed to care more about me than his own life was making more of an appearance than ever before.

"Guy, I have something for you." Cyril's voice was quiet as he opened the door in the early morning.

I wanted to say something back to be nice but nothing sounded right in my head. So, I stayed quiet.

"Please, Come to the living room. Join me when you're presentable." He closed the door.

I opened my eyes and looked around. Presentable? Did that mean there were people in the house? I didn't feel like being social. Not now. Not ever. I closed my eyes and rolled back over in bed. Maybe if I pretended it didn't exist, the world would melt away and leave me in this bed for the rest of eternity.

There was a knock at the door. "Guy, I promise this will make you feel better." Cyril said with a plea in his voice.

Nothing would make me feel better. I swung the blankets off from me and put clothes on. I stopped into the bathroom and looked at myself in the mirror. What a joke I had become. My blonde hair was long and tousled in a mess in front of my face. When I pulled it back, I found two battered eyes staring at me from behind the glass. My face was sallow and malnourished. I felt like I was staring into the face of a ghost. Someone who was not fit to live anymore.

I splashed myself with water and forced my feet to carry me into the living room. Before I could look around, I felt the pressure of another body press into mine. "Stranger!" A woman's gasp made my mind break.

"Laurel!" I pulled away from her and looked her up and down. "What are you doing? I thought you were still being held captive by Tony?" I realized as I said it, that this was a very peculiar thing to say. Probably even more peculiar to consider the truth behind it.

"He's kind of taken a step back." She said, scratching her chin. "I brought you something to cheer you up." She stepped aside to reveal a beautiful black, upright piano. "It used to be Peggy's…" Her face twisted into tears. "I thought you would want it."

I couldn't stop myself from mirroring her. We shared a moment in silent gasps of breath. "Peggy had a baby grand." I said softly after a minute, sinking to the floor.

"This was from her mother's house. It was the piano she learned to play on." I helped her up from the floor and sat her next to me on the piano chair. "Cyril said that he would find space for it. So, I brought it over."

"I thought it was a delightful idea. I thought it would help brighten your mood." Cyril stood on the other end of the piano and tried to smile at us. "I think if the two of you worked at it, you'd make a good team, musically." He added after another minute of silence. "I still have some connections in the media. We can take this somewhere great!"

"Oh, no. I don't think I'm ready to do anything of the sort right now." I said to the two of them, hoping I wasn't bursting any bubbles. "I'm just lucky if I can force myself to get out of bed in the morning."

"That's fine. You can take your time." Laurel said. "Listen, I miss Peggy just as much as you do but she wouldn't want you sad like this. She'd want you out there, singing. Bringing music to people. We're in the middle of an age of tyranny and I think we can change it all with our music. We can't let the ASL win."

I let her words settle before I spoke. "I'm just not ready."

"That's fine." She repeated. "Did you want to play something?" She nodded to the piano.

I played the only thing I could think of at the time. Claude Debussy's Suite Bergamasque. It was a bitter sweet sound that I needed to hear. It cooed me into a relaxed but yet cold state. The room felt strangely empty as I pressed the final keys of the song and silence took over.

I saw Laurel almost every day from that point on. Each time she came over, she brought more and more sheet music with her. "I wrote this after you left for Paris with..." She knew I hated to hear her name. "Anyways, it's a nice little piece about setting out into the world and making something new of yourself. I couldn't quite finish the lyrics but I think the music is coming along sweetly." She placed it on the piano top in front of me.

I was sitting at the piano chair, sipping on the tea Cyril left me before he headed out to take care of business. "Let's give it a go."

We were beginning to sound like a good pair. I was afraid to get on the subject of Robby but when I felt strong enough to ask questions about the world, I asked her, "When was the last time you saw him?"

"Who?" She asked.

"Robby."

My words gave her mixed messages. "Guy, I'm sure he's wanted to come see you. He just feels guilty about everything that happened." Her voice was soft and concerned.

"That's not what I mean." I said. "I was asking about the two of you."

"It's not the same, really. A lot has changed since... Well, since the last couple months. I've only seen him a few times. He's busy. Everyone's busy. Though, honestly, I can't complain. It gives me the freedom to pursue other things."

"What happened to you? I went a long time without seeing you. Did he hurt you?" I asked, remembering the black eye she was sporting at Robby's speakeasy.

"Not directly. This is all very complicated to explain, Guy. Tony is a nice person. He's just very emotional. He has a lot going on." She looked up at me from the sheet music. "Even though he's done a number of things to me that most people wouldn't be able to forgive, I do."

"What's he done?"

"For starters, he pretended to love me from day one. I don't think that man ever loved me the way he wanted everyone to believe he did. He did love me. Just not in the marital sense. He was infatuated with me. With my energy. My spirit." She smiled and furrowed her eyebrows at the same time. "But he never did love me." She turned and looked into her lap.

"I'm sorry. I didn't mean to..."

"No, it's okay." She said, looking back at me once more. "I fell in love with Tony on day one. My mother thought he would be perfect for me. What's there not to love? A perfect, full-toothed smile, lots of cash and quite the charmer...

"I was a fool. I never saw what was right in front of me. First, Morgan, then you." Her eyes intensified. "He loves you more than any human I've ever seen love anyone on this planet."

"I'm sorry." I said once more.

"Oh, it's not your fault, honey. It just happened." She said as she pulled a cigarette from her handbag on the carpet and placed it in between her lips. "Things just happen. That's why I was so furious before you left with—" She stopped. "Before you left to head South." She corrected. "Everything was coming out at the worst time and I threw every bit of anger I had at him. I fell into alcohol and he caught me before I fell completely. I owe him my life. Which is why I never bothered leaving his custody. He was doing it for my safety."

"Laurel, people deserve their freedoms. You shouldn't have let him do that to you." I tried to tell her.

"No, Guy, you weren't there. There was so much more to it than what I'm telling you. I don't think I could ever explain it in a way that would make you understand. Understand me. Understand him." She looked out the window at a bird that landed on the branch of the tree. "He is a fantastic man. He's just living in a time that doesn't suit him. Just like all of us in this game."

"Then let's make it our time." I said.

"What?"

"Yeah, let's take back this city from them. Make them pay for it all."

CHAPTER 20: LET'S DO IT

"I'm sorry, Guy." Cyril placed his hand on my leg. It was an ordinary morning. Tea had just finished brewing and light poured in through every window. I found myself resting my head against the back of the couch.

"For what?" I lifted my head and took a cup from the tray. I attempted to keep my voice calm and emotionless.

"You had another nightmare last night. I could hear you in your sleep." Cyril patted his hand on my leg and took the remaining cup from the table. "I just wish there was something I could say or do to help you with all of this."

"Cyril, you've been here this whole time. That's more a person could ever do. Hell, that's more than anyone else in my life has done. Sometimes I feel as though they are all avoiding me. As if they didn't listen to me and it's too late."

"That's the most you've spoken in weeks." Cyril said with an awed face, tipping his cup to his lips.

"I know. It's not been easy." It was like losing my mother all over again. "I've been working out plans with Laurel. We're going to try and take down the ASL."

My words made a concerned expression splash his face. "Guy…"

"I know you're going to tell me that I'm being foolish but I know what I'm doing. This is for Peggy." I tried to keep my voice convincing.

"I have been in a battle to keep you alive since I met you and here you've been placing yourself in every dangerous situation you can find." He grinned faintly. "I wasn't going to call you foolish. If anyone can take down that organization, it would be you." He paused. "I just wish it were someone else. You've endured too much already."

"Thank you. Your words have always pulled me through my troubles." There was so much I wanted to say but the words evaded me. "I want them to pay for everything… You know I don't believe what they're saying, right?"

"I know you don't."

"Then stop feeling like you have to prove it's false to me.

There's no way you could have shot her." I was referring to the piles and piles of newspapers that the ASL plagued with stories of her death being planned by Cyril to frame the ASL into crimes for them to be shut down.

He nodded, looked down, then back up again. "Before you meet up with Laurel today, would you accompany me to the docks? I wanted to enjoy one more day in the sun before the autumn leaves litter the streets." He helped me up from the couch and put an overcoat on by the front door.

"If you find me a nice, big hat." I smiled.

Laurel and I began to play shows every week. Tony began to appear at every single one. At first, I felt like he was doing us a kindness by making his presence known which quickly became a topic of worry between the two of us.

"Do you think if Robby finds out about us doing shows, he'll show up as frequently?" I asked her after finishing a set.

"I'm not sure. I just hope one of these nights, that bitch from the ASL shows up." Her face was angry. "I want to run her through."

I turned and smiled from the fire in her eyes. I didn't even care that she sounded slightly insane. She was the only other person who understood me now. Cyril was nice company to have but he had only touched the surface with Peggy. Laurel and I had known her unlike any other.

"Do you think Tony's going to start tightening your leash?" I gave her a quizzical look but kept my voice light.

"Who knows." She rolled her eyes, then looked in his direction. He was sitting at the bar, staring over at us. "I think the only reason why he's lightened up so much is because of Morgan."

"Morgan?"

"Yeah, he cares what Morgan thinks and I don't think Morgan is a fan of him locking me away. Months ago, I allowed myself to be locked up while I put myself back together. So many things were changing for me. I was lucky to have Robby. He would come in and take me away. He'd remind me that there was still so much life left to live.

"Now, Tony is on the edge of his security with people." She fixed the sparkly bow in her hair and looked back at me. "I think he's afraid of running out of people to trust. I think he's pissed off enough of us to the point of us fighting him back. He's losing his grip."

"You really think so?" I looked over at Tony again. He had a hardened expression on his face and two drinks in his hands. "Is that why he's allowing us to do these shows at his clubs?"

"I'm not entirely sure. I just know that he's been a bit off lately."

Her words pierced me like a knife. I couldn't help but feel sorry for Tony. At one point, I even understood Tony in ways I don't think he even did. He was a very complex person. "Maybe he's feeling the effects of everything he's done to people." I thought again of Oliver and his lover, who had now been lost to time. "Maybe he's feeling guilty for once."

"Maybe." Laurel began, batting her lashes as a reporter approached us and bared her gapped teeth in a beautiful smile.

"Laurel Reynolds. One of New York's most enigmatic women. What brings you out tonight?" The reporter asked. He was a large gentleman with a bowler hat and glasses. His teeth were showing as he spoke.

"Didn't you just catch the performance?" Laurel gave him a distinguished look.

"Of course, but you disappeared from the lime light for years and you're just now coming out of your shell. We still remember you over at The New Yorker." He was practically salivating.

"Apparently. Well, I'm very flattered. I've been working with the talented Guy Linister over here." She waved in my direction. "He's pulled me out of a very large slump." She batted her eyes again.

"You guys make quite a pair." I could tell his tone was meant to be cynical. I ignored him and walked to the bar.

"What are you drinking?" Tony asked as I sat next to him.

"Nothing. I quit the stuff." I raised my eyebrows.

"Nonsense. You don't quit the stuff." I could tell by his face that he was trying to decide which emotions to convey to me.

"Well, I do." I patted his hand on the top of the bar.

"Wow, you really loved her, didn't you?" His face split, on the verge of tears. I pulled my hands into my lap.

"I did." I looked down, somberly into my open palms.

"She was quite the lady." His words drifted into his own memories, coming to life in the room. "When I first met Laurel and Peggy, they were quite the dream. I remember just how young and enthusiastic they were. Wanting to become famous. Talking like they already were." He turned his body to mine. "I met them in Harlem. They were doing a show at a bar Morgan and I were thinking of acquiring. I felt like I had struck gold that night.

"The two of them looked incredible. You should have seen their dancing. Their movements matching one another like magic. Like electricity in a wire, those two. I couldn't just let them leave the bar without talking to them. So, I flashed a bunch of cash and sat them down at a table. I could tell Laurel was nervous. Peggy, however, had the most disinterested look on her face. She thought I was full of it. Just trying to pick them up." He laughed.

“That’s when I fell for her.” His smile faded. “I messed up pretty badly, my friend. I didn’t know who I was just yet and I let myself get carried away in her magic. I ruined her.”

“She forgives you, you know.” I said after a moment, placing my hand back on his. “We’ve talked about you.”

“All good, I hope.” He smiled again.

“Yes, Tony, all good. She understands why you did everything. I do too.” My mind wandered. This seemed to be the only time to ask him. I pulled out my confidence. “I just have one question for you. I need to know, Tony.”

“What’s that?” He was looking me in the eyes.

“Before me, did you…” I tried to find the right words to ask it. “Was there another man you were in love with?”

“Yes, Guy, you know about Morgan and I.” His face turned confused and bunched up. “But you know that I didn’t love him. It was just a closeness that we had.”

“No, Tony, I mean, before him even.”

“No.” He broke eye contact.

“You can tell me the truth. I won’t judge you. Even if you—”

“Alright but it was a long time ago and things were turned completely around. I don’t know where to begin with the whole thing. I was much younger and—"

"So, it's true..." I mouthed to myself, realizing that all this time, I was painting him out to be a lost and tortured soul. He was really a murderer. Sure, he's come a long way since then and probably regrets it but I never thought I would ever be in this position with him now.

"What? Guy, what's true?" He was shaking his shoulders defensively.

"You've killed someone." I shook my head slightly, not trying to start an argument in public.

"What!?" He jumped up from his chair and glared at me. "What on Earth—"

"Tony, you don't have to lie! I know everything!" I said, loudly.

"I don't think you know what you're talking about!" He shouted back.

"I met with Oliver. He told me all about Christopher. Tony, you can tell—"

"Who?" He took a large gulp of one of his drinks. "I've never heard those names in my life!" He stormed away from the bar, leaving me angry and disgruntled.

...

The day burned brightly through the windows. I had barely sat down at the piano with a cup of tea that Cyril had made me when the front door blew open like a gust of wind.

"I told him that we're not doing it. Did you?"

"Told who? What? Laurel, what are you talking about?" My fingers were barely grazing the keys.

"Robby… He wants us do a performance at his self-named joint." She lit up a cigarette and sat next to me.

"Laurel, I told you, no cigarettes around the piano. It's not good for it." I waved my hands around the swirls of smoke.

Laurel got up from her seat to find the ashtray. "Oh, honey, lightened up. It's just a thing." She caught my expression and sat back down. "I'm so sorry, I forgot." Her eyes welted up. "I'm just so frustrated with Robby. He knows what this will look like to Tony if he gets wind of it and nearly everything you and I do gets out to the public."

"Didn't that place close down that night with the raid?"

"Yes, but you know Robby. He purchased another place." She rolled her eyes.

"What? Did he call it 'Robby's?'"

"Not quite. He called it 'Robert's.'" She wandered about the room, looking for the ashtray again.

"Wow, how stupid can you be?" I thought that it must have been Robby's old business partner James who had bought it from the state.

"Oh, I know, honey. They're a bunch of baboons." She waved her hands around like she did not want to put the cigarette out and leaned on the other end of the piano. "Play me something sparkly!" She said in a dreamy tone.

"Laurel!"

"What?"

I made a gesture to the cigarette.

"Fine..." She grumbled and put it out in the ashtray on the coffee table.

"I didn't want to show you this but I feel like you should see it with me and not wonder about it yourself." Cyril's words blustered along while we set the table for dinner.

"What's that?" I asked, placing the forks on the left, the way he liked.

"They're trying to add to the story of that night by including you. I bet they're pissed about you walking freely around New York with Laurel at your side, doing shows at more illicit places." He dropped a newspaper in the middle of the dining room table.

I read the headline and few paragraphs. "They're blaming me now for Peggy's death!?" I shouted. "That's absurd! What cowards!" I took that paper and ripped it to shreds.

"I know, I know, but Guy, please don't lose your head. They're going to say whatever it takes to get to you rally against them. This way you'll become an easier target." He sat on the other end of the table from me. "Think about it. Think about how many times you were able to get away from them. Think about how you used your connections to get both of your pals out of jail. You're a threat to them."

"You're right. Maybe I will rally against them."

"Guy." He warned.

"No, I mean it but in a smart way. I can get some materials printed and we can start spreading a counter message to the people of New York. I'm sure everyone's been waiting to hear the real story. Hear how they've been filling their heads with lies this whole time. I bet my story will shock and enlighten the masses." I was struck with inspiration.

"Alright, fine." Cyril laughed. "But could it at least wait until after dinner?"

"Guy, you have to do it." Robby had to make an appearance after Laurel told him off. He wasn't showing any proof of being shot in the shoulder just two months ago. "You realize that he won't stop controlling her unless we make a plan to get rid of him."

"Robby, what are you talking about? How does this have anything to do with Laurel and I performing at your place?"

"She's still under his control. She will hardly speak to me and I don't feel like it's the best idea approaching her first with Tony lurking around. I could get her in more trouble." He walked around the room, pulling at his hair.

"Stop that. Are you saying that you want her to show up and risk everything with Tony because you want to see her? Because you're not talking to her so she won't get in trouble. Yet, you're perfectly fine with her doing a performance at your club. A performance that you know Tony will find out about." I said it all in a rush, trying to invoke some guilt. "She's not talking to you because of several other reasons. It has nothing to do with Tony." I explained.

"Were those her words?" He asked.

"No, not exactly."

"Exactly, Guy. That's because there's more to it than you think. He likes you. That's why he's allowing her to do shows with you at his places."

"You're being ridiculous."

"And you're being naïve, as always." Robby grinned and sat at the piano chair next to me. "Come on. It will be just like old times. You, me and now Laurel." He made a gesture to make me look at him. "You know you want to."

"Even if I did, Laurel would never go for it. So, forget about it."

"What if I told you that this will be the show to end all shows?" His voice was still carrying its amused tone.

"You'd be wasting your breath. You realize what happened last time you had something up your sleeve, right? You're not exactly the best planner." I shook his hand off my shoulder and walked into the kitchen.

"This will be your key to freedom." He continued to be enthusiastic.

"I don't want freedom anymore." I stared out the window into the backyard. "I don't deserve it."

"Of course, you do. We all do. I don't know why I didn't listen to you before, but Guy, you have to trust me with this. I know what I'm doing this time."

"I don't think anything you say can change this." I shrugged him off again and walked through the back door. He followed. "If Laurel doesn't want to do this show, then I don't either."

"So, it comes down to her, does it?" He smiled and walked back into the house. "I'll give you a ring later." He called.

"I'm just unsure." Laurel confessed after a brief interrogation.

"You said that you didn't want any part of his schemes anymore. Why are you on the fence again?" I asked her, trying to get her to see reason.

"I'm torn because I like Robby. He makes me feel things that I never did with Tony. I just can't get mixed up with him again. We'll be caught. Ruth may not be around anymore but that won't stop Tony from doing something about our… relationship." She began to pull books off the shelf and examine the covers.

"If you really want to do it, then we can but I don't think it's wise." I told her.

"I don't think it is either but I don't want to lose him. I think he's playing the same game as Tony now." She turned to watch my expression.

"But Tony hasn't shown any of his usual signs. Maybe he's not a threat anymore." I said.

"I want to believe that but I keep thinking about things he's done in the past and it's like my mind is stuck. I'm a scratched record on the needle. I can't let go of all of the terrible things Tony has done to keep me in his clutches." Her melodramatic words took a second to sink in.

"I'm willing to do whatever you deem fit, Laurel. I don't think that performing at Robby's is a good idea but I'm tired of pretending like I know what I'm talking about. After all, I'm in this mess because I listened to myself." I closed the lid to the piano and walked to the bedroom.

After a few moments, I heard the door creak open. "Are you alright?" I could tell she didn't want to have to ask.

So, I replied with, "I'm fine. It's just been a hard couple of months. You understand." I sat on the bed and crossed my hands over my legs.

"I do. I'm sorry. I've been a terrible friend trying to get you out and put you in a better place. I just wish I had better judgment." She sat next to me.

"Laurel, I just want you to follow your heart. I don't want to see you upset anymore. You meant so much to Peggy and you've come to mean the world to me. I have little to hang onto and I want to make sure that you have the world, even if I give everything up."

"Thank you for that." She paused and sighed. "You're a great person. You were perfect for her. I wish things would have ended differently." She took a long time to think. "Let's do it."

"What?"

"Let's do it. What is life when your cautious? Neither of us have anything to live for anyways! Let's do it!"

I didn't bother arguing. She was driven. I could tell from the beginning of the conversation.

• • •

The day before the performance, we were invited to a small get-together at a place in Brooklyn. Tony wanted us to meet a few possible investors in his business. He basically wanted to show us off.

This was fitting for Laurel, who dressed in an elegant cocktail dress full of shimmery patterns and complete with large, pearl earrings. I wore a regular suit and tie and had Laurel pick me up.

The place was an extravagant number, painted in all white interior with silver and gold lighting fixtures, like lamps and wall hangings. Each piece of furniture was a simple black or grey and the dining room was covered in lace draperies.

I found Tony in the parlor room near the entrance. His face was paler than usual and little gaunt. It was off-putting and made me jump and startle upon greeting him. He must not have been sleeping, or possibly he was drinking too much.

We met a few persons, whose names I couldn't remember minutes after speaking with them. Tony gave a toast to the room and winked in our direction. "We're all in." He said at the end of the speech.

"In for what?" Laurel stood next to her husband at the end of the long table.

"We've decided to help the two of you take down the ASL." Tony smiled through his pale face.

I turned to Laurel. "You told him of our plans?" I asked her, under my breath, though, I'm sure the whole room could hear me.

"A while back, yes. I didn't think it could hurt for him to know." She gave me a fake smile and turned to the rest of the group. "I think that's a lovely idea. We've begun to make plans for printing propaganda in retort to their advancements." Spoken like a true politician. I gawked at her.

"Yes, we've heard." An older gentleman cleared his throat to my right. "Tony has offered up a better plan."

"What's that?" I asked trying to be part of the loop.

"You two are to get on Robby's good side, perform at his place this weekend and we'll take it from there." Tony's voice was prepared and practiced.

So, this was his game. He would knock out two birds with one stone. He would have the ASL shut down along with Robby. Possibly killed. And now, since Laurel and I were playing both sides, we would have to go along with it.

CHAPTER 21:
THE ONE WORTH SAVING

"You shouldn't go." Cyril was helping me untangle my tie when I got home from the party.

"You know I can't do that." I shook my head, inches from his face.

His eyes pierced through me. "Every time you do one of these events, something crazy happens and I have to bail you out." Cyril was finally taking on harder qualities to express his distaste for my decision-making skills.

"I get that Cyril but— Ouch!" He pinched my neck in the fabric. "Be careful! That's my skin!" I hollered.

"I wasn't trying to lynch you! It's not my fault you wanted to turn yourself into the human rubber band ball." He laughed.

"That's me. The jumbled mess." I said without any tone in

my voice.

"Oh, come on, Guy. You have to admit you do some pretty stupid things. Bold but stupid." He pressed his lips together. "Half the time I try to make bets with myself on what kind of drivel you'll be caught up in next. You know, for someone who's extremely blunt, you have a hard time communicating what you really want with people."

"I get it! Could you stop?" I slapped his hand away from my neck.

"Fine, get it off yourself." He shrugged and walked back into his bedroom.

I followed, still trying to untangle the piece of fabric. "I meant stop badgering me. I still need help with this thing!"

"How on Earth did you manage to get it tied this tight?" He stood from his bed and began to work at it again.

"I don't know. I was so frustrated on the way home, I guess I got carried away." I huffed.

"I guess!" He twirled his hand in circles. "Tada! All done." He slipped one side of the tie through my collar. "You're welcome." He sneered and walked passed me.

"Thank you!" I called and sat on the bed, sighing.

He appeared in the doorway again with a cup in his hand. "Please don't be mad at me when I say this but, I'm not going this time."

There was a pause like the two of us were frozen to our places. I stood up. "That's fine. I wasn't expecting you to be glued to me for the rest of your life." I told him.

"That wouldn't be so bad." He smiled, flirtatiously.

"It really wouldn't." I agreed, thinking back to all of the times Cyril was there for me. "Why do you feel the need to look after me so much?"

"I couldn't tell you that. It would ruin everything." He said, closing his mouth tighter than a hem of pants afterward.

"Ruin what?" I asked.

"Ruin this. Ruin us. I like how we are around each other. I like your company. You're a very genuine human being. You're probably one of the nicest people I've ever come encounter with in my lifetime. I just like you in my life and I don't want to mess that up with things that don't need to be said." He turned to leave but then turned around again. "Perhaps, that was saying too much as it is."

"You wouldn't be so wrong with that notion, Cyril. You're a great guy too. You've been here for me without asking for anything in return. I've complicated your life and you've not once felt the need to express the hardships I have placed in your lap. You're—"

"Like you." He said, with a smile returning to his face. "I'm simply continuing your gestures. I like people to be happy. That's why I joined the police. I used my connections to make sure that truly innocent people were let loose."

"Really?" I asked with a grin.

"Well, not entirely. I joined a long time ago because there was another agenda I was part of when this whole eighteenth amendment bullshit started. I don't think it was the best place for me. A man that I fell deeply for took advantage of me and I had to walk away from it. I've honestly been afraid of him walking back into my life ever since." He explained.

"May I ask who?"

"It's not as if you would know him, Guy. This was years ago. Part of a different place and time." He looked at me. "His name was David. He was very rich and very powerful. Just like Tony was with you. There was something a bit different about him though. Unlike Tony, who has some sort of semblance for the feelings of others, David was a psychopath. He, would use peoples' emotions against them. He liked high staked games like that. He was a true monster."

"You really think that Tony is a good person?" I asked.

"No, don't misread what I'm saying. Tony probably does care about people. That doesn't make him a good person. Your actions are what make you a good person and he doesn't do well by them.

"You, however, are a good person. You make your actions

count. You mirror your actions with your intentions and never mislead people. You are a true aspiration to others. It's the reason why I have tried to protect you from harm and it's the same reason why I think you shouldn't go this weekend. Call it off. Become sick. Break a leg for Christ's sake, but don't go." He got closer and pleaded.

"I don't think it's wise either but there may be a way to end all of this without any of our side being affected." My mind flew in multiple directions as I thought of the possibilities.

"What are you saying? Are you going to try and murder Ella?"

"That was one thought." I said, grimacing.

"I know you, Guy. I don't think you could ever kill another human being." His words were soft.

"You know me too well." I made a dull smile and looked into his dark ocean eyes.

"Maybe I will have to come then." He smirked, drawing in closer.

"Cyril. I think the whole idea is trying to keep people from going. There's nothing I could say to convince Robby not to go but I would think you would listen to me. I don't want you hurt." I said it in contrary to how I truly felt. He always knew what to do and I knew that he would be fine. I just didn't want to risk anything anymore.

He said my name aloud and drew even closer to me. "You are the one worth saving."

A pattering of raindrops began to hit the roof above us. "I'll be okay. I just couldn't bear the thought of losing you. Not after everything you've done for me." I found myself pulling my face closer to his. I didn't know what I was doing but I felt a great deal of affection for Cyril and I felt as if he was one of the few people who understood me and understood what I was going through.

I knew deep down that no other woman could replace Peggy, but Cyril wasn't a woman and he had my best interests at heart. He cared more about me than anyone and without asking for anything in return.

He drew in closer and closer until our lips touched. It was like an electric shot had blown a fuse between us. He sprang apart in an instant and looked me in the eyes. "I'm sorry. I can't." He left the room.

There wasn't any friction between Cyril and I during the following days. I could tell that he felt guilty about the kiss. He said that it was because of Peggy but there was more to it that he wasn't ready to discuss with me. I didn't mind either way. I didn't intend for the kiss to happen to begin with. Being so wrapped up in the moment, I gave into what felt like a natural reaction.

I grabbed a postcard from the maildrop on the way into the

house and met Cyril in the kitchen. "You received a postcard from Billy George." I set it on the dining table.

Cyril grabbed my shoulder gently. "Did you still need assistance getting ready?"

He helped dress me for the night and gave me a big hug at the door. "If anything happens, take this card and call this number." He tucked a white card into the pocket behind my lapel and patted my chest.

"Who is it?" I asked, taking the card out and looking at it.

"It's me. It's the number for the phone I'll be stationed at tonight. I'll be a few blocks away." He smiled with a tear forming in his eye. "Did you think I was going to let you go without some form of security?"

"Cyril…"

"I won't actually be there. So, I won't get hurt." He gave me another hug as Laurel pulled up.

"Thank you." I said before closing the door behind me and getting into the vehicle.

"Hi stranger." Laurel smiled. She was wearing a coat made of bulbous fur and black lace gloves.

"You look like you're trying to weather a storm." I commented on her outfit choice.

"It's just the overclothes. I've got a hot little number I'm hiding under this jacket." She gave me a flirtatious look.

"So, did Tony tell you what was on the agenda for the night? Is the ASL showing up at some point? How is this going to work?" I asked her a flurry of questions.

"Hold your horses, sheik. Take me to dinner first." She giggled. "I don't know a thing but I trust Tony. If this whole operation is in his hands then we have nothing to worry about." She hiccupped.

"Laurel, did you drink?"

"Maybe a tad." She laughed.

"And you're trying to drive us?" I asked, disgusted.

"Oh, come on, Guy. Like you're never done it! Besides, I needed something in my veins to get me through this without the nerves taking over." She hiccupped again.

"Aren't you worried that Tony is going to have Robby turned into the bulls? Or even worse, killed?" I asked, trying to sober her.

"I'm still sitting on the greener side of the yard." She said, vaguely.

"Don't you care about Robby?"

"He hasn't bothered with trying to make sure that I'm okay. He's only called upon me when he's wanted me to perform for him. I'm not his show-monkey." Laurel had a little venom in her eyes as she stared at the road in front of us.

"You both seem to have communication issues because I'm hearing the same thing from both of you and for your information, he's taken a step back because he's been afraid of getting you in trouble with Tony. He told me that a few days ago."

"Then why is he trying to get us to play this show?" She asked.

"I wondered the same thing but it's because he thinks that it will make Tony show up and he can get Tony arrested or something. At least, that's what I got from what he said to me."

We both looked at each other. "So, that means that they both knew about the show and the both invited the ASL to the event." She said, suddenly sober.

"It's a huge trap. They're both going to get arrested."

"Not just them, Guy but us too!" Laurel gave me a petrified expression as she flew through an intersection without stopping. "We can't go. We'll all get thrown into the slammer!"

"We have to go. We have to warn them."

"That won't work. When was the last time either of them listened to us?" She asked.

"We have to figure something out. If we can even leave with one of them, it'll be worth going." I said, regretting it instantly. I remembered what happened with Peggy and I didn't want that to repeat itself. I wasn't sure that I was okay with the idea of either of them going to jail though. It was a matter of their lives versus ours. Sure, I could leave town with Laurel and Cyril now, scot-free but, I would feel forever guilty for having the ability to do something about two other peoples' lives and not.

"We can do this." I took her hand. "We said it before. We're throwing caution to the wind now."

"You're right." She said, mostly to herself.

"Do you have a flask?"

"I thought you quit drinking?" She asked, musically.

"I did but I'm going to need to chug a bit before we get there."

"That's my boy." She smiled and pulled a flask from her beaded hand bag.

Robby's new place wasn't what I expected. The sign wasn't lit up and the front windows were dark. There wasn't anyone on the streets outside either. It was like the whole block had taken a vacation. The shrubs along the sidewalk were left to die in the coldness of autumn and the two trees that sat on both sides of the front door were almost vacant of any leaves.

I took her hand in mine. "Listen. There's quite a bit I have to say to you." I told her.

"Guy, we don't have to do this. You and I are getting out of this thing alive." Her voice was steady enough to believe.

"We don't know. I didn't think anything was going to happen that night and I regret it every day. If I would have known, I would have said so many things to her that night." I tried to keep my composure.

"Guy, you proposed to her that night. She knew how you felt." Her eyes were beginning to fill with tears. "I know it sounds a little stupid to say after all of this time but I always secretly wished it was me you ran off with that first time. I didn't know my feelings then and I didn't think you had any interest in me. So, I gave up on you. I put all of that focus into Robby. I think he could tell that I was infatuated with you. It was the way he would react to little things I said." Her words were confessional and honest. She used a soft tone to calm herself out of an oncoming onslaught of tears.

"I never knew." I said to the night air, which was almost cold enough to see my breath. "I always liked you from the beginning too but Tony made things a little difficult for me. Who knows where we would be if you would have come with me in her place." I felt like a terrible person to admit that but I didn't care. It was the truth.

She laughed a humorless laugh. "Isn't that a kicker?" She smiled through her bleak expression. "What a world we live in." She shook her head. "Well now we can enter this thing with a clean slate. With any luck, it'll go out with a bang!" She made a firework effect with her hands before taking mine in hers again.

"Well, hopefully it doesn't go out with a bang." I said as the door sprang open.

"Marvelous. You're both here." Robby said with his hands stretched out like a conductor. Then, his eyes caught our hands tied tightly around each other. He grew silent.

"Robby…" I started to say.

"I don't want to hear it." Robby said quietly and turned back into the building.

"That won't do well with our argument." Laurel's face turned pink as she pulled her hand away.

"Robby, we weren't holding hands with any ill intentions." I told him as I entered the building. "There's something we have to talk to you about."

"What? You guys are together now!?" He said through gritted teeth. He led us over to the bar and loaded a cart with empty glasses. "Save your bullshit, boy. I can't believe you." He sighed. "I'm not letting this get to me. Tonight is going to be a good night." He talked to himself.

"Robby, I'm serious! Tony knows you're leading him into a trap. He's leading you into one!" I yelled at him.

"I don't want to hear it, Guy. Buzz off." He shot me a look

and turned with the cart to walk into the dancehall.

"You have to listen to me this time! You're going to end up in jail. He's really coming with backup!" Laurel stayed a couple paces behind me while I continued to shout at him.

"I know, Guy." He turned to look at me with the tray in his hands. "I told him to come. I tricked him." He was smiling.

"What?" I looked bewildered between him and Laurel behind me.

"So, are you guys in on some counter trick?" He smirked. "Here to take us both down. So, you can run off into the sunset?" His voice turned into a sharpened knife. "I don't fucking care anymore. You're only here to be entertainment and bait anyways."

"I'm leaving." Laurel turned around and headed back towards the bar.

"She can do whatever she pleases." He shrugged and placed the cart of glasses behind the bar, next to the stage.

"Robby, we're here for you. I promise." I said, agitated, trying to level with him.

"Is that what you told Tony?" He forced another irritated sigh. "Look, it's either me or him and I know you are only doing right by him because he's playing you. I know it. You know. So, stick around, I've got something up my sleeve that's going to not only blow your mind but set all of us free."

"What is it?"

"If I told you that, you'd try to do the Guy thing you do and walk out of here with both of us. That's not how this works. You can only live with one of us. So, who's it going to be? Your best friend of ages or some lounge lizard vampire?"

His words were cold. I guess it didn't matter how long we had gone without talking, he knew me better than I was anticipating. This meant that the game had switched to trying to get Tony to stay away from the venue.

I walked away without saying a word and found Laurel outside, leaning against the car. "I almost left you!" She huffed through a cigarette. "Let's get out of here."

"We can't do that."

"What? You're not serious." She exclaimed, dropping her arms to her sides.

"Laurel, Robby has something planned for Tony. He's pretty positive in his plans of avoiding the cops. That means that the real target is Tony. We have to stop him."

She took a long time to reply to me. I could tell what kind of position she was in because I was in a similar one in the past. Stuck between two people I had history with but didn't necessarily love. At the time I didn't know what to think when I first got back from the south with Peggy. Everything was so new and I was confused about Tony.

She must be having trouble deciding who's worth saving. "I know you must think I'm crazy for caring for either one of those men." She finally said after a few minutes.

"No, actually I don't."

"Guy, how could you ever understand how I feel about Tony? Sure, Robby's been in your life longer than anyone but Tony is a different story." She said, probably recollecting something in her memories as she spoke.

"I understand because everything everyone thought about he and I was true." I finally confessed.

"What?" Her eyes flicked open like someone had pushed her out of the sky.

"Well, except for the sex part. That I could never understand. It didn't happen but I did feel a great affection for Tony. He's always had some sort of hold on me."

"He's a charmer." She said with a whimsy smile.

"Yup." The plosive of the letter "P" was drawn out to dramatize my reaction. "Do you think ill of me now that you know? I've been holding it in for so long because it's not something normal to talk about casually."

"I don't, actually. I always sort of knew. I just wasn't sure." She had an expression that I couldn't read. It was a mixture of amusement and the air of seriousness that contorted her face in an inexplicable way. "And to be honest, it is a normal thing to me. I've been with Tony for so long and seen some things. Not everything is black and white, Guy. To be completely open with you, since you're confessing things to me, a long time ago..." She began in a whirl of breath. "I used to love Peggy in a way that wasn't normal..." Her face rotated through different expression until she settled on pressing her lips together like she was waiting for me to scrutinize her.

"Really?" I had so many questions. "Did she return the sentiments?"

"Yes." She smiled. "You see, sometimes people just love people. It has nothing to do with being a man or a woman."

"Did you guys date?" I asked, trying to keep my voice merely interested.

"No. Nothing like that, Guy. We tried things and cared for one another very much but we're very different people. I think we both realized that it wasn't going to work for us. We both wanted husbands and children."

"Can a person be attracted to both?" I asked, stupidly. "I mean, sexually?"

"Yes. Of course. Aren't you?" She chuckled to herself.

"I mean, do you think Peggy was?"

"Attracted to you? Honey, that is a very dumb question.

Peggy wouldn't have just picked you to have with children with her. That's not her style. She knew what she wanted and she went for it. That was the type of person that she was. She was in love with you." Her voice cooed me back into the moment.

"What a crazy tangle of emotions." I said after a few silent moments.

"You bet." She said, eyes stirring in dramatization. "Well honey, are you ready for the show?"

"What do you mean? We're doing it?" I asked with a half-smile.

"Seeing as Tony isn't arriving until it gets loud and busy… The show must go on." She winked.

CHAPTER 22: YOU WIN

Laurel grabbed my hand once more. “Are you sure about this? Doesn’t this piss off your boyfriend?” I asked.

“I belong to no man tonight.” She tore away from me and opened her car door.

“What are you doing?”

“Proving a point. I’m here for me. Not them.” And with that, she tore her diamond ring from her ring finger and tossed it into her vehicle, slamming the door with an immense crash.

I couldn’t help but beam at her with an air of jealousy. She was so carefree. Just like the night I met her, with her light hair and slight gap between her teeth. Making fun of my drink order and putting my heart through somersaults.

Having Laurel by my side and knowing things about her

that I would have never known gave me a new sense of confidence. It lulled me into the right kind of mood that I needed. I still felt panes of guilt to think about going on and living, knowing that Peggy couldn't have that luxury.

I let the thoughts leave my head before opening the door for Laurel. We had one night to pull off something impossible and I felt like, in that moment, I could do anything.

The flocks of people arrived in small batches of cloaked individuals. I think people were beginning to be wary of the raids. Thus, hiding oneself became an obvious trend that I was seeing more and more often. It must have taken some work on Robby's part to get people to come back to his joint after last time. I read in the paper that almost two hundred people were taken into custody.

"Hi Guy. I'm actually surprised to see that you made it here." Markel poked his head out from the side of the stage as Laurel and I arrived in the wings to get ready.

"Of course, I made it. I'm too worried about what would happen if I didn't show." I gave him a courtesy smile to compliment my joke.

"I would have thought that after Robby told you what was happening, that you wouldn't have wanted to come." His words were causal.

"What's happening, Markel?"

"He didn't tell you?" His eyes widened and his face turned beat red.

"What's going on, Markel?" I grabbed the sides of his sleeves.

"I know I shouldn't tell you but I feel a stronger loyalty to you than to him. So, please don't repeat this." His words were shaky.

"I won't." I said, eagerly trying to get him to continue.

"Robby wanted the two of you on the bill tonight to lure the ASL into the club as well as Tony, right? Well, Robby's been working in secret the last couple months with a... Let's just say persuadable police force." He twiddled his words around.

"Why?"

"He's going to have his main hands take down the ASL, then arrest Tony." His face turned contemplative.

"But Markel, aren't you part of his main hands?" I asked in horror.

"Hey, business is business. They took down Peggy. This is war." I flinched at the mention of her name. His voice changed to a tone that I had never heard from him before.

Part of me agreed with him on Peggy's account but I don't think she would want anyone killed for her. "How is he going to manage that with all of these people around?"

"Did you see everyone here? It was sort of the theme he was banking on. Everyone dressed up in secret. We're going to be doing the same. That way no one knows what's going on."

"You realize that you could end up hurting an innocent person in the process, right?" I was trying to scare him into rethinking his plan of siding with Robby.

"What are you two talking about?" Laurel asked after pulling her dress down and finishing her makeup in the mirror.

I explained everything to her.

"That's just madness." She remarked to Markel as he stood there during the explanation. "It'll never work. Tony is going to be surrounded by his people tonight." She instantly looked at me, regretfully. She just told one of Robby's men of Tony's plans and I could tell she felt terrible about it.

"Don't worry. Markel is different. He's not going to tell Robby." I turned to him and gave him a fevered look. "Are you?"

"No, sir. No, ma'am." He made a salute and turned back to his position in the wings.

"Guy, this complicates things."

"You're telling me. They both have their own people and you, me and the ASL are caught in the middle of it." I looked around the backstage area for any extra doors besides the one to the right of the stage. One that would make an easier getaway but there was nothing there.

"The second we notice anything fishy, we'll bail." She smirked.

"I think you're right this time." I caved in.

Robby flashed his face from the side of the curtain. "Are the two of you ready?"

I jumped out of surprise. "Yes... Whenever you are."

"Good. All of the guests have arrived." His eyebrows shook up and down in excitement. Without saying another word, he tore away from the curtain, leaving Laurel and I in panicked silence.

The music began to queue and we heard the booming voice of James. "Ladies and gentlemen. Robert's is pleased to present the world renowned, local talents of Guy Linister and Laurel Reynolds."

The music grew louder and the curtains slid open quickly. I took her hand and sat at the piano while she approached the microphone. "Hello, everyone. Wow, a lot of gorgeous faces out there tonight. I'm honored." She smiled, modestly. "Well, we're going to sing a few songs for you if that's alright." She began to nod to egg on the crowd.

Everyone cheered and when the horns died, I pressed my fingers onto the first chord of a slow song. She sang in a mournful coo that dazed the faces of the already drunken men in the front of the crowd. I watched her eyes graze the audience. Like me, she was looking for Tony, his people and any sign of the ASL's arrival.

I felt like we would know if they arrived. They usually made their presence known. I wondered if Robby told them to be there at a certain time or if he was even the person who alerted them. It would have probably raised suspicion if Robby was the one to say anything. I know I wouldn't trust it if I were in their shoes.

We finished the first song and were deafened by the roar of the clapping hands and hollering hoots. I stood up and bowed. "We've got another song." Laurel whispered to me from a few feet away.

"I know but we may not get a chance to bow." I nodded to the right, where two men were standing on the edge of the crowd with guns pulled out from their long coats.

She spotted them and quickly bowed along with me. "Should we leave?" She asked, pursing her lips.

"And create suspicion?" I asked in reply.

"Exactly. Maybe they'll scatter." Her eyes became focused on the audience even harder than before. The crowd continued to cheer.

"Alright. I trust you." I said, returning to my microphone at the piano. "Hit it, boys!" I shouted to the horn players at the foot of the stage. I watched within a few glanced seconds, the appearance of Ella and Kamila, as well as four dozen policemen arrive through the door at the other end of the room.

There was a drum roll and the band began to play. Laurel ran up to me, grabbed my hand and we flew into the wings. I could hear her breath pushing and pulling as we huffed to the secret door off the right of the stage. "We did it." She smiled.

"I know but—"

"You're still worried." She laughed. "I know."

"Not so fast!" Ella came into the room behind us, grasping a gun tightly in her hands and pointing it in our direction. She was followed by Kamila, mirroring her action.

Before we could say anything to her, they were both knocked off their feet by Alvah and Markel.

"Not this time!" Alvah said to Kamila. She began to lift herself from the ground and the two pointed their guns at one another while Ella continued to point hers to Laurel and I.

"Are you going to shoot me?" Kamila looked a little shaken at her husband but had an estranged stare to her expression. One that made her appear as though she had lost her mind.

"Are you going to shoot me?" Alvah asked her back.

The two began to circle as another person entered the room in a clatter. Two guns went off.

They shot each other.

Their bodies fell in mirror to one another and Ella screamed in panic. There was a quiet moment that took over the room as Tony stood in the doorway.

"Tony, get out of here!" Laurel shouted at him while Ella kept her hand steady in our direction. Markel was pointing his gun at Ella with a feared expression.

"Put that down." Tony said, his voice thick with his accent.

"I'm not leaving until all of you are apprehended." Ella's voice was even more snotty that I remembered. "Any second now my backup will be here with handcuffs and you're all being taken in." She smiled.

"No, they're not." Tony smiled back at her. "I had a few very talented people take them out for me."

"You monster!" She shouted, shaking the gun slightly.

"Don't worry, they're not dead. Just... distracted." He laughed.

Ella turned her gun and shot at Tony. Tony and Markel both let off a shot a quarter of a second later. She clasped a hand to her chest as her knees hit the floor before she crumpled.

"I didn't know what to do!" Markel said, frantically. He was beginning to shake. "She was going to shoot you." He turned to Tony, who was on the floor but not seemingly injured.

"It's alright, kid. You did good." He smiled. "Come on. Let's get out of here." He got up from the floor and began to walk up to us.

Markel crouched down to his partner's body. "He's dead."

We all froze, looking at one another. "Come on! They're coming!" Robby ran into the room and passed Tony and Markel, getting closer to Laurel and I.

"Through here!" I yelled as I turned to the alleyway exit door but before I could put my hand on the handle, Robby's hands encased me and he put a gun to my head.

As Tony pulled his gun up, Robby yelled, "Drop it, buddy! Or he gets it."

"Robby, what in the hell!?" I shouted as the cold metal pressed against my temple.

Markel's face turned pale from the floor where he was still crouching. Tony took a few seconds to react but flipped his gun around his palm in surrender.

"Alright, Robby. What is it you want, huh?" Tony's voice huffed. "Money? Laurel?" He offered like they weren't a thing.

"You." He smiled as four armed policemen entered from behind Tony. "Turn yourself in or Guy's brains paint the walls of this room." His voice was deep and evil.

"You don't have the guts." Tony said with vibrato.

Robby cocked the gun. I could hear the barrel clicking into place and I watched as Tony's eyes widened in shock. He dropped his gun and threw his hands into the air. "You win." Tony's words were broken and feeble.

I watched as the four cops cuffed him and dragged him out of the door. Robby slowly released me. I pushed him away and turned to look at Laurel. Her face was battered with tears. I looked over at Markel and saw his face sallow with an air of brokenness.

"Are you happy, Robby? Look at this! Look at what you've done!" I shouted. I forced myself to keep tears from welling up in my eyes, though I felt the emotions breaking through me as I stared back at him.

"You should be thanking me!" He yelled back. "He's gone. We can live our lives now!"

I shook my head over and over trying to stop all of the thoughts that kept ringing in it. The room felt as though it was about to shake out of my view and into oblivion.

"I feel sorry for you." I said after a beat. "You're going to have to live with this night for the rest of your life.

"Fuck you, Guy. Who needs you." He spat on the floor and walked out of the room.

Markel raised his hand. "Don't, Markel. He's not worth it." I said.

Robby turned to see Markel holding his gun. He pulled out his and the two stood with guns out at each other. "Gentlemen, stop!" Laurel's tear-stricken voice screamed.

I walked between the two and ushered them to put their guns away. "Come on. There's been enough violence for one night. Get out of here." I said to Robby. "Come on." I turned to Laurel. "Let's go."

I walked to Laurel's side and opened the door. "Are you coming?" I turned to Markel. He was crouching down again with his hand on Alvah's chest and tears flooding his eyes.

Laurel and I met up with Cyril at the phone he was stationed at and went back to the safehouse. We rode in silence after giving a brief explanation of the events of the night to him. Laurel stared out the window with steady streams caressing her cheeks like lonely rivers.

Cyril opened the front door for us with a morose expression. We all sat at the couch. The room's essence took me in and brought me back to every moment I spent on that couch.

We used this place as a safe haven. As our place of refuge. There were so many smiles and laughs that took place here. Confessions and arguments. I had come to the realization that all of my attempts to get everyone to get along were a waste.

I came out of my period of solitude, opened up to a group of complete strangers and drove my life into spirals over the course of a year. Here I was now, with almost nothing to show for it. I knew that suggestions to get Tony out of jail were out of the question. I knew that even trying to make a plan to do anything now was a waste of time.

I stayed silent. Everyone stayed silent. No one looked at one another. I could tell that we all shared one mind at this very moment. It was a strange feeling. The three of us had never wanted to hurt another person or be the head of any operation. We just wanted to live and be free.

There was a sense of freedom in the air now but it was dampened by the events of the prior months. It felt wrong. The world was continuing on while we sat here in this forever moment that swallowed us whole. The world that continued just like the many men and women whom walked below the window of my cheap apartment, making music with their movements.

So much had changed. I wanted back then to get out of my life and experience something worthwhile. In doing so, I nearly lost my life. I felt like without Peggy, I had lost everything. This night had solidified that feeling.

I was ready, when Laurel showed up at my door, to throw myself back into it. Possibly even, to commit acts of rage and revenge. I was maddened by the turnout of my life. I was reckless and scheming and I still screwed up. I felt like a failure.

It didn't matter what I did. I was always wrong. Peggy was

right, when she said months ago, that I would regret not listening to her. It was like she knew. She knew something would happen to her. I was kicking myself now. Missing out on hours of sleep, circling the house. Living with the ghost of her and my decisions. I blew it. I ruined everything and everyone. Everyone's lives were sitting in my hands this whole time and I destroyed them ever having a chance at happiness.

"Somebody say something." It was Cyril. His voice broke my reverie and sent me falling back into the present.

"What is there to say?" Laurel's voice was broken.

"She's right..." I looked into my hands, folded into a circle on my lap. "We messed up... I messed up. I ruined everything." I began to confess all of the ponderings that ran in and out of my head in the last ten minutes. I couldn't stop myself. I was ridden with guilt and the feeling of defeat.

Cyril and Laurel both put their hands on each of my shoulders. "You can't think like that, Guy." Cyril said slowly. "That isn't fair to you or anyone else. You carry too much weight all of the time. You hold yourself responsible for everyone around you. You realize that's how this all started?"

"I know. I fucked up." I sighed through the beginning tears, trying to push them back.

"No. That's not what I mean." Cyril replied. "I meant that, you feeling like this, has never done you any grace. What you did wasn't wrong, Guy. You felt the need to do something and you did it. That's more than most can say about anything. It's not your fault you couldn't change the minds of those around you. You're not in control of what people say and do." He patted my shoulder, trying to get me to look at him. I refused.

"You don't get it. I could have made them follow me. They were relying on me." The words left my mouth before I could think of them.

"That's drivel." Cyril waved his free hand. "You're just beating yourself up now. Come, come on. Let's get you some tea."

"I don't want any tea!" I shouted, getting up from the couch and walking into the bedroom.

Laurel followed me and closed the door behind us. "Hey, Cyril's only trying to help."

"I know." I sighed.

"When I showed up that day with a piano in his yard. He didn't know me. I was a complete stranger to him. I explained the situation and who the piano belonged to and he helped me push it into the living room for you." She sat next to me on the bed and pulled my face to hers with her hand. We were an inch away now. "He really cares about you. If I didn't know any better, I'd say he loves you." She smiled slightly.

I didn't know how to reply to that. So, I didn't say a word. After a few seconds of looking at one another, I pulled my face away. "I'm just so angry with myself. I feel like there are a mess of colors swirling around in black and white in my head."

"That sounds beautifully depressing." Her face brightened a little more. "Maybe you should paint." Her head turned to the side.

"How did you—" I began to ask.

"You told me, remember? The night we met at Eddie's? You kept telling me that you were a painter." She giggled.

"I did." I said slowly. "Yeah, that was the night that I was talking about doing music with you for the first time."

"Yup and look at us now." She tried to get me to smile. "See? The world's not over. I know I'm no Peggy and I could never be but I'm here. Isn't that something?" Her eyes began to fill up again.

I placed my hand on her chin and looked into her eyes. "You're right." I knew it would be a very long time before I could ever manage to love another person in the same way that I loved Peggy but if there were to be another person, Cyril or Laurel were both more than I could ever ask for.

The next morning, I woke feeling a presence in the room. I startled a bit, then turned to find Laurel passed out still a few inches from me. She was in her night gown and slippers. We had been talking before bed.

I felt a little better as I looked out the window at the morning light hitting the trees in the neighborhood. I apologized to Cyril and the three of us talked about an array of things to keep our minds off the current events.

I tip-toed into the living in my night clothes, heading to the kitchen to make coffee. There was a steady knock at the door.

I had grown to the idea that visitors were bad news. So, I ignored it, walking into the kitchen and scratching the small patch of stomach hair below my bellybutton, yawning.

I went to open the refrigerator, when the knock continued. I tried to ignore it for another minute but this person was persistent. Hoping it wasn't the police, I pitter-pattered into the living room and swung back the curtain to the patio slowly. It was Oliver.

I opened the door to his bright and glowing face. "Get dressed, friend. We have somewhere to be."

CHAPTER 23:
HE USED TO BE YOU

My mouth unintentionally fell open for a few seconds. "Why are you here?" I finally asked after a long moment.

He continued to smile. "I've been here for a while now. Hurry, get dressed. I have something that will cheer you up."

I raced to the bedroom and quietly changed, making sure not to wake Laurel. I tied my favorite tie around my neck and grabbed a top hat. I don't know why I wanted to look my best.

We got in his nice car and drove left then right, over and over, through the city streets of New York. The sun's light was touching everything in such a surreal way. Maybe it was the circumstance that I was currently in, making its way into my perception. Maybe it was just the season changing right before my eyes. The sun, not wanting to give up its reign of the Earth just yet.

“We’re here.” He said as we pulled to a stop in front of a large, grey building along the docks. I had passed this building a few times that day I was looking for Peggy.

I instantly grew suspicious. “What is this place?” I asked him.

“Don’t worry. It’s just a boat house.” His voice had a cocky smirk in it.

“Why are we here?” I asked as we approached the main door.

“This is my private boat house.” He said, without answering my question.

“Are we going for a ride on a boat?” I asked with my eyebrows raised.

“No. Just follow me.”

I did what he said and followed him down dark hallways, past ships that were docked on the right. We arrived at a room at the end of the hall that was guarded by two men. “After you.” He swung his arm out and one of the men opened the door.

I walked in as my heart dropped into my stomach and I felt it twisting and turning inside me. I didn’t know what to think. The room was dark and I was basically with a stranger. I followed him here because of what I remembered of him but he was acting strange now.

The room was dark and I tried to feel along the wall for a light switch. “Don’t bother.” Oliver said as I heard a muffled sound on the other end of the room. He walked inside and passed me.

In another second, there was a click from a beaded draw string and light filled the space from a hanging lamp above us. Below it was Tony, bound and gagged on the floor.

"Tony!" I shouted, looking between him and Oliver. "Oliver, let him go!"

"I knew that's why you didn't listen to me. You like this son-of-a-bitch!" His voice was maniacal now. "You hear that, Tony!" He shouted down at Tony, who was barely opening his eyes. "You've got yourself a little fan over here!" Oliver's voice bared a striking resemblance to Tony's now, riddled with an Italian accent. He began to kick Tony on the floor.

I ran over to them and tried to intervene, but Oliver punched me in the face, knocking me off my balance. "What is wrong with you!?" I shouted.

I was conflicted again. I knew what Oliver's anger felt like. To be mad with someone who took the life of a lover but to execute things in this way was wrong. He should have let the authorities deal with Tony and his crimes.

"Oliver, it's not too late. Turn him over to the police. You don't have to act this way. I know how you feel, trust me. I lost Peggy." I tried to reason with him.

He began to laugh a sharp, dry laugh. "Oh, Guy, you really don't see anything, do you?" He continued to chuckle through his words. “My name’s not Oliver. There was no Christopher.”

I stared in shock at the stranger that I once cared about. I looked down at Tony’s beaten and battered body and felt a horror run through me like I was falling into the snow. Gooseflesh ran across my body in waves and I collapsed back onto the floor. “What?” Was all I could manage to say.

He laughed again. “My name’s David Rockefeller.” He smiled. “Pleased to meet you. I used to be Tony’s boss.” He looked down at Tony again and gave him another hard kick in the stomach. I heard Tony let out another muffled yell of agony. “That was ages ago though.

“Back when we were trying to strike up this Speakeasy business in Chicago.” He continued smiling. “Tony and I used to have a little thing going on back then.”

I thought about Tony being with David in that way and my insides squirmed. David began to twist in my head like a nightmare now and I was completely useless once again. Stuck in a poorly lit room with a monster and his prey.

“You’ll find this hard to believe but I loved little Anthony here.” David’s face was distorted into a fury that made his features look inhuman. “I was willing to give up my life for this man. I did everything for him.” His voice was growing louder now. “But he didn’t want me, did he?” He asked Tony on the floor. “He would rather steal my ideas and start a monopoly in New York!” He kicked him again.

"Stop! Please, stop!" I begged.

"I couldn't let that happen." He shook his head back and forth like a madman. "So, I let him have his game for a while. Even let him marry that slut, Laurel. Sure, he paid his way into the light of New York and probably made more money than he deserved but I was always in the background waiting. Waiting to take it all away from him.

"I tried to get Laurel to do my bidding for me. I thought if his own wife stabbed him in the back, it would break him more than if I stepped into his life again. I thought it would crush his soul. Which was more satisfying to me than shutting him down but she refused.

"I suppose, I started my plans too soon. She was still madly in love with him. Falsified by his sheer charm and wit. It was disgusting." He rolled his eyes in a menacing manner.

"So, I found another person. A man who came into this country with nothing. He was well spoken and charming. I worked with him on securing positions in many places in New York to allow him the power to shut Tony down. Again, thinking of things on the inside.

"He was to charm Tony and lull him into doing business with him. Maybe even fall in love with him. Then break him from the inside." He paused to look up at the light, then he began to pace the room. "But that backfired. I made this poor fellow fall in love with me to execute the plan but he was too good of a person to go through with any of it. He's next on my list." He spoke mostly to himself.

"That's where I came in, huh? You ran out of options and got lucky when you saw me working with him."

"Oh yeah." He smiled, raising his eyebrows. "You were perfect. I knew from your dynamic with Tony that there was something going on between the two of you."

"Oh yeah? And how did you know that?" I got up slowly and started counter pacing against his pace. I was looking around the room for any other doors or windows.

"You haven't guessed it by now?" He grinned an evil grin. "I used to be Tony and he used to be you."

I felt a flipping feeling in my stomach like I had eaten something curdled. "What?"

"Yeah." He drew the word out dramatically. "He was lucky. He got away from me... Or at least, he thought he did." He continued to circle the room on the opposite side of me.

I began to feel even more worried as I realized that there weren't any other means of escape. The only other thing in the room was a small pile of boxes with full wine bottles next to them. I swallowed hard and looked down at Tony again.

"No one gets away from me. He thought after all these years that he was safe... What a fool." He laughed again. "I hated that you didn't bother doing anything about him even after my story. I thought I pegged you as the heroic type. Empathetic and caring for others in need."

"I didn't know you. That was your mistake." I told him. "You were a complete stranger and I luckily had Peggy there to tell me not to trust you or I would have done something stupid."

"That harlot. I forgot about her. Good riddance." His face was mechanical. I felt an anger growing inside me. "It was sheer luck that I found Robby." He continued. "I was meandering around New York deciding my next move when I ran into him after one of your performances. All I needed was a new name and motive and he was all mine."

I thought back to the night Robby and I got into our fight. I remembered the strange figure with the mangled voice taking orders from Robby. "James?" I thought the question was resounding in my head but I spoke aloud in fear.

His smile was all the response I needed. "When I found out that Tony wasn't arrested that night at Robby's I decided to take another approach with your friend. I told him that I could have Tony taken care of and he listened. He wanted to spearhead the Speakeasy operation and found Tony to be in his way.

"He was easy to manipulate. I told him that I had tried to reach you and Laurel and it was no use. You guys were lost to Tony's cause." He started to laugh. "He ate it up. It was like he had believed it before I said it... So, I told him to throw one final event at his place and I would handle everything."

I let him continue talking as my mind did a circle of quick thinking.

"And I did." He said with a flash of victory on his face. "I had my men take Tony once and for all. That part with Robby putting a gun to your head wasn't my idea but I wish that was." He smiled.

I turned quickly behind me and grabbed a wine bottle from the storage area, breaking it on a crate. I turned back to David.

"Oh, oh, oh! Let's not get hasty, boy." His voice seemed amused. I saw Tony's eyes glare up at me, fully conscious.

"I know you have a gun, hand it over." I said loud enough to try and evoke fear in him but not loud enough to alert his henchmen.

"Actually, I don't." He put his hands up.

I edged closer and closer. "I know you do, David. You wouldn't be that stupid."

As I walked closer to him, he drew the gun from a side-pocket in his jacket and it went off. The gunshot hit me in the shoulder. I paused for a moment to check my wound in disbelief. There was no pain. My adrenaline was running too hard to feel anything.

I lunged myself at his body and caught him off guard, causing him to fall and drop the gun. I scrambled for it and grabbed it. I held his gun hand tightly in my left hand while my right hand with the broken bottle reach toward his neck. I had maybe ten seconds to do this before the others entered the room.

"You wouldn't dare." I could hear a smile in his voice. It enraged me even more.

"You don't know me, remember?" I said, as I slit his throat with the glass bottle. There was a look of shock that took over his face as one last gurgle escaped his mouth and his body went limp.

The door flew open in a flash. I fell into the darkness on the other end of the room and fired at the man on the left. I thought I hit him but I missed. I had never shot a gun before. I was out of luck.

I saw a flash of light as the man on the right shot in my direction, narrowly missing me by inches. I returned fire with another shot and got lucky, hitting the gun-hand of the man on the right. He toppled over in pain as the man on the left turned to run through the open door.

The other man rushed to his side. "He's already dead. Let's go!" The guard helped the injured one up and they ran off. A few seconds later, a car engine growled and was followed by screeching tires.

I let out a huge breath and dropped the gun, dashing over to untie Tony. I unmuzzled his mouth. "What's a matter with you!? Get the gun! You can't leave more evidence here."

"Don't you want me to untie you first?"

"Quickly!" He yelled.

I pulled at the tightly bound rope around his hands with no luck. They were thick and tighter than anything I've ever tried to untie. I turned around, grabbing the glass bottle from the floor and tried to use it to rip the rope.

"Be careful, Guy. I'm pretty fond of my wrists, ya know." He said, musingly.

"Relax." I said as the rope snapped.

"Nice firing by the way." He said as he limped into a standing position, rubbing his wrists and spitting on the floor. "Let's get out of here. With any luck, we're alone." He walked to the doorway. "Slowly now."

"Here, take this. I'm a terrible shot." I handed him the gun as I continued to handle the glass in my good hand.

"Good idea." He took it and we slowly paced our way through the dark boat house to the front door. I glanced outside at an empty dock.

"I think we're clear." I whispered.

"I think you're right." He nodded in agreement.

We dashed to the car, who's keys were still sitting in the ignition. "What a terribly arrogant man." Tony said, as he took the passenger seat next to me and I kicked the machine into life.

"Yeah, I couldn't believe half of the things he just told me." I said in amazement, trying to get out of the dockyard without hitting anything. My fingers were still shaking from the events that had just taken place.

"Believe it, kid." He spat out the window. "He's a terrible human being that I tried many times to leave."

"But you did… Successfully." I smiled.

"Not so successfully." He said, pulling his left hand out of his coat pocket. It was missing three fingers. "Seven more hours in there and I wouldn't have any left."

"Tony, you're bleeding!" I yelled, almost hitting a wooden post. "We've got to get you to a hospital!"

"I'm bleeding? You've been shot!" I could see Tony staring at my right shoulder from the corner of my eye.

I had completely forgotten about being shot. Now that we were in the car and the danger felt long behind us, the pain in my shoulder sprang through my entire body.

"Why did you do all of this?" Tony asked me, staring at me with his pale face. He still looked like he wasn't eating or sleeping or both.

"Why wouldn't I?" I asked back, with an obvious tone. "You would have done the same for me."

"You're right." He smiled and went to place his hand on my

driving hand. Then stopped, realizing that he was still dripping blood.

"Tony, I just have one thing to ask after all of this is over with." I said, trying to sound serious.

"What's that?"

"Leave me the hell alone." I wanted to keep the disbelief out of my tone. So, he'd believe me.

"If that's what you wish. I'll be gone." His smile faded and he looked out the window, defeated.

After dropping Tony off at the hospital, I went back to the safehouse to tell Cyril and Laurel everything that had happened. Before I could get into any of the details, they both noticed all of the blood on me. I wasn't just covered in my own blood. There was also a substantial amount of Tony's and David's blood as well.

Cyril refused to listen to anything until the wound was cleaned up. So, we compromised. I let him fix my shoulder while I poured over details of David's deception.

"That's right. I remember that whack-job." Laurel's voice was quizzical. "He was quite a strange man." She mused. "I thought he had lost his mind."

"What kind of a story did he give you?" I merely glanced over at Cyril while directed my question to Laurel. His face was sallow and pale.

"He was trying to tell me something similar to the one he told you. He told me to divorce Tony, tell the world who and what he really was and to get him arrested." She scoffed. "The problem with his story was that, I didn't know that Tony liked men at the time. We were only married for a year at that point and he was very deceiving."

"I'm just glad you're alright." Cyril said after a few seconds of silence.

"Yeah, I'm fine. I'm not very pleased with myself… But I'm okay." My eyebrows furrowed into a look of indignation.

"Why's that, honey? You freed Tony. You freed us all." Laurel said. "Who knows what would have become of us with that lunatic wondering about."

"She's right. He was a terrible man. One of the worst kinds of people." Cyril said. "Trust me. I know…" He fell silent.

I looked at him. "How would you know?"

"I came to this country with nothing…" He began. Thoughts instantly began to flood my brain. "I had no future. I came here to find my mother. She left my father after I was born. When he died, I found it to be my duty to find her and reunite. I never knew my mother…

"When I met David, he promised me that he would help me

find her. That all I had to do was take this Tony character down. I believed him at first and felt a sort of affection for him. I was willing to do anything to find my mother and he seemed like an endearing man whom just so happened to be affected by the decisions of this monster, as he put it." He stopped for a second, probably trying to read my expression. I could tell that I didn't look happy about what he was saying.

"I was sympathetic to his problem and tried to go along with it for both of our sakes." His face turned sad. "But it was wrong. I knew it was wrong. I tried to convince him that there was another way to handle it but he became mad with power and started to scare me. I feared for my life. So, I used the connections that he made for me to disappear for a while..."

"That's why you wanted to help me when you met me." I realized aloud.

"Exactly!" His face was solemn. "I didn't know what to tell you at first and I didn't think you would believe me if I told you the truth. So, I kept it simple."

"All this time, you were trying to protect me." I said, feeling a sense of something that I had never known I could feel.

"That's beautiful, Cyril." Laurel said, as tears filled her eyes.

"I felt like a tornado in the middle of everything that was going on and... I wanted to tell you, Guy, I really did but as things got crazier and crazier for you, I just never found the right time to tell you. I thought in the back of my mind that David had disappeared, after all, and I didn't want to invite that energy back into my life.

"I'm sorry that I never said anything." He was looking at me with an expression that gave me chicken skin. It was the most honest face I had ever seen.

"It's alright, Cyril. You've been more of a friend to me than Robby, whom I had known my whole life." I put my hand on his thigh.

"There's more, Guy." He said with a smile.

"What?" I asked.

"I can't tell you. I want someone else to give you the news." His face continued to beam.

With everything that had happened over the last half a year, nothing went back to normal. Robby continued to do business. I'm pretty sure that Tony did as well. The only things that did change were Laurel and I quit performing music and I was able to secure my old, dingy apartment under a pseudonym.

I began to paint again. I felt more inspired with my paintings than ever before and my apartment began to be filled with canvases. Most of my work was dark colors and faint, vague shapes of people and strange figures. I never submitted anything to galleries and I kept to myself mostly.

Once or twice a week, I would be visited by either Cyril or Laurel. We'd play the upright piano and sing or have coffee. Very rarely would we make dinner, unless it was Laurel who cooked. I was still terrible at preparing food.

Markel came to visit one day with a single rose in his hand. He left it on the top of Peggy's piano. "I'm very sorry for everything." He said. "If I could go back, I would change it all. I hope you're not mad at me."

"I'm not mad at you, Markel. You did what you needed to do." I tried to comfort him, even though the sight of the red rose on the top of the piano was tearing away at me.

"I'm not working for him anymore." He said, point blank. "I'm starting over. Moving back to Germany. Going to be a free man." He made a sad smile and edged closer to me for a hug.

I pulled him into a grasp and said, "I'm happy for you. Go make something of yourself."

"I will. You'll see." His smile got wider as we pulled apart.

My days began to drag on into a melted mess of time that was indiscernible from itself. I often thought back at those times when I was with Peggy and we owned the world. Everything was ours. I let those times overtake me. They were the most beautiful and precious moments that I had and I never wanted to let them go.

I knew that there was nothing that I could do to bring her back but I saw her in every painting that I painted. Every song that I would sing and every face that smiled back at me. There were still moments that I couldn't live with myself and I hated every bit of it but it made me feel more and more human somehow and I eventually grew used to them.

I was lost in my thoughts, as always, painting another piece. This one was a first for me. I was attempting to recreate Peggy's face on the canvas. I was terrible with real people but I thought that I would need to start somewhere.

Before I could finish work on it for the day, there was a knock at the door. I knew that if it was Laurel or Cyril, they would come in anyways. So, I didn't bother with it.

There was a creak from the door and I heard heeled footsteps enter from behind me. "I think the hair is all wrong."

A ripple shot down my spine and every hair on my body stood on end. I turned to see a woman, wrapped in a dark, black coat with sunglasses on and matted black hair.

The image of the woman confused me. The voice was so familiar but her appearance gave me a start.

"What?" She asked. "Seeing a ghost?" She pulled off the sunglasses to reveal an indescribable hue. It was as if I had rediscovered color for the first time. She was magnificent.

EPILOGUE I | PEGGY

“It’s not going to work.” I told him, his eyes digging into me with frantic edges.

“Peggy, listen to me. This is the only way.” Cyril’s voice was fear shaken. “Once you die, there will be a disconnect in him that will force him to take the proper actions needed to leave this whole mess. Trust me.”

“It’s just not going to work.” I repeated. “I’m going to have to be killed. In a way that’s believable.”

“I can handle that.” Cyril’s reply was so blasé that it was convincing enough.

“But how?”

“I’ll accompany the two of you to this event on Friday. When I find an opportune moment, I’ll have to shoot you.”

"Like really shoot me?"

"Like really shoot you." He shook his head slowly.

I gave him a look.

"I'll shoot at a place that won't hurt immediately. The adrenaline will help you with the pain and the drugs will take over after that. Don't worry, I'll take care of you."

"Shh." I covered his mouth. "Sorry." I let him go. "I thought I heard Guy."

"No. He sleeps in." Cyril smiled like he was going to laugh.

"Alright, I trust you." It was the last plan I had left.

"After you recover in the hospital, you'll have to flee to Paris. Set up your life and come back for Guy when everything's been solved and organized. It has to be at the right moment." He said in a blur.

"Two problems with this plan, Cyril." I told him.

"Hmm?"

"Firstly, what about my funeral?" My voice felt a little sarcastic and teasing.

"I'll handle that. I'll tell Guy that It's too risky to have one and we'll do something here at the house in honor of your memory." His smile faded and he looked down.

"You're already feeling guilty?" I lifted my eyebrows and sighed loudly. "This isn't going to work." I sang.

"Yes, it will. I'll keep a perfect poker face."

"You'll be guilt ridden the whole time, though!" I lifted my arms in frustration and took a large gulp of the booze on the coffee table.

"What was your other complaint?" He asked, trying to keep me focused.

I took a second, collecting my thoughts. "How will I know when to come back?" I sat next to him again.

"I'll send you a postcard." He said simply.

"The only problem with that is I don't know where I'm going to end up." I shrugged.

"Peggy, you have my address. Send me one first." He laughed.

"But what if Guy sees it?"

"Make up a name on it. Say Billy or George." He continued to chuckle.

"Alright... We're really doing this, aren't we?"

"You are." He smiled.

"Oh, thank you, Cyril, you're quite the friend." I exclaimed, hugging him deep into the couch.

"Just promise me that you two will be happy if I do this." He said as I pulled away from him.

"We will." I beamed.

EPILOGUE II | GUY

I combed the canvas with my brush stroke absentmindedly. I was too mesmerized by the sunlight dancing in the water of the fountain below my balcony. Our Paris apartment had an enchanting view of a garden space with two old fountains that I adored.

I was trying to finish up the last three pieces before my exhibition on Saturday. I was presenting a series of work that I had started when I moved here eight months ago. They were faces. I was getting pretty good at painting colorful works of people I once knew.

I loomed over the painting that I made of Tony. His face was eager for something that wouldn't fit on the canvas with him. He had his familiar spark in his eyes that made me curious. My heart sank as I touched the drying paint with my finger tips and moved along to the next painting.

Robby's face stared back at me from a two-dimensional acrylic styled mess. It was conveying a pain behind his stern, unwavering expression. He refused to break his gaze with me. Determined to be the better man. I let go of the gaze before him and passed the corner of the room to arrive at Cyril's painting.

His smile was true to form. All knowing like a saint. The colors used in his painting made him stand out in an ominous glow that I could feel in my chest as I smiled back at his beautiful blue eyes. He had never asked for anything and neither did this painting.

Next to his was the golden glow of Laurel's presence. She was dressed in the same outfit that I had met her in. Silver with sequins flashing in the light from the distance. The gap in her teeth was prominent in her effervescent smile that made the room want to dance. She was sitting on a barstool, looking up into the stars, waiting for her queue to hit the stage.

I moved along to Markel. He was standing with a stern posture. Confident and unmovable. Knowing what he wanted but not wanting to harm anyone in the process. His lapel was a bright red in contrast to his outfit. He was a true soldier. A man of action. He showed reliability right up to the end.

Alvah's painting was dark and gloom. I left the shadowed

figure of a woman in the background as a ghost of his past. Haunting his every move. I used very little color and tried to convey his expression but felt like I failed to do so accurately.

The rest of the room was filled with paintings of Peggy. From paintings of her red locks, spinning in the atmosphere to cheeky smiles of her with black hair from the days that we reunited before moving to Paris. Her life was the true spirit of the room and I couldn't help but get lost in each one of the painting's eyes, glaring down at me from all of their locations.

"We've got another postcard from Laurel. She said that her and Cyril are coming to visit next month. They're excited to see us." Peggy entered the room with her short, red hair bobbing against her shoulders.

"I can't wait. It's been too long." I turned to give her a big squeeze.

"Jeez. Lay off that for a bit, will ya?" She smiled and pulled away, dropping the postcard onto the floor.

"I'm sorry, honey but after I thought I lost you, I just never want to let you out of my sight." I smiled into her face.

"I get that. You've been saying that a lot this past year." She sighed.

"Well, what would you do if you thought you lost me?" I gave her a cheeky smile and wrestled my nose against hers.

“You’re right, I get it. I’m sorry.” She pulled away again and curtsied her sarcastic curtsy. She straightened up a moment later and looked around at the room. “Honey, are you sure you don’t want them all in the exhibit? This one of Laurel is incredible. You really captured her.” She shook her head approvingly at the painting against the easel to our left.

“Yes, I’m sure. It’s hard to explain but I don’t think I’m ready for the world to know about my past. I just want to celebrate my happiness and achievements.” I told her. I knew she would never understand or maybe she would understand all too well. Either way, I knew she knew there was no changing my mind.

“Alright. Well, I’m happy for you. You’re first big exhibition!” She cheered.

“Don’t be so happy for me. We both know how I got this gig. Your French really saved my ass!” We laughed.

“I still can’t believe you traded the words for show with ass.” She laughed, picking up the postcard from the floor.

“I know.” I replied, trying to keep a straight face. “Excuse me, monsieur. Could I put a few of my paintings in your ass?” I repeated in English. We both fell into each other with laughter.

The day of the exhibition came. They set the venue up with dozens and dozens of red roses on my request. Irises were my favorite but there was something about the effect of the red rose on Peggy's piano that Markel left that day that never ceased to give me hope.

We walked into the place, hand in hand, passing painting after painting. I turned to see Peggy blushing slightly. I felt her arm steering me in a particular direction. I had a feeling of what was coming. The one painting that she wasn't shy with.

I stood there, feeling Peggy's hand unlock from mine and wrap itself around me. I bore up at the impossible eyes on the canvas. Their hue was indescribable yet, not exactly how I saw them. I could not perfect them but they were close enough. However, this face wasn't Peggy's. "I still think they should be green." She said in a singsong voice. "To match yours."

Instead of arguing with her, I simply placed my hand on her stomach and met her dazzling eyes.

"I suppose we'll find out who's right in a few months."

A special thanks to all who believed in my book and who donated on Kickstarter. Without you, this would not have been possible.

Melissa Windham, you are a saint.

Very special thank you to Ali Husseini, Will Laws, Jonathan Mercado, Vanessa Negata, Renate Norris, Timothy J. Perry, Shannon Ford, & Adam Yeager

ABOUT THE AUTHOR

Growing up, Andrew Michael Yeager never saw himself becoming a writer. His creative outlets always spanned the arts, but he often found more creativity in artwork, both visual and musical. He started dabbling in poetry and short stories, but never found a character whose story was compelling enough to continue. With the completion of this novel, however, his craft took a new turn. Andrew's passion for *Prohibition* was fueled by the division in the United States that came with the 2016 presidential election. As a supporter and advocate for the LGBTQ community, Andrew felt a strong pull to tell a story that is relevant in current society in many of the same ways it was in the 1920's. This project was initially backed on Kickstarter and was selected as a "Project We Love" by the staff. Andrew resides in Seattle, Washington with his mischievous 22-toed cat, Arnold.

Made in the USA
San Bernardino, CA
23 December 2018